THE GLASS PEARLS

THE GLASS PEARLS

———

Emeric Pressburger

This edition first published in 2022
by Faber & Faber Ltd
Bloomsbury House, 74–77 Great Russell Street
London WC1B 3DA

First published in 1966 by Heinemann, London

Typeset by Typo•glyphix, Burton-on-Trent DE14 3HE
Printed and bound in the UK by CPI Group (UK) Ltd, Croydon, CR0 4YY

*This book is a work of fiction. Any references to historical events,
real people, or real places are used fictitiously. Other names,
characters, places, and events are products of the author's imagination,
and any resemblance to actual events or places or persons,
living or dead, is entirely coincidental.*

A CIP record for this book
is available from the British Library

ISBN 978–0–571–37104–4

10 9 8 7 6 5 4 3 2 1

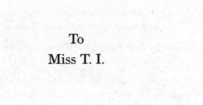

To
Miss T. I.

FOREWORD
by Anthony Quinn

Emeric Pressburger's name will forever be entwined with
that of Michael Powell. Together they formed one of this
country's most vital creative partnerships, to rank alongside
Gilbert and Sullivan, Morecambe and Wise or Fortnum and
Mason as a byword for a certain British distinction. Under
the aegis of their production company, The Archers, Powell,
the director, and Pressburger, the writer, hit a streak from
the late 1930s to the late 1940s that was unsurpassed in our
native cinema: *The Life and Death of Colonel Blimp* (1943),
A Matter of Life and Death (1946), *Black Narcissus* (1947)
and *The Red Shoes* (1948) are notable milestones of that or
any other era.

Powell, acknowledging the telepathic bond between
them, likened their partnership to a marriage. But to
read his two-volume memoir, *A Life in Movies*, one might
have assumed it was not a marriage of equals; as the more
introspective, less flamboyant of the two, Pressburger was
sometimes mistaken as the ancillary to Powell's overweening
talent and personality. That misapprehension was corrected
in a 1994 biography of Pressburger by Kevin Macdonald,
who had a personal mission to set the record straight: he
was Pressburger's grandson. When the 'marriage' broke up
towards the end of the 1950s both men struck out on their

own, with mixed fortunes. In 1960, Powell's extraordinary *Peeping Tom* was released to almost universal obloquy; it would take years for critics and audiences to recognise it for the sick masterpiece it was. Pressburger took the ill-advised step of directing a film himself, *Twice Upon a Time* (1953), about which little is remembered aside from producer Alexander Korda's snap verdict on seeing the rough cut: 'Boys, I could eat a tin of trims and shit a better picture.'

In fact, it was in another art form that Pressburger found his métier. His first novel, *Killing a Mouse on Sunday*, was published in 1961 and won instant acclaim. Set during the aftermath of the Spanish Civil War, it tells the story of a Loyalist living in exile in France who resolves to cross the border back into Spain, despite the peril to himself, to visit his dying mother. Glowingly reviewed and translated into several languages, it was also adapted as the 1964 movie *Behold a Pale Horse*, directed by Fred Zinnemann and starring Gregory Peck. Not bad for a debutant, and all appeared set fair for the publication of his second novel *The Glass Pearls* in 1966. Yet its fate would be almost an inversion of the success of his first. Having barely sold its initial print run of four thousand copies it disappeared very soon after, its only review a stinker in the *TLS*.

That may surprise us today, though perhaps at the time the story of a Nazi on the run would not have held such great appeal. While the Second World War as a subject of 'heroic' conflict was gripping British and American cinema, Holocaust literature lacked a commercial profile in the mid-1960s. *The Glass Pearls* now looks like an outlier in this regard, and its remarkable daring still reverberates. Set in the summer of 1965 it attends to the character of Karl Braun, a slightly built, unobtrusive piano tuner who sets up home at a seedy bedsit in Pimlico Road, London. Neighbours speculate on the new arrival, though his apparent ordinariness hardly rouses curiosity. Braun is just another loner in the vast impersonal city: 'He enjoyed a good book, a good play, a good concert, a good talk. What else does a man want from life?' One answer to that might be peace of mind, for this man is not in fact 'Karl Braun' but Dr Otto Reitmüller, a brain surgeon who conducted unspeakable experiments on concentration camp inmates and is now hunted across Europe for war crimes.

That Braun's terror of discovery is handled with such empathy and tenderness betokens his creator's moral imagination. Pressburger, a Hungarian émigré, spent hungry years as a freelance film writer in Berlin during the thirties and came to love both the place and the people that gave him a home. When the Nazis rose to power he was forced to flee, first to Paris, then to London, yet he never forgot his affection for the 'ordinary' Germans he lived alongside. He took an early opportunity to express it in a propaganda film, *49th Parallel* (1941), that he co-wrote with Rodney Ackland about a six-strong band of Nazis on the lam in Canada after their U-boat is sunk. His nuanced portrayal of one fugitive, a baker in peacetime Germany, underscores the tragedy of decent men coerced into Hitler's war machine – as the gentle elder of the village where they hide out asks him, 'How can you get mixed up with such a lot of gangsters?' More memorable still was the scene in *Blimp* when German officer Theo Kretschmar-Schuldorff, played by the brilliant

Anton Walbrook, poignantly describes the loss of his two sons to the Nazi Party – as broken by that as he is by the death of his wife.

In *The Glass Pearls*, however, Pressburger essayed his most troubling study in spiritual corruption. Karl Braun is a civilised man, an accomplished violinist who enjoys concerts at the Festival Hall, romances a young woman named Helen and mourns the loss of his wife and child twenty years before in an Allied air raid on Hamburg. Back then he was a doctor and 'a fanatic' who researched the brain's capacity for storing memory: 'He put a person under hypnosis, bid him tell his personal story in great detail and then he operated. As soon as the patient recovered, he heard his story once again, noted the discrepancies and operated again, cutting out another minute colony of cells. *Ad infinitum*. Or rather: *ad finitum*. The end came soon enough.' A monstrous crime, and yet Braun doesn't consider himself a monster. Nor, mysteriously, do we. When later he reads a newspaper report describing him as 'vain, ruthless, ambitious, self-centred', he is genuinely offended and baffled by the charge, regarding himself as one who 'loved his work', adored his wife and child and prayed to God. How can this mild-mannered fellow be a sadistic killer too?

When he is contacted by a fellow Nazi who urges him to flee to South America and join 'the Brotherhood', Braun's old fear that the net is tightening revives. But does the fear have any grounding in reality? Pressburger's trick is to keep the reader guessing. Braun/Reitmüller has to bear in mind a recent and notorious example of a criminal run to earth: 'The pursuers of Eichmann knew the date of his wife's birthday, they observed him taking a bunch of flowers home and that was the final proof of his identity.' His suspicions, already heightened, become febrile. He believes he is being followed by two men. He wonders if Helen, the object of his desire, is collaborating with the police in their hunt for him. This uncertainty lends the latter stages of the book the morbid tension of a thriller. When Braun takes Helen for a weekend to Paris, he recounts to her his first experiences of exile – of his escape from Germany, his arrival in Paris and his struggle to secure a residence permit, his favourite café the Brasserie Lorraine, the apartment on the Rue Quentin-Bochart where they used to throw parties, and the little green oysters they used to feed to their guests.

The particularity of these reminiscences is key to Braun's invented backstory, and yet they carry a more disturbing resonance – for they are Pressburger's own. As Kevin Macdonald has pointed out, it is quite extraordinary that a Jewish writer, having lost his own mother and other close relatives at Auschwitz, should choose to graft his own identity onto that of his murderous protagonist. Pressburger could not forgive himself for what happened to his mother, for not having taken her to England when he still could. Confronted by such traumatic memories most writers would probably have cast their narrative from the victim's point of view. But Pressburger wasn't 'most writers'. Instead, he focused upon the guilty man hiding in plain sight, which lends the novel its strange, wrong-footing power. At some level we hope that Braun will escape his pursuers, and simultaneously we long for him to be caught and punished. Perhaps he represented to Pressburger a chance of expiation, twisted into an unexpected shape. It is a portrait conjured from pity, certainly, but also from a cold-eyed acknowledgement that the perpetrators of the Holocaust were not some inhuman aberration. On the contrary, as Hannah Arendt wrote of its principal architect: 'The trouble with Eichmann was precisely that so many were like him, and that the many were neither perverted nor sadistic, that they were, and still are, terribly and terrifyingly normal.' *The Glass Pearls* bears out that observation with artful and chilling exactitude.

THE GLASS PEARLS

CHAPTER ONE

1

ON THE FIRST Saturday morning in June, a large van pulled up in Pimlico Road. Mr Mulholland who kept a stationery shop and also sold and delivered newspapers, came to the door to see the cause of this unpredicted eclipse of the sun.

'A piano!' he announced to his wife. 'Who's getting a piano?'

She went on counting newspapers in the back of the shop, acknowledging but not answering his question. But when she reached the next round number, she joined him to stare at the van. Usually well-informed on matters concerning the neighbourhood, this time she had to admit defeat. With sullen faces they watched the intruders.

First the vanman, a veritable giant, stepped down from the driver's seat. He smoothed his green baize apron which, like his peaked cap and both sides of the van, displayed in bold letters the ownership of apron, vehicle and man. 'London Pianos' said the writing on apron and cap. The sides of the van gave further information: 'Tuners of West London. Tuning, Polishing and Removals of Piano-fortes.'

Presently a second man descended from the front seat, hatless, with a bow-tie, greying hair, slight in build, not at all the type who could carry half a piano. He smiled at the Mulhollands and nodded a friendly greeting towards them. This made the couple turn on their heels and retreat into the depths of their domain which was richly draped with rolls of toilet-paper, sheets of greaseproof, pads of notepaper and greetings cards for every occasion except the one at hand.

When a moment later Ken, the delivery boy, came in and Mrs Mulholland asked him if he knew whose piano it was, Ken replied:

'It's not a piano. It's Mrs Felton's new tenant.'

The boy was right. Instead of a piano, several suitcases and a large rolled-up bundle emerged from the back of the van. The slightly built gentleman shook hands with his giant friend, watched him depart and caught another glimpse of Mr Mulholland, who had reappeared in the door with the object of securing the custom of the new resident, and this time managed a rusty smile not unlike the flat chord of a long-forgotten piano.

'Ken!' Mr Mulholland called, loud enough for the stranger to hear. 'Give the gentleman a hand!'

The boy, polite and eager to please, went running and when ten minutes later he came back, he reported that Mrs Felton's new tenant was a foreign gentleman who worked in a piano factory, and the bundle in his luggage was one of those continental bedspreads which he called an eiderdown. He needed no stationery at present but he read a fair amount, wished to take a morning paper and two Sunday papers, and his name happened to be Mr K. Braun, spelt the continental way. Mr Mulholland nodded several times, once especially to his wife who entered Mr Braun's name in the delivery book.

'Did he give you anything?' Mr Mulholland asked the blushing boy.

'Half a crown.'

'Very generous,' nodded Mr Mulholland once more, exchanging a glance with his wife who knew its meaning by telepathy. If ever the boy wanted a rise, the topic of generous tips was to be brought up immediately.

2

Two floors above the stationery shop, the new tenant stood dumbfounded in the open door of his room. He had completed the first stage of his moving in by carrying his belongings as far as the lobby and was now ready to proceed with the second: moving his luggage into the room proper. But was this his room?

Geographically, it appeared to be: first door right, next to the telephone, the lamp-post in front of the window. But where was the polished mahogany table which had taken his fancy when Mrs Felton showed him round? And what had become of the green velvet settee? The effrontery by which it had been replaced was covered with a faded flowery chintz with spots on its lower parts, while its upper regions were clouded over darkly – a legacy from countless tenants, gone for ever, who left behind coffee-stains and hair-grease as pockmarks of their private worlds by which to be remembered.

A friendly voice, coloured by a strong German accent, called from behind:

'Welcome, Mr Braun! Let me share and endorse your bewilderment. I am Leslie Strohmayer.'

The new tenant turned to behold a big man standing in the bathroom door, belabouring his long mane with strong, ruthless fingers, a conspiratorial grin on his thick-set lips. He wore a quilted dressing-gown, much too short for him and once of blueish hue. The toes of his right foot had broken out of their prison – a grimy sheepskin slipper. He went on cheerfully: 'I'm sort of Proconsul here. Representing Mrs Samuel Felton in her absence. It's my job to be here when the meter is read; I collect the rent and the pennies for the telephone calls, and I'm responsible for the furniture.' He sighed happily. 'But I am corrupt to a large extent. I conspire against Supreme Authority.' He slouched across the hall, wiping his hair-oily hands on his dressing-gown, pleased that he had succeeded in mellowing the new-comer's black mood. 'Pardon me,' he said. Braun had to step aside to let him pass into the room, and watched him proceed to the oval table which had gone through such a disastrous metamorphosis since he last saw it. There, with a spectacular snatch, the Proconsul pulled off the lino cover held in place by strong elastic bindings. He seized the shabby chintz at one swoop, he stripped the settee in similar manner and hurled the whole tatty lot up on to the top of the wardrobe. He was panting from the effort as he pointed through the window. 'She lives there – on the fourth floor above Bains the chemist. She keeps watch on us through her ex-husband's binoculars. He used to be purser on a big liner, and left her a tidy sum and the binoculars.' He went to the window, pulled down the blind and adjusted it expertly about half-way down. 'In this position she can't see a thing and I pledge my word that she never will. Mind you, it'll cost you something.' He screwed up his left eyebrow as a sign of conspiracy. 'Are you getting a morning paper?' He waited for a nod, enjoying the puzzled look on his fellow-conspirator's face. 'When do you read it?'

'At breakfast.'

'Splendid. You leave your newspaper for me every morning. In exchange I undertake to look after your window, blind and all. And I give a good report on your behaviour. What do you say?'

'Agreed!'

'Shall I help you with your cases?'

'No, thanks.'

'I won't charge you for that.'

'Really, I can manage.'

'I hope you don't get me wrong,' he grinned. 'We all have to live. When do you want the bathroom?'

'Seven-thirty, if possible.'

'That'll be fine. Kolm will follow you. Will you be using the kitchen?'

'Not much. Why?'

'I'm a first-class cook. Whenever you want dinner, just say the word. On the basis that I get the left-overs.'

'How do you know there will be left-overs?'

'Trust the chef.' He laughed roguishly. 'Live and let live.'

The new tenant, having now completed taking possession of his room, wished to terminate the conversation and be left alone. Strohmayer's last offer had touched his heart.

'Why not prepare my breakfast, Mr Strohmayer, on the same basis?'

The first-class chef's face clouded over.

'At what time do you have breakfast?'

'Eight o'clock.'

Strohmayer shook his head sadly.

'I never get up before nine-thirty.'

He managed another sly but rueful smile and left the room.

3

By noon, Braun had finished unpacking. When all three suitcases were empty and his four suits, his dark brown overcoat, the fawn dressing-gown and his six neckties were neatly arranged in the wardrobe, he unrolled the voluminous eiderdown, stuffed it into the largest suitcase and shoved it under the bed. Each spring when time came to store the eiderdown for the summer, he said goodbye to it as to a trusted friend, a benevolent monster who withdrew into its cavern to hibernate. On each occasion, it occurred to him that one does not hibernate in summer, but he couldn't remember the proper word for it, nor could he find it in the dictionary, and he forgot about it till autumn was round once more and he had to wake up his chum – the friendly brute. Every so often he had to disturb its sleep prematurely when, like now, he decided to change his address out of season. On such occasions, he never forgot to apologize in his thoughts and, consequently, to smile at his own folly which he attributed in turn to senility, or

to childishness, abhorring the first and taking pleasure in
the second.

Hidden among the soft folds of the eiderdown he kept
a small cardboard box. Whenever things had looked really
hopeless, he opened the large suitcase and dug his hand into
the eiderdown to feel for this box. He didn't have to withdraw it, the mere touch satisfied him. Just knowing that
it was there gave him confidence. Still, on rare occasions,
he did take out the box and open it. It contained, wrapped
in cotton wool, a spare set of four false teeth, mounted on
a slender bridge, similar to one he always wore. On such
occasions he might slip it on to see if the clamps still worked.
But he never wore it for any length of time.

Under the half-drawn blind he could see the busy street.
Conspicuous, their red coats glittering in the sun, two Chelsea
Pensioners were moving stiffly among the shoppers, never
exchanging a word, just marching to a soundless beat.

Suddenly, without the slightest logical explanation, Mrs
Taylor came into his mind. He tried in vain to discover the
link responsible for the association. There she was, haunting
his mind, thin-chested, her legs a shade heavy for the rest
of her body. She couldn't be more than twenty-eight, her
face arranged into cool studied indifference, her dark eyes
glancing towards the clock on the wall belying her calculated apathy – as he first saw her at Thos Harrower & Co.,
Estate Agents about four months ago. As he came through
the door, hurrying from work to get there before closing
time, she turned away and began rummaging in the filing
cabinet, hoping that her blonde colleague would take on the
new client. But the blonde was absorbed in scratching her

newly filled ballpoint pen on a piece of cardboard to induce the flow of ink, and Mrs Taylor had to leave the filing cabinet. She returned to her desk with a sigh.

'Yes, please?'

It sounded half a question, half a reprimand for disturbing the peace. With it she enrolled him among her very own branded customers. She asked for his name, present address, the amount he could afford to pay for a room while her thin inky fingers crawled to and fro on the printed form. She handed him two addresses, but he didn't call at either of them. That was the night Hein turned up out of the blue, making his blood run cold, forcing him to delay moving, not knowing which was less conspicuous: to stay put or to move, since he had already given notice to his landlady. It was not the unexpected encounter with Hein that scared him but the ease with which Hein managed to find him.

'Stop worrying!' Hein pleaded with him. They were travelling in an otherwise empty carriage on the London Underground. It was not yet six o'clock in the morning. 'Stop worrying, remember it used to be my job to ferret out people. I had been trained for it. Finding people is second nature to me.'

'What do you want from me?' Karl Braun asked.

'Two things. I'm returning to Argentina in a month's time. Come back with me. We have the same old discipline, all of us old comrades. We don't have to watch every step we take, we often talk of old times, read *our* kind of books – you'll be happy there among us. We had a German doctor but he died. We need another. A man can learn to drive a tractor, mend a fence, milk a cow, but he can't learn medicine. Not at our age and not on a lonely farm. You come with me to Zürich, we'll draw our money – money always comes in handy. It's still there? You haven't drawn it? Why should that money rot in that Swiss Bank in Zürich? We need it on the farm. We've had several bad years and we've decided to take the small risk and get the money we had tucked away. I've put up your name and they have voted – unanimously – to accept you. You pay in your share of the money and you'll be happy in our Brotherhood till the end of your days. What do you say?'

'I'm happy here.'

'How could you be happy here? They are after you. You are on the list. On top of the list. "Tuning pianos", indeed! A famous doctor like you!'

Braun shook his head.

'I'm not going. What else?'

Hein studied his friend's face for some time before he answered.

'I, personally, need you.'

'Need me for what?'

'You cured me in '44. You said yourself it might come back. It has.'

Karl shook his head again.

'You must go to somebody else. When you are in Zürich – there are excellent doctors there.'

This made Hein wild with indignation.

'How can you expect me to go to a stranger? You treated me with hypnosis. Imagine a stranger poking about in my mind! God knows what I would blurt out!'

'I'm not going to do it,' Braun repeated and hoped that it sounded firmer than the previous time. 'I won't risk it. I forced myself to forget about that money in Zürich and I don't wish to be reminded of it. I have lived for twenty years according to self-imposed rules; it wasn't easy and I'm not going to change my ways now. I denied myself everything I used to enjoy most. You said yourself before we parted: "The more you like to do certain things, the more difficult it will be to give them up, but the more useful you'll find doing so to hide your identity. You are a heavy smoker," you said, "don't ever smoke again. You like playing the violin, from now on never touch it. Medicine's your very life – don't even read about it!" I never did. And I'm not going to take any risks now with only a few more weeks to go.'

'What do you mean?' Hein asked as if he wouldn't know.

'The twenty years are up in May. On the 8th May to be exact. The war ended on 8th May, 1945. Twenty years added makes 8th May, 1965. That's exactly twelve weeks and two days from now.'

'Aren't you reading the papers, man? Haven't you heard that they're postponing the date?'

'Don't talk rubbish.'

That was when Heinrich von Stampel went berserk. His face became flushed. He seemed deprived of all power of voluntary motion. He sank into a coma. No doctor could help him any more. Braun did what little he could and got off the train at the next station. Amazing how the brain works in an emergency. Without the slightest recognizable logical process, it absorbs the facts, selects a favourable chance and makes you act accordingly. It made him do what little he could do for Hein. It drove him to leave the train and board another. A few minutes later he changed once more. He sat glued to the window as the train passed station after station. At Liverpool Street he saw the crowd and guessed what had happened. He got out, took yet another train, travelled to Edgware Road and from there walked to the factory. Two days later an inquest was held – he found a tiny paragraph in the paper about it – the cause of death was diagnosed as natural. They buried him in the Argentinean corner of the Brompton Road cemetery and, with the corpse, they buried Karl Braun's predicament, too. Ten feet of earth covered Hein's body and time shovelled one day after another over his memory.

No newspaper mentioned his name again.

If Hein was wrong in assuming that his friend could be talked into abandoning a clandestine life for the safety and cosy companionship of the Brotherhood, he was right about the intention of the West German Parliament. Early in March the English papers reported that the majority of members in the Bundestag voted in favour of extending the deadline for the prosecution of alleged Nazi crimes.

The news hit Braun with cruel ferocity. Most people can bear anything as long as their ordeal is limited. As long as they can count the days, the years; as long as they know they are progressing towards an end of their tribulations. Only if the suffering imposed upon them appears to be limitless do they go to pieces.

As in the first weeks after his escape, Braun began to have nightmares. But while twenty years ago his nightmares were confused and came in jumbled shreds (like experiencing being handcuffed, or sitting in a room and suddenly hearing the key turning in the lock, or being chased into a cul-de-sac), now his nightmares came in towering proportions, well-developed and orderly, as if they had grown to this size throughout the years, in the dark cavities of his mind. Now, they always started in a law court, where he was to be tried. Each time in his nightmares, he had to go through the whole rigmarole. They kept him below in a windowless cell, while above the High Court assembled. At last the prisoner was led up the concrete steps and stood in the dock waiting. It seemed they were waiting for the Lord Chief Justice to appear, the most important single person in the proceedings. But the prisoner pretended to himself that he, the prisoner, happened to be the most indispensable person here, for even His Lordship waited in his robing room to be told: 'The prisoner is in the dock, My Lord.' Then His Lordship adjusted his wig, his two dressers smoothed down his ermine robe, and he swept through the door.

'Everybody will rise!' the court crier cried. The people in the galleries rose, the photographers stood up, the pressmen, the jurors, the counsels, the warders got to their feet – everybody did, except the accused who had never sat down in the first place.

The preliminaries took some time. Nothing was hurried so as to give the court an air of importance. The jurors were sworn in. The wings of the heavy carved doors were heaved open, so that the people from the surrounding streets could enter. They began to file across the court, lowering their heads as they passed the prisoner's catafalque-like dais. They made their way up to the judge's platform and out again through the four small doors into the corridors and down the stairs into the back streets, beyond.

In his opening speech the Lord Chief Justice would explain that, according to the wish of the People, the court would sit open to everybody. The ritual allowing the German people to file through this court-room symbolized the people's wish: to be judged by its own conscience and thus purify itself of the deeds of the past.

Now it was the State Prosecutor's turn. As he read the indictment he drew the High Court's attention to the world beyond Germany waiting to see how the German nation would deal with the problem of war crimes and the criminals who perpetrated them.

'We have a national responsibility to discharge,' he began. 'A number of our fellow-citizens have committed dreadful crimes. Some of them have been caught and punished. Others have not been found as yet and have escaped punishment. Why should such resourceful criminals profit from their craftiness? Criminals who say to themselves: Keep under cover just a little longer. A couple of months and no one will be able to touch you.'

Counsel for the Defence jumped to his feet.

'I protest, My Lord. This is a German court and as such it should not concern itself with how foreigners judge a defendant in our courts. Twenty years have gone by since the end of the war. According to the Statute of Limitation, twenty years is the deadline for the prosecution of crimes.' He paused like an experienced actor who knew the value of timing, and scratched his head. 'Which presents me with another basic problem, My Lord. Hasn't the time come to find a new definition of the word "crime"? What is "crime"?

Who is a "criminal"? What is "duty"? If the majority of the people elect a government and a leader, this elected government, this elected leader, are the proper authorities to define where the citizens' duty lies. You have got to obey, or you are an enemy of the state with the obvious consequences. Now assume: a few years later the government is defeated – they all are, sooner or later – you're told you shouldn't have obeyed them. What you did was *not* "doing your duty" but you have committed a crime for which you'll be hounded and, if caught, tried like a criminal. More than that! Although there is a legal limitation to prosecuting a crime, there is no such limitation for *your* crime! My Lord! If the accused here is a criminal, so are we all. We should close the exits and keep all these people entering here. The clerk should read out the names of all of us. A hundred million names! And then we *shall* have to extend the deadline, if for no other reason, to enable the prosecutor to name all of us hundred million war criminals.'

In the commotion that followed, Karl Braun heard the distant voice:

'Release the prisoner!'

Each time he woke up, trembling and perspiring – a free man. Only to be rearrested the next day by his imaginary pursuers in another nightmare, and only to be acquitted again. Every night he tried himself and every night he acquitted himself.

As often before when he got desperate, he brooded upon suicide. He had the means and – he thought – he had the strength to do it. But as days and weeks passed and nothing out of the ordinary occurred, he convinced himself that he was safe. In late March, he read that the Bundestag in Bonn had adopted extending the time limit for the prosecution of Nazi crimes until the end of 1969, just another four and a half years. He could count the months, the years, as before.

Above all, sheer exhaustion had claimed him, snatched him from the claws of his nightly pursuers and hurled him into bottomless, dreamless, healthy sleep. All through April and May he had been lying low. Then – it was the last day in May – he went back to Thos Harrower & Co., Estate Agents.

The girl with inky fingers greeted him as an old customer and gave him Mrs Felton's address in Pimlico Road. That was the occasion when he learnt her name. Her boss had called through the half-open door:

'Mrs Taylor?'

'Yes, Mr Valentine?'

'Aren't you supposed to be in Ebury Street by five o'clock?'

'Yes, Mr Valentine.'

'If my watch is correct, it is 4.58 now.'

'I'm on my way, Mr Valentine.'

She rose at once, giving Braun an apologetic smile, watched by the mousy little man through the gap in the door. She pressed Mrs Felton's particulars into his hand and was gone.

He wondered who *Mister* Taylor could be?

On the street below, a car hooted, another took it up and a moment later pandemonium broke loose. Vehicles stood bumper to bumper as far as Chelsea Bridge Road. Just one of the things one would never think of when taking a room. He loved cars. Not under these circumstances, though, waiting frustrated in the narrow street, advancing a few inches every now and then. He used to adore driving along the Autobahn back home. My God, there they knew how to build roads! Here, in England, people were proud of every paltry little by-pass and the Hammersmith fly-over passed for a miracle of engineering. If Hitler had invaded England in the forties, the English would now have proper trunk roads, too. Failing to invade England, the Führer should have stopped the war when he had the whole of Europe at his feet. His name would have gone down in history as the greatest road-builder of all time. Greater even than the Romans.

Now, here was an example of logical thinking. It evolved, step by step, from the hooting of cars to the traffic jam, the narrow street, the wide Autobahn and the man who built it. You could always trace a logical progression in thinking, when one thought rationally. And when there was none, you could bet your life against a farthing that you were involved in something irrational, like getting infatuated with a woman. Happily some people had developed a built-in thermostat against such overheating of the blood.

4

At first he intended to ask Strohmayer about the shops, but dreading another commercial proposition, he decided against it. He found a dairy, placed a standing order for a pint of milk, bought a dozen eggs and a pound of sliced bacon. Everything was slightly cheaper than in Bayswater. He calculated that with his room costing fifteen shillings less, plus about 5 per cent saving on food, he could cut down his weekly expenses by almost a pound. When he returned to the flat, he bumped into Strohmayer.

'How much?' Strohmayer asked, pointing an accusing finger at the bacon. When told, he shook his head in disgust. 'I get it ninepence cheaper. Allow me!' He unwrapped the greaseproof paper and shook his head again. 'Mine is better quality. I make a deal with you. I get it 20 per cent cheaper, you pay me 10 per cent in kind.' He saw the bewilderment on his victim's face. 'If there are twenty rashers, you give me two. And what are your hobbies? Sport? Boxing? Rugby? Soccer? Tennis?' When Braun said, 'Sorry,' he went on: 'First Nights? Concerts?'

'Both.'

'Splendid. Do you mind going with Kolm? He's crazy about concerts.'

'I don't know him.'

'You'll like Kolm. Works at Bains the chemists. Come, I will show you your territory in our ice-box.'

He took a great deal of trouble to allocate the available space with scrupulous fairness. Each of the three tenants had his own little plot in each section: a small-holding on the top shelf – the coldest part, Strohmayer called it 'the Arctic circle' – another tiny allotment in the 'Temperate Zone' and a spot in the least cold territory, the narrow strip carved into the door itself.

'I can get you the best seats for any concert. You pay less

than a quarter of box-office price. Twenty-five-shilling seats for six. How's that?'

'Ten-shilling seats are good enough for me.'

'Nonsense. Nothing's too good if you can have it.'

'Really, I assure you.'

Another conspiratorial grin lit up Strohmayer's face.

'The truth is I can only get the most expensive seats.'

'Fine,' Braun said. 'Let me know which concerts.'

'Any concert. You name them, I get them.'

He helped Braun to stow away his stores.

'I can get you cheaper soap, too. Razor-blades, tooth-paste. Same arrangement. I get them 20 per cent cheaper, you pay me ten, in kind. One razor blade from ten.'

'You don't expect me to buy ten tubes of tooth-paste?'

'Of course not. You pay when you have reached ten. And don't worry, I do the book-keeping. You can pay me in advance if you like, I don't mind.'

'I'll think about it.'

Strohmayer laughed.

Shortly after one o'clock, Kolm came home. When he heard that the new tenant had moved in, he knocked at his door.

'I'm Jaroslav Kolm,' he introduced himself. 'I work at the chemist's the other side of the road. If you need any toilet articles – soap, razor-blades, mouth-wash, tooth-paste – I can get them 20 per cent cheaper.' He saw Braun smiling and understood. 'You've already met Strohmayer, I see. He gets part of his merchandise from me.' The old man sighed. 'If only he would consider working. With all his flair for business and using only part of his inventiveness to dodge work, he could make an honest living for himself.'

'How does he get concert tickets so cheaply?'

'Cheaply? He gets them free. Concert Agencies, Sports' Promoters, Stage Producers are sending him tickets gratis. He and a man called Anthony – I forget his other name – have founded a thing called "International Press and TV Information Service". They have no offices and no Service, but they do have very impressive notepaper. Strohmayer reads about coming events in the papers – not *his* papers, mind you – and writes in for tickets.'

'Don't promoters expect to get results? A cutting from a newspaper?'

'From a weekly in Palermo, Sicily? From a Norwegian provincial daily?' Kolm chuckled. He took off his glasses, wiped them with a spotless handkerchief which he kept in his breast pocket and, though he reported on Strohmayer's shady exploits with critical undertone, he could not hide a certain admiration for him. His lips quivered slightly as he balanced censure with true affection. He sniffed and snorted in short bursts, a sign of his qualified adoration. He replaced his pince-nez in the shallow groove that the connecting link had worn into his nose and released another short burst of snorts. 'Anthony, the second founder member, a barman in a Chelsea dive called the Temple Bar is, of course a great help. Every so often, Strohmayer invites Public Relations people for a drink, and he is met with great reverence by Anthony. You know how it is with barmen, Mr Braun? The barman of a saloon, where you happen to be a "regular", knows more about your background than your own mother. If a barman greets you with "Hallo, Mr Strohmayer, sir!" and pours you your "Usual" without asking, you're a man of substance. For good measure, Anthony throws in a few asides like "I hear, sir, the First Lord wasn't too pleased with your 'naval review' in the *Cape Town Times*." Strohmayer then stares darkly into his glass and mutters: "First Lords shouldn't be pleased all the time, Anthony. It's not good for them." Anthony winks at the P.R.O. You must go there one evening, Mr Braun. It equals any performance at the Old Vic.'

It was past two o'clock when the old man rose to go. By then, they had established that they liked the same kind of concerts, both played chess and both liked to walk. When you crossed Chelsea Bridge, you were a stone's-throw from Battersea Park. Strolling there on summer evenings, with the din of the Pleasure Gardens in your ears, the glitter of the river beyond the trees, could be magical.

Left alone, Braun sat on the green velvet settee, contemplating the months lying ahead. Life was not too bad. He did not mind tuning and repairing pianos. Visiting other people's homes, watching their relationships, could be quite amusing. He made enough money for his needs, he even had a little in the bank. He enjoyed a good book, a good play, a good concert, a good talk. What else does a man want from life?

Across the street, almost opposite his own window, a dark girl came into the bathroom and began brushing her hair in front of a wall-mirror. Soon she got so absorbed in her task that she relaxed controlling her pretty face. It now seemed years older, surprisingly harder and curiously ugly. If he had moved the blind, if she had become aware of somebody watching her, she would have instantly resumed her vigilance, her face would have changed in a flash to the well-tried, carefully studied expression she knew suited her best. The whole complicated procedure perceiving the warning in the brain, deciding to act, flashing orders to those tiny controlling muscles of her face – all this would happen in the fraction of a second. And there was more to it: the action of every single hair-thin muscle had been pre-set, like the tabulators of a typewriter. Dozens of such tabulators were working at the same instant and working with the greatest precision. The nervous system and the brain! What magnificent creations they were! How much work had to be done to understand them. And how little one knew about them. He couldn't resist the temptation. He switched on the bedside lamp and saw her face react immediately, even before she glanced up.

Suddenly he felt hungry. According to Strohmayer, there was a fish-and-chip shop just round the corner; the chef was supposed to be an Austrian friend of Strohmayer's. 'You get a double portion if you mention my name,' he said. It was more likely that he collected a bonus after every customer he sent there.

The girl who had been brushing her hair had appeared now in another window, holding a tablecloth and flicking bread-crumbs into the street. She saw him and, realizing that he had caught her red-handed, offered a smile for a bribe.

In the lobby, he stopped by the telephone. The sheet of notepaper pinned on the wall already had a blank column headed by his name to record his calls for future accounting;

a column which would remain blank since he never made any calls. Nobody ever called him either. He reached for the S–Z volume of the directory. There were nine pages of Taylors in it.

By the time he stepped onto the pavement, the traffic jam had cleared. Instead of looking for the fish-and-chip shop, he crossed the bridge and strolled into Battersea Park. He found no magic there, only a multitude of screaming children and scores of rollicking dogs, and he returned home.

Sunday, he wanted to sleep late but, shortly after six, muffled voices in the hall had woken him. His ears were set to perceive faint sounds, like the ears of animals of the wild; they let standard conversation through undetected, but as soon as somebody began to whisper, his senses instantly sounded the alarm. It reminded him of his childhood, when he used to go hunting with his father in the Black Forest. In the small hours they often stumbled on a distant herd of deer grazing in a clearing, his father picked one out with the long-range rifle, the shot reverberated tenfold in the mountains, one of the herd fell, the others went on grazing. The crackle of a twig would have sent them into a stampede.

He got out of bed, tiptoed to the door and stood there listening for a while. He heard the door-chain slide from its furrow and a woman's voice whispering:

'You could have offered me a cup of tea, you're mean.'

'You get one at the coach terminal. And close the door downstairs, there's a good girl.' It was Strohmayer. The female voice challenged him:

'You don't mind me walking about in this get-up, do you?'

'I do very much. Don't forget the door downstairs.'

'When shall I see you?'

'I'll ring you tomorrow.'

'You haven't got my number.'

'I'll get it from Anthony.'

'He wouldn't give my number to you, he's a gentleman. It's Fremantle . . .' The rest was lost in the creaking of the door. Her high heels began descending the stairs. Once they paused and she said quite aloud: 'You're a drip.'

Strohmayer laughed and called after her in a hushed voice:

'Remember to close the door.'

He slid the chain on, his slouching slippers played a short duet with the clip-clop of her descending feet, followed by a solo performance of her high heels as they reached the pavement. Braun twisted the blind, but she kept too close to the houses for him to see her. It was pouring with rain.

The bed felt warm and friendly, but he was unable to fall asleep again. He wondered what Mr Taylor looked like? Couldn't be much of a man if he let his wife work at that Estate Agent's. The mousy Mr Valentine wouldn't pay more than twelve pounds, if that.

He turned on his back, stretched his legs, folded his hands and prayed. It was a short, childhood prayer, the sentences trailed each other, his lips had learned to form the words automatically, like fingers could memorize a piece on a musical instrument. Only once in a while the meaning of the words penetrated his anxious mind. While he prayed, he pondered: where, in the brain, did these robots reside?

He prayed every single day. He felt insecure if he forgot to do so. When he could not remember whether he had prayed yesterday, he reassured himself by saying the text twice over, once for today and once for yesterday. Each time he finished praying in general terms, he petitioned the Lord for special favours, like finding a suitable room, getting a certain job; he might ask for the successful outcome of an interview, the passing of any kind of peril, in fact, for everything. Though he believed firmly that every action carried its own reward or punishment, he attributed a sort of giant computer to the Almighty into which all relevant facts concerning his person and relating to the subject of his special request were fed, and a single second later out came a 'yes', a 'no' or a qualified answer. Nobody knew of this praying habit of his. As a child, he had an open mind on the effectiveness of praying. He did it only to be on the safe side. Later he got more and more possessed with the power of praying and got firmly convinced that if he missed it, things could not possibly go right that day. Perhaps there was no more to it than self-hypnosis, but he knew enough of the power of that and took no risks. All through the pagan years in Germany, he went on praying. During the first year of the war, he shared a room with Dr Schumacher, the anaesthetist, and waited night after night till the lights were extinguished to say his prayers in the dark, forming the words in silence with his lips. Once, home on leave, Ilse asked him in the middle of the night: 'What are you muttering?' He lied that he couldn't go to sleep because of the heat and was trying to remember a poem by Schiller. She wanted to hear it but he couldn't think of one and recited 'the Lorelei' by Heine. It was quite safe as she had never heard of it before since

Heine was a Jew and had been eliminated from schoolbooks a long time ago. She found the poem lovely, wished to hear it again and again, but the baby started to cry. They listened to it, holding each other tightly, and so he fell asleep. Next day, he had a telegram recalling him to the camp, thus missing one of the most severe air raids of the war. When the news of Ilse's and the baby's death reached him, through the haze of dull pain, it shot into his mind: he had forgotten to finish his prayers that night.

CHAPTER TWO

1

THE PIANO FACTORY which employed Braun – and two other tuners and repairers – occupied the best part of an ancient building not far from the little bridge in the district passionately called 'Little Venice'. On one side of the bridge, the Regent Canal widened to a pool where painted boats anchored and where, on a tiny island, swans nested. The private life of these swans made up a considerable part of the conversation in the administrative offices whose windows overlooked the pool.

Mr Parsons, the junior partner – junior in precedence of accession, not in age – began the day's routine by going over his mail and asking his secretary:

'How's the sex-life of the swans this morning, Miss Hall?'

Each time he thus teased her, a blushing Miss Hall patted her unruly greying locks with nervous fingers and burst forth: 'Really, Mr Parsons!' And each time, she proceeded to give a detailed account of the number of eggs laid overnight, reported on fights fought among the birds, how a cob kept chasing a pen, 'For sheer nothing, Mr Parsons! Just to assert his superiority! His brute strength, Mr Parsons!'

The junior partner, now totally submerged in an ocean of letters, mumbled:

'Asserting nothing. It's carnal passion, Miss Hall. Down-right lewdness. Take a letter to Brockhurst, Birmingham, re three baby-grands, delivered so and so, get the date from Jack, Dear Sirs!' He went on reading and answering his mail, interspersing passing remarks on the libido of swans destined to shock the spinster's virginal touchiness, knowing too well that she simply loved it. When, after this morning ritual, she withdrew into her own cubicle, pleasurably bewildered, to start pounding away on her typewriter, she was convinced that she had a boss, worldly and charming, for whom to work was more exciting than for most. Once or twice, she stopped firing long bursts of black words on to the white sheets in her machine, to call Jack Cartwright, the accountant:

'Jack, be an angel, and give me the delivery date of three baby-grands to Brockhurst, Birmingham.'

'May 10, '62, Lilian,' came the booming voice from the intercom, well before she even finished the question. 'Have you seen that tiny cygnet, Lilian?'

'Let me get on, Jack, there's a dear. I'm trying to get through my mail before midnight.'

'Could we lunch, Lilian?'

'Lunch! Heavens, Jack, I'll be glad if I find time for supper tonight.'

'Perhaps tomorrow then. I'll try tomorrow.'

'Do that, Jack.'

Just before lunch-break, the three repair men telephoned to check on any cancellations in their afternoon appoint-ments. Two of them were dull men, with little more interest than getting through the day somehow and collecting their pay-packets on Friday. The third was different.

'This is Braun, Miss Hall. Anything for me?'

She answered in her sweetest voice:

'Yes, there is, Karl. Wait a mo', will you? I know there is something, I wrote it down.' She had her pad right in front of her, the message clearly written on it in her strong masculine handwriting, but she went through the motions of searching for it, chattering all the time. 'I thought you might pop in during your lunch-break as you are in Maida Vale. You *are* there, aren't you?'

'Yes, Miss Hall. In Clifton Court.'

'I told you you may call me Lilian. Everybody does.'

'Sorry, Lilian.'

'I can't find my pad, isn't it infuriating? Are you lunching? As you are so close to the office, I might join you and I'll have it with me. It must be right here on my desk.' It was. She picked it up, turned it over, shifted the book she used for checking her spelling.

'I've got sandwiches,' he said, 'but I could call again after lunch.'

'Oh, well,' she snapped, 'it won't be necessary, I've just found it. The name is Tastichoke. They are out this afternoon. Can you make it tomorrow instead?'

'Can be done. I'll bring forward Mostyns, they're always in a hurry. I know Tastichoke. Delman Mews. I was there before. It's not far from the place I've moved to. Time?'

'Between four and five.'

'Do you think I could go straight home from there?' He added quickly: '. . . Lilian?'

'I suppose so, Mr Braun. You've got your book full for tomorrow?'

'I do.'

'In English you don't answer a question of "have you" with "I do".'

'Yes, sir,' he said smartly.

'And I'm not a sergeant major!'

'You sound like one. How are the swans, Lilian?'

She laughed.

'I'll tell you when I see you, Mr Braun.'

'Till tomorrow then, Lilian.'

'Goodbye, Karl.'

She replaced the receiver and contemplated her own little Universe. Elsie Cartwright loved her Jack, she would not give him a divorce for all the tea in China. Jack Cartwright was in love with Lilian Hall and Lilian Hall was crazy about Karl Braun. Here the sequence came to an abrupt end since nobody knew anything about *him*.

2

When, the same evening, Braun got home, he found a message stuck on to his door handle. It read: 'A Mrs Taylor from Thos Harrower, phoned. She sounded rather intriguing. If you need more than one ticket (opera, play, concert, etc.) let me know in time! – Leslie Strohmayer.'

Braun read and reread the message, but could not find the key to it. Why should Mrs Taylor phone him? He made a point of telling her that he had taken the room at Mrs Felton's; there was no outstanding business between them he could think of. If only Strohmayer were here, he could cross-examine him . . . 'sounded intriguing' – what did Strohmayer mean by that? She must have said something personal to sound 'intriguing'. Of course there must be a simple explanation. Somebody had left a bunch of keys at the office and she was now trying to locate the owner. If so, she would have mentioned it on the phone. His watch showed twenty to six. With a little luck she might still be there. Now was the time to call her, with Strohmayer out and Kolm not yet back from work. He stood in front of the telephone undecided what to do. He swallowed, cleared his throat, dialled the number, all but the last digit, and paused. He took a deep breath and completed the job. He heard the bell ringing. A male voice answered.

'Excuse me,' Braun said and felt his throat thicken again, 'can I speak with Mrs Taylor?'

'Sorry, sir. Mrs Taylor has gone. Can I help you?'

'No, thanks. I'd better ring tomorrow.'

'Who's calling?'

'The name is Braun.'

'I'll make a note, Mr Braun. Thank you for calling.'

He felt a strange relief. Like a hungry fish that took the bait but somehow managed to wriggle off the hook. The poser for the fish remained: to eat or not to eat. An empty stomach sharpened the senses, while satiety made them dull. Still, on balance, more hungry fish were caught than those who had eaten their fill.

He went into his room, threw Strohmayer's message into the waste-paper basket, and began to study the monthly programme of concerts at the Festival Hall. He would have to invite Lilian Hall to one of these concerts. Not only out of courtesy, but also as an act of self-preservation. She could be a powerful ally or a venomous adversary who ruled arbitrarily over the repairers' daily bookings. It depended on her alone whether they finished off their working day with a job close to their lodgings, or at the opposite end of town. He remembered his conversation with her that morning which, in turn, reminded him that he had not marked his call on Strohmayer's account sheet in the hall. While he did this, he heard somebody panting and climbing the stairs. A key turned in the door and Kolm's arrival took charge of the evening.

'And how's Mr Braun tonight?' the old man greeted him, in his most generous mood. 'Is Mr Braun going out to dine, or would he care to share a splendid fish with me?'

Braun stood in the kitchen, watching him gutting his splendid fish.

'What made you come to England, Mr Braun?'

'The same that made you, Mr Kolm: Hitler.'

Kolm produced a pair of scissors and clipped all the fins. The dorsal fin gave him some trouble. He looked like the proverbial Wandering Jew in person. But only his eyes seemed tired, his hands moved swiftly. He sighed.

'I had no choice. I *had* to come. But *you* are not Jewish.'

'No.'

'I do admire those who left out of political conviction, Mr Braun. Which part of Germany do you come from?'

'Freudenstadt.'

'Fine place. I was there in 1928. We had been on a walking tour through the Black Forest, my poor wife and

I, newly married. I don't know why I am saying "my poor wife". Really she was rather lucky. Died of tuberculosis in '31.' He lit the oven, tore off a generous piece from a roll of grease-proof paper, buttered it, ground some pepper over it and added some salt. 'You don't mind fennel, Mr Braun?'

'No.'

'Good. Did you come straight to England?'

'To France, first.'

'Which year?'

'In '33.'

'Oh, you are one of the early birds!' He squeezed a piece of butter into the cavity of his splendid fish, making it look more splendid every second. 'I had great difficulties, Mr Braun. In Prague we believed he wouldn't dare to invade Czechoslovakia with the guarantees of the allies. When I found out that there was only one guarantee for safety: to get the hell out of the country, it was too late.' He wrapped his fish in the paper, making a tidy elongated parcel of it, tied string round it and put it into the oven. 'Just as this fish can't escape from this oven, so it was with us. No exit permit for Jews. Not even for money. Certainly not for somebody called Kohn as I was then. No official dared to risk it. I had sold everything I could and sat in the Café Central, day after day, waiting for a miracle. You are not a Jew, Mr Braun. You have left for more noble reasons than I wanted to leave for. I was just scared. Sitting in the Café Central, listening to the horror stories, drinking coffee, frightened to go home . . . Have you ever been in the Café Central, in a street called the Graben, in Prague, Mr Braun? No? Commercial people, students, bring all the gossip. It is an establishment where you could get all the important papers from all over the world, local and foreign. And in every one of them, on every page, it had been stamped: "Stolen in the Café Central!" – because people used to slip the papers from their frames and take them home.' He washed his hands and the scissors over the sink, asked if his guest minded eating in the kitchen and showed him how to lay the narrow table by the window. Braun had to remind him to conclude his story.

'How *did* you get away?'

'Ah, yes! How, indeed!' His lips quivered, he snorted several times just like he did when telling of Strohmayer's exploits. 'One day somebody brought the news that you could get an exit permit after all, for money. For 200 dollars. I bought 200 dollars on the black market. The money I had wasn't sufficient so I sold my winter coat. It had a very smart wild-marten lining, very popular with S.S. officers for their great-coats, you know. Well, I had the dollars, but back came the intermediary – sort of exit permit broker – the crooked official didn't dare to do it. Not for somebody called Kohn. You know, Mr Braun, Kohn used to be the most Jewish of all the Jewish names in Central Europe. So there I was, sitting in the Café Central, with all those dollars sewn into the lapel of my jacket, listening to their rustle and to all the rumours. Every day another bunch of my friends was sent off by cattle-trucks, with one-way tickets. Until one day an idea came to me. You know how it happens? When you are pressed, when you are desiring something very much something always happens. Only when you have given up every hope are you lost. All those Jews who perished, they all had given up every hope, that's why they were lost. Well, I cursed my name. I wrote it down on a piece of paper to spit on it, to insult it. And suddenly I realized that, if I wrote it down like this—' He took pen and paper from his pocket and demonstrated with his beautiful calligraphy. 'Can you see, Mr Braun? K-o-h-n! Now, if you doctor it slightly, if you transfer the end bit of this "h" to the "n" that follows, with a little bit of goodwill you have created from that "h" an "l" and from this "n" an "m"! It's not "Kohn" any longer but "Kolm"! It certainly looks "Kolm" to a crooked official who wants your 200 dollars and is afraid to give a permit to somebody called "Kohn". I got it. There it was, stamped into my passport! The next day I left Prague for Switzerland, stopped on the Bellevue Bridge in Zürich and asked a passer-by which way was East – you know, Jews always turn East when praying. I did pray there, on the bridge, thanking the Lord. And now we're going to eat!'

3

Karl Braun walked along the wet pavement of Eaton Square, turned into Elizabeth Street and by ten to four stood in the door of a new building called Delman House. One entered it from the Mews, through a glass door framed in copper, indicating that people of substance lived there. The Mews still had a few of the old-fashioned houses left on either side, one-time stables rebuilt into garages with flats above them. On one of these, at the very end of the cul-de-sac, Braun's eyes were caught by the hoarding of Thos Harrower & Co., Estate Agents, offering 'This Desirable Property with 44 Years' Lease For Sale'.

He felt tense while he worked on Mrs Tastichoke's piano.

He spoke not a single word to the Spanish maid, who pretended to be dusting the furniture to justify her presence, planted there by her mistress to keep an eye on the piano tuner. Once or twice he glanced at her and received, if not encouragement, at least qualified interest. No, she couldn't be an informer. Nobody could have known that he and not one of the other tuners would come to do the job. Except Lilian. And the idea that Lilian might be spying on him was simply absurd. Mrs Taylor couldn't be an informer either. He met her at the Agency the day Hein arrived in London. He mustn't lose his sense of proportion. He must be careful, that's all. But he had always been careful.

He found several keys out of tune, adjusted them, played chord after chord to test their pitch; his fingers flew over the keyboard. He only realized that he had actually produced a melody when the Spanish maid turned and stared at him as if he had transgressed his lawful authority. And all the time, he couldn't escape the notion that Mrs Taylor might turn up in the Mews, showing a prospective buyer around, wishing her to come and also hoping that she wouldn't, thus not involving him in new situations. Each time he approached the window under the pretext of examining a tool, or a piece of wire, he could overlook the whole length of the Mews. He wished now that he had a car. She would be glad to accept a lift, a bit bewildered, perhaps, by the coincidence of meeting the very man she had telephoned and who had failed to return her call, but glad nevertheless to find shelter from the drizzle.

Exactly at five o'clock, he saw her coming through the archway alone, holding an umbrella over her head, the collar of her raincoat turned up. Only when she reached the door of the 'Desirable Property' and lowered her umbrella, did he realize that it wasn't Mrs Taylor at all, but her blonde colleague. He returned to the piano disappointed, but reasonably cheerful. He finished the job without hurry, let his fingers run over the white keys and then over the black ones. The Spanish maid watched him admiringly, forgetting to dust the shining surface of a marble table. He closed the lid over the keyboard, completed the form in his order-book by the window, glanced down at the drenched cobblestones, just in time to see the blonde locking up and departing.

'Will you please ask Mrs Tastichoke to sign this?'

The Spanish maid hesitated. Her instructions were not to leave the piano tuner alone in the room. To her great relief, the dining-room door flew open and a little girl of seven stormed in, followed by her very pretty mama. The lady had a lovely voice – not unlike a clarinet, the piano tuner thought.

'Is it all right now?' Mrs Tastichoke asked, touching the polished mahogany of the piano.

'Yes, madam.'

'You can start practising, Sissy.' She smiled at the child as if she had outwitted her and wished to rub it in.

'Oh!' Sissy piped up, annoyed by the prospect and hating the guts of the man who had finished repairing this instrument of torture much too soon. She opened the lid and banged it down as hard as she could. She knew she had gone too far this time. She looked anxiously at her mother, now busy signing the piano-man's book. After she handed it back to him, the lady turned to the maid.

'No TV for Sissy this afternoon, Maria.'

Sissy started to howl. Mrs Tastichoke looked out of the window.

'Still raining,' she said.

'Goodbye, madam.'

'Goodbye. Say goodbye to the gentleman, Sissy.'

Instead of saying goodbye, Sissy uttered several dark threats, serving notice not to eat a single bite for dinner, not to go to school tomorrow, and not to come back from school if she went. Her beautiful mother waited patiently, no doubt with many trump cards up her sleeve.

Braun had no hat – he never wore one – he didn't mind the rain. To walk home from here didn't take longer than five minutes. He felt better now. The sensation of uneasiness had gone. He smiled to himself about offering a lift to Mrs Taylor in his non-existent car when, under the archway, he found himself face to face with her. Like Braun she had no umbrella. Her whole attention was taken up with watching her steps among the tiny puddles. Then she noticed the man staring at her. The dim light of recognition began to flicker in her eyes. How he wished he had that car now!

'Aren't you the man . . .' It took her a second only to place him. 'You've taken one of Mrs Felton's rooms.'

He wondered whether to remind her of her phone call, and said his name.

'That's right,' she concurred, as if it needed confirmation. 'Have you seen Miss Truman? My colleague from the office.'

'She left about ten minutes ago.'

'Are you sure?'

'Positive. I saw her. I was working up there.' He raised

his tool-bag to supply evidence and nodded at the building.

'Can I give you a lift?' she asked, turned and started to run across the street. He couldn't follow immediately, for a bus and two taxis got between them, splashing him with a fine spray of water. When the going was clear, he spotted her on the other side of the street holding the door of a dilapidated two-seater open for him to get in. He thanked her while she fumbled with the switches. She remembered the address of Mrs Felton's flat.

'Do you like it there?'

'I do.'

'Good.'

She turned into Ebury Street. They floated towards Pimlico Road in the cold-blue light from the B.O.A.C. building, reflected by the low clouds and the wet asphalt.

'Isn't it oppressive?' she asked. It sounded more than just dislike for colour and light.

'What is oppressive?'

'Oh, never mind.'

'Is it the shade of the blue? Is it the kind of light? Or is it B.O.A.C.?'

She turned her head in surprise.

'What made you say that?' When he remained silent, she answered his question. 'Perhaps you are right. On Saturday I took somebody to London Airport, somebody very dear to me.'

'I hope whoever it was will come back soon.'

She sighed.

'Ten weeks.'

'Almost half of one week has gone. One twentieth of your

waiting is already over.' She looked at him again and this time she smiled. He went on: 'Only unlimited waiting is unbearable. When you can't count the days.'

She slowed down. They were in Pimlico Road.

'Say where?'

'Where!'

She made for the kerb. He watched her hands holding the wheel. The car brushed Ken's bicycle but it didn't fall over. It seemed to him too silly to ask her if he could see her again. He got out, went round to her side. She let down the window.

'It was kind of you,' he told her.

'We are encouraged by Mr Valentine to give lifts to clients in rainy weather. 'Bye now!'

At this moment a big fat apparition rushed out of the house, swept past them, wheeled round a second later, and Braun recognized it as Strohmayer. He wore a heavy, strangely cut dark green overcoat, a hat of the same colour with a very wide brim recalling the photographs of actors of a bygone time. Before he addressed Braun, he bent low to see who the lady was in the car.

'Wait!' he commanded her. He remained in this half-folded position, but twisted his fleshy neck. 'Braun! I've just received two tickets for Oistrakh! Festival Hall! I thought I'd let you know before your charming lady takes her leave. Otherwise you are stuck with Kolm. My name's Strohmayer.' He untwisted his neck and was facing the driver of the car again.

Braun mumbled her name by way of introduction, but Strohmayer had sharp ears.

'Your servant, Mrs Taylor. I had the pleasure on the

telephone.' He doffed his enormous hat and straightened up. 'I must hurry. I overslept.' He bowed to Mrs Taylor, doffed his hat once more, and was gone.

'Would you?' asked Braun.

'Would I what?'

'Come with me to a concert?'

'A concert?' she repeated as if she didn't trust her ears. 'No, I don't think so.'

He pushed up the blind from what Strohmayer called its 'safe' position and sat in the semi-dark on his green velvet settee. The shimmering blue light that flooded the room was strong enough to throw a shadow of the window crosspiece on to the wall, and showed up the raindrops as they slipped, in endless procession, down the window-pane, turning them into fantastic living cells as they would appear under the microscope.

All his suspicions were crazy. Hein had found him because he had been searching for someone whose name was known to him and whom he knew to be working in a piano factory. Otherwise Hein couldn't have found him either. Anyway, they buried Hein three months ago. The police would have done something by now. They wouldn't give three months' start to any suspect. Certainly not to one who had a valid passport and could leave the country any day.

He wondered who Mrs Taylor had taken to the airport on Saturday? Was it her husband, or was it her boy-friend? And *why* did she telephone? He should have asked her. But if he had, there would be nothing to phone her about now. A moment ago it seemed stupid not to have questioned her about it. Now it provided him with a legitimate excuse to get in touch with her again. This eternal uncertainty between action and effect, between conduct and consequence, always fascinated him.

The following day there was another message from Strohmayer. 'Thos Harrower is after you again! – Strohmayer.'

Without hesitation he dialled the number.

'Can I speak to Mrs Taylor?'

'Mrs Taylor speaking.'

'This is Karl Braun.'

'Oh yes, Mr Braun!' She sounded quite pleased. 'How was the concert?'

'It's tomorrow. I have kept your ticket.'

There was a pause. Then she asked:

'Do you really mean it?'

'I do.'

'All right.'

'Begins at eight o'clock. Can we meet at twenty to eight?'

'Where?'

'Main entrance to the Festival Hall.'

'Is that by Waterloo Bridge?'

'Yes. I'm glad you can come.'

'I must warn you. I've never been to a concert.'

'How's that possible?'

'No one has ever asked me.'

CHAPTER THREE

1

THEY SAT VERY grandly in the third row of the stalls, he in his blue suit, talking of the music they were about to hear; she in a mauve dress that accentuated the paleness of her almost translucent skin, mildly curious about what he had to say. She spoke very little. After several unsuccessful attempts, he had given up trying to gauge her profundity. To everything he said, she had no more than the minimum of comment to offer.

'Do you like going to the theatre?'

'Yes.' She studied the programme he had bought for her and he didn't dare to ask her what she liked or disliked.

'It was nice of you to phone me.'

'I never phoned you.' She thought for a moment. 'Perhaps it was Ann. One of Mr Valentine's salesmanship rules. To ring up and ask the client if he is satisfied.'

'Giving your name?'

'You were my client. I often do the same for her.' She must have felt guilty about blocking the conversation, for she offered an opinion though not of her own.

'Dan used to say: only old people and unattractive people went to concerts and to opera. Dan's my ex-husband.'

'Sweeping statement,' Braun said.

She realized that she had offended him. Trying to untie the string of her words, she only got more enmeshed in it.

'He meant: people who couldn't do anything else. You know?'

'Like what, for instance?'

'Like dancing. Or bowling. Going to parties.'

'I see,' he said, but he did not. She thought: he would have been equally amazed by other views of Dan had she not, wisely, kept them to herself.

She found the size of the orchestra most impressive.

He reminded her: 'Would you like to read the programme note on the Leonora No. 3?'

She hushed him to silence.

'I'm counting!' A moment later she announced the result of her labours. 'One hundred and six! Fancy coming all the way from Russia. Think what the fare must have come to! What does *he* want?'

She was referring to the good-looking young man who appeared on the platform to inform the audience that there would be a change in the advertised programme. The Leonora No. 3 would be replaced by Weber's *Oberon*. A general 'Oh!' went up in the hall. Braun was one of those disappointed. She could sympathize with him since he had told her a lot about this Leonora and now all his trouble would be wasted. He had, in fact, made her quite interested in this Leonora Overture. One of the bandsmen was supposed to play a signal on his trumpet in an entirely different part of the house.

The music turned out to be strange but far from unpleasant. ('You must have long hair, long ears and hair growing in your ears, to enjoy it!' Dan had said and was, as usual, wrong.) The conductor came on the platform, acknowledging the applause, bowing right, left and centre. The most famous conductor she had seen up to now was Duke Ellington who hardly moved his arms and still every single member of his band followed him like recruits follow a drill-sergeant. Unlike this big fellow, who pointed, waved his hands, beckoned, nodded in every direction and pleaded almost on his bended knees with his men to play softer. She wondered if Duke Ellington was really a duke? Perhaps some African king had elevated him to the peerage. This one will never be a duke, partly because he had none of the dignity a duke is supposed to have and, partly, because in Russia they have stopped having dukes for some time now.

Suddenly the music took a new turn. Gone was the slow, long-winding phrasing. A melody with rhythm replaced it. So much rhythm, in fact, that she found it easy to waggle her head to it. A very old gentleman with a rich, silver mane, who sat on her right, turned and stared, as if he considered such visible proof of her audience-participation out of place. She stared right back and discovered that the man had, indeed, tufts of silver hair in his ears.

She hoped that the famous Oistrakh would not be replaced. Braun knew a lot about him too, he had even some inside information about Oistrakh's family circumstances. He had a son who played the fiddle like his father. Or almost like him.

When, to a new burst of clapping, the soloist appeared on the platform, she took to him immediately. He reminded her of her father, somewhat stout with a warm smile, and very purposeful. The conductor turned to him, Oistrakh nodded his consent and the orchestra began to play. They played on their own for quite a while. She tried to find the name of the composer in her programme, but the silver-maned type stared again and made her postpone her quest till the interval. By now, her 'father' on the platform got impatient with the proceedings, understandably too, since he had been billed as the star of the evening and they gave him next to nothing to do. He raised his fiddle shoulder-high and brought his chin to rest on it. His look seemed to say to the conductor: If you and your band won't shut up, I'll walk right off the platform! The conductor understood, nodded, signalled to his lot to stop and gave Oistrakh the freedom of the place. His playing was absolutely tops. She had never heard anything like it. Silver thread on black velvet. She closed her eyes and for no reason at all, it made her see the walled garden of her childhood. The garden belonged to some big-shot, a foreign ambassador perhaps, whose flunkeys used to chase away brats like herself when she and the other urchins put out their tongues at the ambassador's kids. She saw this walled garden often in her dreams. Secretly, she wouldn't have minded going inside just once. To see how it felt playing there, touching the rhododendrons, stroking the shimmering rays of the fountain, waving to her chums who had hoisted themselves on top of the wall and now stuck their tongues out at her.

The music stopped. She opened her eyes. There was some concentrated breathing and coughing, as if the whole audience had held its breath for half an hour. But not a soul applauded. Braun grinned, rather patronizingly, she thought, as if *he* and not Oistrakh had fiddled for the last thirty minutes. He took her programme and showed her the page which dealt with the Second Movement. She could now read the name of the piece: Violin Concerto by Johannes Brahms. She repeated it several times to herself and knew that she would never forget it.

They left during the interval. He told her that the symphony, the work of a contemporary Russian composer which made up the entire second part of the programme, might be just a little too heavy-going for her. She went for him at once.

'I know more about music than you think!'

'I'm sorry.'

'My ex-husband was very musical. Played the guitar like an angel.'

'Angels play the harp.'

She laughed.

'You're German, aren't you? Are Germans musical?'

He felt a tiny pang. A spark had switched on a danger signal. They were sitting in her car, driving out of the parking lot, chock-full of vehicles, but deserted of people. He told her that he did come from Germany, the Germans were indeed musical, and changed the subject.

'Where is Dan now?'

'I don't wish to talk about him.' They drove in silence across Westminster Bridge. Then she asked: 'Do you play a musical instrument?'

There it was again. Another spark lit another warning light in his mind.

'The piano. Not very well. Not more than a piano tuner has to.'

'Have you always been a piano tuner? I mean, back in your own country?'

Now there were three danger lights burning. Nobody wishing to pry deliberately would be that careless. He switched off all three.

'I was a photographer.'

'Portraits? Or fashion?'

'News-photographer.'

'Couldn't you do it here?'

'When I came to England, I spoke no English at all. I didn't know anybody. I didn't know my way about in London. Tuning pianos – even blind people can do that.'

'When did you come here?'

'Nineteen forty-six.'

She said nothing for a while and he knew she was trying to add up the years to figure out his age. She knew of a Chinese restaurant in the King's Road. She kept looking curiously at everybody and everything while they were led to a small table in one of the cubicles. Suddenly, she stopped.

'That old waiter there! He's serving that couple near the kitchen door! Watch him when he sees me!' She turned to the manager: 'Can we have Papi to serve us?'

'Certainly,' said the man, and handed them each a thin volume containing the list of food and drinks. Braun opened his.

'What do you say to "122" preceded by "109" and half a portion of "147"?'

She felt cheated.

'Do you know Chinese food? Have you been here before?'

'I don't and I haven't.'

'I don't believe you.'

He explained that he had opened the thin volume where he felt a little gap between the pages, a sure sign that many a customer had held the booklet open there before ordering a meal. It was a well-known trick. She thought it rather clever but it spoilt her own act, for some years ago she used to eat here daily and knew the menu by heart.

'You can cross-examine me. Go on. Ask any number. I'll tell you what it's called.' She didn't exaggerate. To top her performance, she declared: 'And I haven't been here for more than two years!'

The old Chinese waiter, called Papi, came, order-book and pen at the ready. She smiled at him but he didn't even look at her. Braun realized at once that the waiter was almost blind. He signalled her not to insist on being recognized and gave the order himself. She spoke only once when she had to remind Karl to order green tea. The waiter immediately knew who she was.

'Excuse me, Miss. I know you,' he said in a hesitating voice.

'How are you, Papi?' She leaned over the table and kissed him on the cheek.

'I am fine. Very fine. You are Dan's girl!' he added triumphantly.

'I *was*, Papi.'

'You got married! I'm old and stupid. You had your wedding-lunch here. I heard you had a little girl. Who's the gentleman with you? Can't be Dan. He couldn't keep quiet as long as that.'

'It's Mr Braun.'

'How do you do, Papi?' Mr Braun said.

Papi stretched out his hand and shook Braun's. He held it for a moment, guessing.

'An artist. Or a musician. Or a surgeon. Very fine hand.'

Braun made a feeble attempt to withdraw it, but thought better of it.

'He's got something to do with pianos,' she disclosed grandly.

'Where's Dan now?' Papi wished to know.

'Sweden.'

'And the little girl?'

'Also in Sweden. Visiting her father.'

'When is she coming back?'

She glanced at Braun.

'Nine weeks and two days.'

'You bring her here, Miss Helen. You see! I remember your name! You order the duck. If you like duck. And if it's not too expensive for you. Twelve and six O.K.? Very expensive but very good.' He tore out the top page from his order-book and wrote a new one. When he had shuffled away, Braun said:

'I never expected to learn so much about you tonight.'

2

The following week, they went out twice. The first time to another concert. The programme consisted entirely of works by Mozart. The music depressed her and the G-minor Symphony drew tears.

'This music is like me,' she tried to explain. 'Pathetic.' She wouldn't enlarge upon it and he let it be.

'Have you heard from your daughter?'

She nodded. She had a letter from her.

'Can she write?'

'Of course not. She's only five. She sent a page full of O-s and X-es.'

'I would call that a sensible letter, expressing clearly what she feels, which is more than most people can do.' It was the interval, they were leaning against the balustrade, watching the river. He went on: 'It shows you how stupidly we treat growing children. At a time when they are more emotional than at any other time, we tell them to forget that X means a kiss and O means a hug. In the adult world – we tell them – X stands for an "unknown quantity" and O stands for "nothing". What is her name?'

'Eve.'

After the concert, he took her to a pub called the Half a Crown where you could choose your steak in the raw. For 8/6 they cooked it, provided a few mushrooms, a jacket-potato, with a small carafe of wine thrown in. Once upon a time, the price used to be half a crown, but only the oldest patrons could remember those days. The publican had taken down the sign of the giant silver coin and replaced it by a halved coronet, thus retaining the name, but not the price.

Due to Mozart, or due to the contents of the carafe, Helen was visibly thawing. She spoke of Eve's heartbreaking departure.

'When the stewardess took her by the hand and said, "I'm afraid we have to be off now, Mrs Taylor", I thought I'd die on the spot. I kept on saying to myself: no tears, not for the next thirty seconds, just long enough for her to pass the Emigration Officer, and be out of sight. I hugged her a last time, told her to be a good girl and ask her daddy to send a telegram. And then I stood there, waiting to wave to her, hoping that she would turn before disappearing. I watched her clutching her doll, stopping by the emigration man. He glanced at her passport and must have made the obvious remark, for she opened her doll's overnight bag, pulled out the doll's passport and handed it up to him, hardly reaching up to the height of his desk. The stewardess made her turn. Eve held the doll high, waving its arm in final farewell. Then she grabbed the stewardess's skirt, pulling it, impatient to get on.'

'All small children are like that,' he said.

'Have you ever had any children?'

He almost told her. He checked himself just in time. Nothing is more inviting to disclose your secrets than to be told by others of their own. Hein used to lecture him: 'When somebody is asking you straight questions, it's easy to be on your guard. But when somebody is telling you his own life story, that's the time to watch your tongue.'

'No,' he said.

'I cried. I couldn't pull myself together. A policewoman talked to me but I just went on crying. I can't forget seeing her, a tiny little thing, setting off, all on her own, a paper-tag dangling from the buttonhole of her coat. This paper-tag was, perhaps, the worst part of it. And then, going home to an empty flat, waking up Monday morning, driving to work without dropping her at the day-nursery and not calling for her on the way home.'

The waiter came with another carafe of cheap wine. He poured a sip for the gentleman as if it had been château-bottled Burgundy. Braun went through the ceremony of smelling it, tasting it, nodding his consent. Then he asked her to go on.

'There's nothing else,' she said. 'I don't know why I'm boring you with it.'

He protested. She raised her glass.

'Do you know that for two years I never went out with anybody?'

'Why not?'

'You see I had great trouble in getting custody of my child.'

'I thought courts were more likely to give the custody of a small child to its mother.'

'True. But I used to be very silly.'

'Silly, how?'

'Just silly. Dan came up with dozens of witnesses. They all testified that I couldn't possibly look after a child, that I was too silly for words, that I had never learnt anything, I could never get a job and if, by some fluke, I got one, I could never keep it.' She sighed. 'Also that I was a liar – which is true. Everything that they said against me was true.'

'What happened?'

'The judge asked me: Do you want your child? I said: Yes. Then he asked: Will you get a job so that you can give her a home? I said: Yes. "I will give you a trial," he said. "When she reaches the age of five, I want you to send her to her father for ten weeks every year. He will pay for her trip and he will also pay maintenance for her.'"

'Is he quite well off?' Braun asked.

'He has a good job. With a tractor factory. Tractors and agricultural machinery. Makes quite good money.'

'Has he remarried?'

'No. But he's got engaged to be married.'

He watched her closely. She didn't seem to mind Dan getting married again.

'Now it's your turn,' she said. 'Tell me about yourself.'

The waiter brought the steaks, the mushrooms, and the jacket-potatoes, and she debited him with his life story. After dinner, he talked of the play they were going to see and went on living on credit.

3

The play was *A Midsummer Night's Dream*. She had not seen any Shakespeare before. It over-awed her even more than her first concert. She seemed parched for all sorts of knowledge. A wanderer in the desert, thirsting for water, and offered chilled champagne: it seemed an entirely un-expected treat to her. He wondered whether, after a while, she would be craving for water again. Nothing fascinated her more than sheer magic. Magic in music and magic in words. Harmonies, whether by Mozart or by Bartok, made the same impression on her. She could listen to Shakespeare with wide-open eyes for hours, enjoying the sound of the words without taking in the meaning of any of them. She told him how her life had changed since Eve's departure.

'I used to get up at seven every morning. I played with her, dressed her, we had breakfast together. I took her to the day-nursery and then went to work. In the evening I called for her, always afraid that I might be held up by a late client. The day-nursery closed at six, you know. We played when we got home; I cooked something, put her to bed. By the time I had cleaned up the flat, I was dead tired. Even if I could have afforded a baby-sitter, I wouldn't have had one. I imagined that the judge had planted spies all over the place to find out how I behaved and, if I had failed, he would have taken her away from me. You know what I mean?'

He did. Especially the last bit about the spies.

Each time they met, he discovered a little more independence and a little more girlishness about her. Released from her adult duties, she grew younger every day. Now he understood what she meant when she went to all that trouble to explain how she used to be before. Even her vocabulary had changed. A concert she used to describe as wonderful, was now 'fabulous'. A letter from Eve: 'super'.

In the third week of their friendship, they were going to a concert and had planned to eat in the Festival Hall Restaurant before the concert. They were to meet sharp at six o'clock inside the main entrance. He waited and waited, but she never came. He called her office, and called her home, but there was no reply. He waited till the very last minute before the concert started and, as soon as the first piece ended, while the attendants performed their clever little routine, pushing in and setting up the grand piano, he rushed outside to have another look.

There she was sitting by the coffee-bar near the stairs, where the commissionaire barred her way. They hurried upstairs, but found the doors already closed. A moment later, they could hear the orchestra playing the introduction to the Emperor Concerto. They pulled up two chairs and could hear the music quite clearly. A little muffled, perhaps, like having water in one's ears. The corridor was empty. On the stairs, a programme seller sat on the top stair, counting her takings and then her unsold programmes.

'What happened?' he whispered.

'I met somebody who'll fix up my holiday,' she whispered back.

'I didn't know you were going on holiday.'

'You don't have to know everything.'

'No,' he agreed.

For a moment they listened silently. She obviously felt in the wrong for she spoke again, in a hushed voice.

'I had no holiday last year. I must take one before Eve comes back.'

'Where are you going to?'

'The New Forest.'

'Why the New Forest?'

'I want to lie under a tree. I'll take my portable with me and play music. There's lots of music on the radio, not only pop. I can't stand the sun. I once had sunstroke. So—' she shrugged as if bowing to the inevitable, 'so I have to have trees.'

'You had a heat-stroke,' he corrected her.

She looked astonished.

'That's what the doctor said. He said: there isn't such a thing as sunstroke. You *are* clever.'

'Your skin is very sensitive. Lots of people with very pale skins get heat-stroke if they are not careful.'

'Not like I had it.'

'When was that?'

'In the summer of '57. The year I met Dan. We went to a place called Bandol in the South of France. Have you ever been in France?'

'Yes.'

'Where?'

'Paris, mostly. I lived in Paris.'

'Well, it can't be as hot in Paris because lots of Parisians go to Bandol in the summer. You see I'm no good at swimming, so while Dan swam – it was our first day there – I hired a mat and fell asleep on it. When they woke me up, I couldn't see anything. Everything was as black as night. They called a doctor. I had a temperature of 108 degrees. I had to stay in bed the whole seven days we were there. And driving home, Dan had to put up the hood whenever the sun came out. He was wild, I can tell you. No sun for me. No, thank you.'

They were not admitted until the interval. After the concert, she dropped him in Pimlico Road, refusing to eat anything. When he entered the flat, Kolm popped out to see who it was.

'I thought Strohmayer had come in,' he apologized. He needed little encouragement to join Braun in the kitchen to keep him company while he fried two eggs for himself. 'Braun!' Kolm began, and he could guess from the timbre of his voice that something momentous had happened to him. 'Braun! I have become a rich man.'

'How come?' Braun asked. He had never before been called just 'Braun' without the 'mister' by the old man.

'I had a letter from my German solicitor. My restitution has come through.' He paused, expecting a flood of questions. When none followed, he answered them anyway. 'One thousand four hundred and twenty pounds, in a lump sum, and sixty every month. After the solicitor's ten per cent I'll still have more than a thousand left. The lump sum is for loss of earnings, the pension is for being sick. Hitler is paying up after all. How lucky to have my kidney trouble. Without it, there wouldn't be any pension and they wouldn't have dealt with my case out of turn.' He pursed his lips and snorted. 'I hope *you* have got a little disease tucked away somewhere. If you haven't, they'll make you wait for years, hoping no doubt that you'll die and they can keep their money.'

'I doubt it. The money for compensation had been set aside as one of the conditions of the peace treaty with Germany. The money is there.'

'Are you claiming a lot?'

'Quite a lot.'

'Who's your solicitor?'

'Dr Schreiber.'

'Schreiber – Schreiber – Schreiber—' Kolm wondered, searching his memory. *'I've* consulted eleven German solicitors in London to find the best. I can't remember a Dr Schreiber.'

'He's in Paris. I used to live in Paris for a while. I had to apply there.'

'That explains it,' Kolm said, happy that he had missed

no opportunities. 'Well, I hope you get yours soon. Still better than my good wishes would be a juicy little ailment. Just a little chronic ailment.'

He went, content, and not guessing that the man he left behind felt equally satisfied with himself for not faltering once under his questions. Braun had been preparing himself for all sorts of answers to all sorts of questions, but he had never thought of being asked about restitution. Perhaps it would have been wiser to admit that he had never applied for it for reasons of pride, or because he had hesitated too long and missed the date by which the applications had to be filed.

He washed up, put away the dishes, gradually forgetting about Kolm and his life-long sinecure. He thought of Helen and would have given anything to talk to her. Who was the person who had helped her to find a place in the New Forest?

When he crossed the hall to his room, he stopped by the telephone and stood there for some time. She wouldn't be asleep yet. But he conquered his longing to call her, went to bed, and petitioned his Heavenly Computer that, somehow, he could persuade her to spend her holiday with him. Not in the New Forest but in a foreign country. There were trees everywhere. No one could take more care of her, and her tendency to suffer a 'heat hyperpyrexia' than he could. That's what she had in Bandol he was certain. The body temperature rising to 108° F. was an unshakable symptom. She had to avoid tropical conditions and alcoholic excess. He could even remember that extra normal humidity in the atmosphere enhanced the liability to this form of heat-stroke.

4

Next Wednesday, they *did* dine at the Festival Hall Restaurant. He fetched her at her office, or rather around the corner in Ebury Street, where she used to park her car. She arrived with Ann, but they stopped at the corner, she said something to her, left her standing and crossed the street alone to meet him. He waved to Ann who didn't seem to see it, just stood there staring.

'What's the matter with Ann?' he asked.

'I don't know.' She unlocked the car, started the engine. He had hardly time to clamber aboard. She turned left into Eccleston Street instead of following the shortest route, and at Eaton Square she turned left once more, so that they were in Elizabeth Street as before.

'What are you doing?' he inquired.

'I want to see if she's still there.'

She was.

All through dinner, he talked of Beethoven and the Ninth Symphony which they were going to hear. She let him talk, asked no questions – rather unusual for her. He knew that she hadn't taken in one single word.

'What are you watching me for?' she erupted.

'Something is the matter with you. What is it?'

'That stupid girl.'

'Ann?'

'She got wild because I was going out with you.'

'Did you promise to be with her?'

'Of course not.'

'Hasn't she got any friends of her own?'

'Heaps.'

'She is a pretty girl. Surely lots of men would love to take her out.'

'She's not interested in men.'

'How do you mean that?'

'Why don't *you* try to take her out?' she asked.

'I've got somebody to take out.'

She seemed in a strange mood. He had never seen her like this.

'Why do you take me out?' she suddenly wanted to know.

'I like you and I like to be with you.'

'Do you expect to have an affair with me?'

'Only if you want it too.'

'Well, I don't. You are like all the rest.'

'Did you expect me to be different?'

She didn't answer. He called the waiter, paid the bill; it amounted to just over four pounds. He would have to go to the bank tomorrow to draw another few pounds from his already depleted savings in order to last out till Friday. Silently, they went into the Hall, now almost full. The very old gentleman with the silver hair who had stared at her so disapprovingly at her first concert, sat next to her again, this time with a fat score on his lap. Between the pages, he had prepared tiny slips of paper on which he had scribbled notes in advance and which he now checked, like a general checks the deployment of his troops just before a decisive battle. He also tried the flow of his pen, planning to make further notes during the performance. Braun was about to remark on it, but changed his mind. She found it a remarkable coincidence to be sitting beside the unfriendly gentleman, but said nothing. She stared in silence, wondering why all those people who sat beyond the platform were divided into groups of ladies and gentlemen, similar to the ferry boat in one of Dan's stories. The boat plied across the St John river somewhere in Canada. She almost started to tell Karl about it, when the sullen expression on his face made her refrain. She returned her gaze to the packed rows beyond and slightly above the platform. Both groups wore black – the men dinner jackets – which added to her puzzlement. There were only a few dinner jackets in other parts of the auditorium. Perhaps those groups belonged to a conducted tour of some kind? Could be foreigners who didn't know the custom at the Festival Hall.

He, on the other hand, would have loved to explain to her that beyond the orchestra were seated the members of the Chorus, waiting for their turn much later, in the last movement of the symphony. The empty chairs in front of the conductor's rostrum were for the soloists who would file in just before the last movement started. For some time, he couldn't take in any of the music. Then, as if it had been claiming him, as if it had fought for him, it did get hold of his senses. It blotted out everything else. Music was a miraculous, bottomless purse: the more you took out of it, the more it kept for you.

She closed her eyes and, once again, she sat on top of the wall of the ambassador's garden. The next moment, she did something she had never experienced in any of her dreams: she felt herself sliding off the wall and landing on the lawn. Nobody bothered about her, nobody prevented her from walking on the springy grass, touching the cool rays of the fountain. She saw her friends sitting where she sat before, sticking out their tongues at her. She didn't mind.

The climax was at hand. Although he knew exactly what would follow, the anticipation engulfed him with breathless expectation. He always felt elated at this point. It had little to do with the score, it was nothing but blatant theatrical effect. He couldn't help touching her arm gently to warn her. She drew her elbow away, the silly goose. Now as at a command, the soloists and every single man and woman of the huge choir rose to their feet. A hush went through the crowded house. She saw from the corner of her eye that his hands were trembling. Only a mere second and Schiller's beautiful words 'To Friends!' will ring out. This little ignorant soul beside him would have no inkling of its meaning, even if she understood the German text.

He arrived home with a tremendous welcome piece of freedom floating on his chest. Both his spirit and his body were aware of its buoyancy. He still felt good from telling her, when he accompanied her to her car:

'I'd rather walk home if you wouldn't mind.'

'I don't mind.'

She drove off, almost running over the parking attendant who cursed, picked himself up and came over.

'Is she a friend of yours?'

'No fear,' Braun said breezily, quoting one of her expressions, and marched briskly towards the narrow path that led to the lane along the river. He adored strolling by the river, especially at night. He loved, when going to the Festival Hall, to get off the bus on Westminster Bridge, descend the few steps and walk along the Thames. The bridges were always alive and so was the shore. But the river seemed dead. The concept of contrast reigned supreme in the Universe. Nothing could be dead without other things being alive. Nothing could be beautiful without others being ugly; no happiness without sorrow, and no freedom without prisons.

He heard the phone ringing as soon as he entered the house from the street. On any other night, he would have run up the stairs to answer it. On this occasion, he took his time. Still the phone kept ringing. Deliberately he picked up the receiver.

'Is that you, Les?' a squeaky voice inquired.

'This is Karl Braun speaking.'

'Karl who?'

'Braun. Who do you wish to speak to?'

'Isn't that Mr Strawmuller's residence?'

'Strohmayer?'

'That's what I said.'

'I'll see if he's in.' Though he knew that someone would have answered the phone before, considering the length of time it had been ringing, he knocked on Strohmayer's door before he returned to report:

'He's not back yet, I'm afraid.'

'Are you the butler?'

'No, I'm the cook-general.'

'What are you cooking at this time of night, mon Herr?'

'What's the "mon-Herr" in aid of?' he asked, mildly amused.

'That's German, mate. You're German, aren't you? I can tell from your accent. Tell your boss in plain English that Anabelle phoned and he can jump in the lake.'

'I will, madam. Good night, madam.' The last bit she must have missed, for she banged down the receiver.

He wrote on the pad kept for messages: 'Madame Anabelle telephoned' – tore off the page and pushed it under Strohmayer's door.

5

There is nothing the logical mind resents more than the fact that logic is totally useless in matters illogical. It is futile to try to prove that a woman is unworthy of you and that, in fact, you are far better off without her. It is no use to argue that problems like People-Starving-In-The-Congo, or Man's-Landing-On-The-Moon-Imminent are infinitely more important than such trivial concerns as 'are you going with Jaroslav Kolm to the opera or with somebody called Helen Taylor?' For some unknown reason, by some unknown process, a bond has been created between her and you, a relationship similar to magnetism, and it cannot be broken by ordinary means. The question of how beneficial it is to a rusty nail to be drawn towards a magnet doesn't arise. Humanity and the Moon are enormous structures, but hold a match in front of your eyes and you can span the Moon.

Braun invited Lilian Hall to a concert.

They were to meet inside the main entrance, twenty minutes before eight. She arrived precisely on time, rather neatly dressed, insisting on buying her own programme and smelling strongly of wilted roses. She knew a surprising amount about music. She liked Wagner, Richard Strauss, and could tell an oboe from a clarinet. She had brought two lots of sandwiches to share: two of salmon, two of chicken.

'Restaurants are so wickedly expensive, the food is over-cooked and everything comes from tins, anyway. Don't you think so, Karl?'

He nodded, remembering Chinese duck and a waiter called Papi.

'If you queue up, Karl, for two cups of coffee, I'll spread myself by the balustrade. That's the best spot for a snack.'

She didn't know that he hated queueing and that the last thing he felt like was to spread by a balustrade in her company. He seriously considered welshing on her when he was out of her sight, leaving her to spread on her own. But then he would have to look for another job and he just couldn't stomach that at the present. He would have to answer advertisements, introduce himself to prospective bosses who would ask awkward questions, loving to poke into another person's private life. As if it mattered a hoot to piano tuning whether you spent seventy years in England or only seventeen. So he did not abscond. He got two cups of coffee and had his snack in the prescribed manner.

He wanted the concert to end, not guessing that the aftermath could be even tougher than what had gone on before. She knew which bus to catch to Pimlico and expressed a bashful wish to see how he lived. He lied that his landlady had laid down, and enforced, a law not to receive any female visitors after sunset. She wondered how such Victorian doctrines had survived in Pimlico and vowed to take matters into her own hands. She threatened to put on her thinking-cap and find a distinguished landlady who would be honoured to accept a paying guest with the qualities of Karl Braun.

'You'd be regarded as a member of the family but nevertheless independent. That's what you want, Karl! People who will look after you, and a room which is really your own, where you do what you please. With moderation, of course,' she added with a glance pregnant with promise. A fat piece of chicken fell out of her sandwich. She hesitated whether to salvage it, then shoved it out of sight with her foot as if she wished to perpetrate a sacrifice to the God of paying guests and their distinguished landladies.

Next week he went with Kolm to Covent Garden. A very pretty Russian soprano, with shapely voice and shapely legs, sang 'Aida'. Kolm let him pay for both programmes – not very generous for a man who had his pockets full of Hitler's money. Kolm also accepted a drink and did not offer a second round; it probably slipped his mind. Braun liked Kolm, the wise old Jew, who also prayed but did not make a secret of it.

'I know there is God, but I don't know what shape He is, and I don't know either *where* to look for Him.' Kolm cleaned his glasses as they took their seats, his lips quivered, he emitted a few snorts. 'Perhaps I'm God in my own right. Imagine, to all those bacteria in my bowels, the germs, to all organic matter in me, I am God. To a certain extent I rule over their fate. I inject penicillin and cause havoc. I might catch tuberculosis, destroy countless numbers of cells and, at the same time, provide happy living conditions for billions of tuberculosis bacilli.'

'Which, in their turn, came from another being. From another world, according to you. That's space-travel for you!'

'Don't laugh! Don't laugh! Do not atoms behave like stars and planets of the Universe? Travelling on pre-arranged courses and making up the chair you are sitting on? Perhaps you and I and also Aida and Covent Garden, London, England, the whole earth, are one single atom, hurtling along its path, adding up with billions of others to another chair, on which another superior being sits thinking that *he* is the hub of the Universe, while he in *his* turn is no more than just an infinitesimal part of another chair, *ad infinitum*.' He looked at Braun sharply. 'There is something the matter with you. Are you ill?'

'Not that I know of.'

'You have changed since I told you about my restitution. Have you taken anything?'

'What are you talking about?'

'I told you of the advantage of having a chronic ailment. You haven't embarked on anything foolish, have you?'

'Of course not.'

The lights were fading out, the last act was about to commence. Kolm lowered his voice.

'Don't do anything without consulting a doctor.'

'I won't,' whispered Braun. The curtain rose and gradually he got absorbed in the action on the stage. Usually he cared little about the story of an opera; he accepted, willingly, everything as a necessary evil, as the framework to

EMERIC PRESSBURGER

the music. Tonight it meant much more than that to him. He watched with fascination the two lovers in their tomb, as heavy blocks of stone were being dragged over the only opening, sealing it for ever – completing their entombment.

When they got home, Kolm made coffee in the kitchen. While it dripped through the filter, Kolm went into his room and returned with a miniature bottle of brandy. The prospect of a drop of brandy made him chummy.

'It's silly you calling me Kolm. Call me Jaroslay. Or, like my old friends used to call me, just Jaro. And I call you Karl, all right?'

'All right.'

'There is not much difference in age between us,' he cackled, spoiling Karl's pleasure in coffee *and* brandy. 'Prosit, Karl!'

'Prosit, Jaroslav!'

Kolm raised his glass, wistfully. Interspersed with his usual little snorts, he chuckled:

'Since I'm a rich man, thanks to Adolf Hitler, I can afford such extravagances.'

Back in his room, Braun sat in the dark and waited for a miracle. He sneered at the notion that he had become infatuated with a woman. Still, if he hadn't, the symptoms could fool anybody. In his despair, and to cut it down to size, he tried to analyse this headiness. He found it sat in the stomach and on the chest, pressing heavily on the one from within, on the other from above. He felt better in the morning, but his condition worsened as the day wore on. As if the microscopic cell in his brain that held her recorded image had swollen during the day to enormous size, obstructing the working of all the other cells – he could think of nothing but her. Almost as disturbing as the ailment itself, was the fact that he couldn't cope with it. To raise his self-respect, he imposed upon himself two conditions: not to telephone her and never to mention her name in his prayers. He stood firm for two long days, but on the third he succumbed and dialled her number. Nobody answered, but this did not diminish his defeat. Miserable, utterly humbled, he sank on his bed and prayed. He prayed that he should be allowed to hear from her. He prayed again unashamedly the following morning.

Nothing happened.

6

The following day, Lilian persuaded him to share her sandwiches at the office. She had news for him. At long last she had found a lovely room for him.

'Only three pounds ten! And all the freedom you want. I'll take you there tonight.'

'Not tonight, Lilian.'

'Why not?'

'I have to see my doctor,' he lied.

'Is anything the matter, Karl?'

She sounded most concerned. He wondered what made him so annoyed about her anxiety on his behalf? She meant well, she liked him, she helped him whenever she could. He made a silent vow to be nice and patient with her. But a moment later he flew into a temper again.

She said: 'I thought you looked rather depressed, Karl.

But aren't we all depressed at times? I have been depressed ever since I came in this morning. And over a trifle.'

'What happened?' he asked, hoping to steer her off prying into his private affairs by relating hers.

'I overheard a man talking to Jack Cartwright. He wanted work. When Jack told him that there were no vacancies, he started to agitate – not against Jack as you would expect – against foreigners in general. Aliens who take honest Englishmen's jobs. "In every firm, wherever you go, you find foreigners getting the plum jobs!" he shouted. He swore, and it was quite impossible to stop him. "It's the same everywhere!" he interrupted Jack who tried to explain. "Especially the Germans! You find them in every office. In every factory. I bet my soul it's the same here!" Jack told him it wasn't any business of his. But I can't stand stupidity. You know how I am, Karl. I told him that we'd got you and you are the best tuner and repairer we've ever had. Better than any of our honest English tuners! And I meant it.'

'What did he look like?' Karl asked.

'Outdoor type. You know, lots of our young men get it from sailing. Sunburnt. Young. Quite intelligent. That annoyed me even more. A real trouble-maker.'

'What sort of work did he want?'

'He never mentioned – come to think of it. I don't think he knew himself. Jack's patience got exhausted, too. At last! You know what an enormous fellow Jack is? When old Jack stood up the chap piped down, I can tell you.'

The afternoon dragged on as if it would never end. He couldn't keep his mind on his work. Who was this man snooping in piano factories? Had the police tumbled on a clue that led them to piano factories so that now they were patiently and thoroughly checking every single one of them? It was the way the police worked. If a taxi-cab had been reported near the site of a crime, they would check every single cab rank to find it.

But there had been no crime! Why would the police be interested? Perhaps the police had nothing to do with it. It could be the work of those bloodhounds in Ludwigsburg: the Central Office for Prosecution of Nazi Crimes. Aren't they offering blood-money to informers? They must have sent somebody over. One of their so-called State Prosecutors . . . No, the man who did the dirty work wouldn't be a German. They had hired a native over here. They'd got plenty of money and there are plenty of Englishmen to do the job. Somebody who knew how to look for a clue and how to follow it up once he had found it. A retired inspector from Scotland Yard, perhaps. Some of them do take jobs with private investigating firms, and, having connections in police circles, get the occasional tip-off from their ex-colleagues . . . No, again. The man who called on Jack Cartwright was a young man. Probably one of those ex-army chaps one hears about. This one had been trained for Intelligence work and was then discarded by the army. Or got out of his own choice to try his luck in a civilian occupation, exchanging an officer's cap for a bowler hat. 'Golden Bowlers' they call them. One of those eager young fellows who happens to know everybody, can open any door, is itching to make good. His name is Johnny, or Mike or Sam. He's about thirty to thirty-two, left the army four to five years ago, tried his hand at a number of things, sold encyclopaedias, insurance policies, and Spanish building sites. Braun knew the type. Easy-going, good manners, rather nice. Has a vintage car and sails a boat. The boat is moored somewhere where he knows the harbourmaster. Now he is selling it – he needs the cash. He put an ad in *The Times*, one of those funny ads, which appeal only to people with similar background. He is very much concerned about the person who will get his boat. To his great disappointment, a foreigner arrives on the London train. Johnny doesn't trust foreigners, but shows him the boat all the same. They sail out of the harbour – the boat is a real beauty – then the stranger decides to show his hand: 'Sorry, I'm here under false pretences. Though I read your ad with interest, I'm not really interested in your "de-bugged, freshly painted, spring-cleaned boat", nor in its "well-darned sail". I'm interested in you. I need a man to do a little investigation for us. As soon as I asked your Colonel McFarlane, he said: Try Johnny, he's the man for you. Johnny has tried every bloody thing since he left Army Intelligence, he couldn't settle down. He's your man.'

Braun could see it all. He could draw the fellow. Tall, good body, strong nose, hard eyes from the sea, bronzed complexion from outdoor life. He would listen patiently to what the man from Ludwigsburg had to say and then give his opinion: 'You say, sir, we've got a corpse – found in the London Tube. But we can't count on Scotland Yard for we haven't got a crime. The police are the same everywhere. Big crime – big effort. Little crime – little effort. No crime – no effort at all. Now tell me from the beginning, sir.'

'On Friday, 12th February, the body of a big man had been found in the first train on the Circle Line of the London Underground Railway. The man had an Argentinean passport, in the name of Enrico Stample. He had arrived by sea from Buenos Aires two days ago, taken a room in a small hotel called the Budge's Walk Hotel. His ship, the S.S. *Mendoza*, continued to Hamburg, where we interviewed the purser and a cabin steward. Both men agreed that Señor Stample suffered excruciating headaches but refused to see the ship's doctor. The Federal Bueau for Investigating War Criminals has a comprehensive filing system in Ludwigsburg, near Stuttgart. We established in next to no time that Enrico Stample was really S.S. Colonel Heinrich von Stampel, Intelligence Officer at the concentration camp in Wittau. His friends called him "Hein". He had his blood-group tattooed in his armpit. Officers of the S.S. did this invariably in case an injury necessitated a blood transfusion. Our files disclosed that there was nothing against von Stampel and we were not interested in him. Except for one reason: he used to be very close to Dr Otto Reitmüller, who happens to be just about the biggest fish we are after ... No, he's not the doctor who experimented with freezing people alive. He was a brain surgeon. He experimented with sawing people's heads open and chopping up their brains. He had research going to discover how brain cells stored memory. He put a person under hypnosis, bid him tell his personal story in great detail and then he operated. As soon as the patient recovered, he heard his story once again, noted the discrepancies and operated again, cutting out another minute colony of cells. *Ad infinitum.*

75

Or, rather: *ad finitum*. The end came soon enough. He was a brilliant young surgeon. A fanatic. A cultured man, a fine musician, an accomplished violinist. Formed an excellent string-quartet in camp. Got married, had a baby. Actually, von Stampel was the baby's godfather. Dr Reitmüller treated the colonel for some nervous ailment. They left Germany together after the collapse of the German forces. Von Stampel turned up in Buenos Aires without the doctor. We had an agent watching him for some time in the hope that he might get in touch with his friend, but he never did . . . Yes, we know what happened to the doctor's wife and kid. They were both killed in an air raid on Hamburg, 24th July, 1943. He has no surviving relatives. His experiments were carried out in comparative seclusion, he got in no contact with persons outside his compound . . . Now, I don't say that von Stampel had come to London to find his friend, but he might have done. Consider the facts. He refused to see a doctor on board the ship. Why? Perhaps he hoped to see a doctor who had helped him before, who knew the nature of his ailment. What made him travel on the Underground at 5.40 in the morning? Perhaps he met somebody. An empty train is a very convenient place for people to meet when they don't wish to be overheard. They can leave at different stations. They can even join the train at different stations . . .'

So, Johnny got to work. He established that the police had notified the Argentinean Embassy, the Embassy sent a minor official to the mortuary who claimed the corpse and the corpse's possessions. Among them Johnny found a torn envelope and on the back of this envelope several telephone numbers. He dialled them all. After the fifth, he announced: 'Well, I'm damned. They are piano factories, the whole bloody lot!'

When he got this far, Braun forced himself to pause. What was happening to him lately? When had he lost his unerring faculty of evaluating things? Heinrich von Stampel died in February. Now it was July. If they had discovered a connection between Hein and himself, they would have scrutinized every possible clue a long time ago. Braun was almost ashamed of himself. Anybody could make mountains out of molehills. He, a scientist, who prided himself on his logical mind, he should know better. The natural function of a logical mind was to *reduce* mountains to molehills, not the other way round.

And when several days passed and nothing noteworthy happened, he settled down to routine activities once more.

CHAPTER FOUR

1

THE FACTORY PLANNED to close down for a fortnight from the last week-end in July. This impending holiday stood, for most employees, as a watershed: it divided the immediate future from the immediate past. Mr Parsons, the junior partner, had bought a small villa in Sardinia unseen, and against the prevailing currency regulations. He and his wife were going to inspect it and spend the first of countless vacations in it. Jack Cartwright intended to plead with Mrs Cartwright, while motoring down to Cornwall, that he yearned to be in the Lake District right now, to pursue the only hobby in his life: climbing the fells there. Lilian Hall would set out to stay with her widowed mother who kept a boarding-house in Windermere, and tell her that she had met a wonderful man in London. Although a foreigner and at present in a rather lowly position, this gentleman had the greatest potentials and if mother would consider parting with two thousand pounds, she could persuade him to start a Piano-Tuning-Polishing-and-Removal business. With Lilian's experience and eternal partnership, such an undertaking would surely prosper and, of course, she wouldn't wear white in church;

she firmly believed white to be unsuitable for any bride over thirty-five . . . Karl Braun had put off moving from Pimlico to that room with all-the-freedom-he-wanted till after the holiday, since (that was his story) he had pledged himself to stay till the end of September at Mrs Felton's place who – he lied – had redecorated his room with the understanding that he stayed at least three months. Even Strohmayer's and Kolm's activities seemed to be affected by the piano factory's vacation. When Strohmayer learnt that Braun might take a continental holiday, he made an offer.

'I'll let your room for the fortnight to one of those distinguished visitors to Britain and we'll go fifty-fifty.'

Kolm immediately protested.

'You can't do that. I know your distingished visitors. They make an unholy mess in the bathroom and talk incessantly on the phone. I want to be able to sleep at night.'

'Why don't you take a holiday yourself?' Strohmayer asked. 'You've got plenty of money. You could go to Prague for a fortnight, sit in the cafés and read all the Russian, Bulgarian and Roumanian newspapers there, stamped "Stolen in the Vladimir Ilyich Lenin Café" or whatever it's called now.' This made Kolm rather thoughtful, and when Strohmayer added, with his roguish grin: 'And I'll let your room too – fifty-fifty!' Kolm said: 'I'll ring the Czechoslovakian Consulate tomorrow.'

When he and Braun met in the kitchen the same evening, he already had news. 'I can have the visa and can go to Prague whenever I like. And . . .' He paused to emphasize what was coming, 'and I have bought a violin!' When he saw the astonishment on Braun's face, he hastened to reassure him. 'Don't be afraid. I won't practise when you are here. I'll do it when I am alone in the flat.'

'I didn't know you played the fiddle,' Braun said.

'There are many things you don't know, Karl,' the old man chuckled. 'I used to be quite a fiddler. On the amateur scale, of course. If you ever come across a small piano and, if the price is reasonable, I might buy it. I know you play it. You could keep it in your room in the window corner opposite your bed. And we could play simple things together, things like the Sonatinas by Schubert, you know: to-de-doooo-ta-da-dam-dam-dam-dam-daaaa . . .' He hummed it atrociously out of tune. Braun knew it well and began to croon the piano part, to Kolm's delight. 'That's it! Isn't it wonderful?'

But Braun's suspicions had been aroused already. Like bubbles in fizzy water, as soon as the bottle top is removed.

'You never mentioned you played . . .'

'I never thought of it.'

'When did you have your last violin?'

'Not since Prague. I left it there. Would you like to see it?'

'No, thanks. I know nothing about them.'

'It's lovely. Like a little jewel. I'll let you hold it if you promise not to drop it.'

'Another time, Jaroslav. I have to go out now. I'm late already. Sorry.'

He got away safely, ran down the stairs, hurried along Pimlico Road. He would have loved to see whether Kolm stood in the window, but he dared not give away that he cared. He felt sure that Kolm was watching him from above.

Perhaps it would have been wiser to face that violin than to raise his suspicions. On the other hand, if that fiddle was meant to be a trap, he wouldn't generate any suspicion. The suspicions would already be there.

They could get Kolm to spy on him because of his hatred for anything connected with the Third Reich. Strohmayer would do it for money. They were offering 10,000 marks – nine hundred and ten pounds! Strohmayer had never seen that much money in his whole life. He would probably denounce his own brother for ninety pounds and he would inform on anybody for nine.

The only person who stood above suspicion was Helen. She never sought his friendship. He wished she did. There was a sudden rush of blood to his head. He turned, went back to the Coach Station, found an empty phone box and dialled her number. Immediately he heard her voice.

'This is Karl,' he began, and had to clear his throat.

'You know, that's funny. We were just talking about you.' She sounded delighted.

'Who are "we"?'

'Ann is here. I just told her that you never ask me out, never even phone me any more. You've probably found another girl, I said, someone prettier and more intelligent than me.'

'When can I see you?'

'What are you doing later? Ann is just going.'

'Would you like me to pick you up?' he asked, marvelling how easily everything went.

'You have picked me up already – in that mews, remember?' She giggled. 'I don't want you to spend money on taxis. I'll pick *you* up.'

'When?'

'Half an hour. I'll hoot downstairs. I warn you, I'm very hungry.'

'Do you feel like eating Chinese?'

'I'm fainting at the thought of it.'

He, too, felt a little faint. If he hurried, he had time to change. He arrived, breathless, at the door of the flat. An unpleasant screeching sound greeted him. A sound that he would have called dismal on any other occasion. Kolm was practising the violin! He was trying to play the Sonatina by Schubert. Earlier Kolm had hummed it in the most atrocious manner, now he played it even more unpardonably. And still it filled Braun's heart with nothing but harmony.

By the time she arrived, it was raining again. She made up for being late by hooting louder and more often than at other times. He thought she looked younger than the last time he saw her, more relaxed and more carefree.

'It takes you a hell of a long time to come down!' she laughed, to avoid being ticked off. She held her cheek for him to kiss; a thing she had never done before.

A young waiter, who looked like a Cypriot, but who pronounced his 'r's the Chinese way, informed them that he had only one table.

'We only need one,' Helen told him. 'Where's Papi?'

It transpired that Papi had been ill and had gone to recuperate by the sea. Not the China Sea, but the English Channel – somehow, she thought, it didn't sound right.

'What about *your* holiday?' Karl asked her, while the waiter led them across the crowded room, and went on probing.

'The table is by the coat-rack, miss.'

They could see the coat-rack but not the table. Only when they stood right in front of it, did they realize that it had been hidden under the pile of steaming raincoats. Whenever people were leaving and lifted off half a dozen macintoshes from the pegs to find their own, eating or even sitting there, proved to be a perilous occupation.

'You haven't answered my question yet,' he reminded her. 'What about the New Forest?'

'Oh, that,' she sighed, 'that's all over. I'm going with Daphne.'

'Who's Daphne?'

'Daphne Hollywell. She's married to Tom Hollywell. We used to know them when I was married. They live near Bagshot. He's crazy about fishing; she's nuts about France.'

'Why don't they go fishing in France?'

'That's exactly what they're doing. You *are* clever, Karl.'

'Where are they going?'

'Have you ever heard of the river Tarn in Southern France?'

'Never.'

'Well, that's where they're going. They've asked me to stay with them. I can share a room with Daphne.'

'Doesn't her husband want to share a room with her?'

'He probably does. But he gets up every morning at 4.30 to catch trout and she's sick and tired of being woken up early every single day on her holiday. So they booked separate rooms, you see?'

'I see.'

'You're not very enthusiastic about it, are you?'

'Why should I be enthusiastic?'

'Aren't you glad that I can go to France for my holiday? I couldn't afford it without sharing a room with Daphne.'

This made him very silent. It was some time before he spoke again.

'When's Eve coming back?'

'August 16th. I'll be back long before that.'

'How is she?'

'Grand. I had a letter from Dan. The first ever. Do you know he can't spell at all? He thinks I'm bringing her up just fine. You don't know how much that means coming from Dan.'

'And what about the sun in Southern France?'

'Oh, Daphne doesn't think it'll hurt.'

'How does she know?'

'She has been there before. Many times. I just have to stay in the shade. Under a plane-tree, if you please! And what about you?'

'I might go to Paris,' he said miserably.

'You don't seem to be very cheerful about it. I'd love to go to Paris if I were you. Do you think I could stop over in Paris on my way to the river Tarn?'

'Are you going with those Bagshots or on your own?'

She gave him a reprimanding glance.

'They are going this coming Saturday. Daphne will fetch me at a station called Millau on Sunday, August 1st. The train arrives at nine in the morning from Paris.'

'I tell you what. You come with me to Paris the Saturday morning and travel to Millau Sunday night.'

'Wouldn't it cost too much?'

'Don't worry about that.'

'I'll think about it.'

He felt that if he could find the right words now, she would do it.

'I could show you all the places I used to go to. The cafés where I sat . . .'

'The girls I went to bed with,' she carried on for him.

He laughed.

'What are you laughing about? What were you thinking just now?'

'I'll show you the Brasserie Lorraine where I used to eat oysters every morning in the season. My God, they were cheap!'

'You weren't thinking of oysters just now. Be honest, Karl! What were you thinking?'

'Oysters. I used to have a pretty little furnished place in the Rue Quentin-Bochart, off the Champs-Elysées. With some friends, we used to invite lots of nice girls and give them oysters. You could buy a small barrel for next to nothing. We bought little glass pearls and concealed them under the flesh of the oysters. You should have seen the girls! One girl would be generous and offer to share the proceeds from the sale of the pearl she found. Others would keep their pearls hidden under their tongues for hours in order to keep their suddenly found riches secret.'

'A very mean thing to do.'

'Yes, but very funny.'

'When was that? When did you go to Paris?'

'Nineteen thirty-three.'

'My God, I wasn't born then.'

He almost asked her when she was born, but it occurred to him that she might put the same question to him, and he kept silent. Instead, he said:

'My first little flat in Paris! With its iron-railed balcony running across the whole width of the building, on every floor, the tall french windows with their grey shutters. And every refugee astonished at my luck to have found it. You know, the shortage in small flats was then even greater than today. No new houses had been built during the war. Nobody could understand how I managed to get a flat. Just walked into a house with a friend to interpret for me, and asked the concierge: Is there anything to let? She said: Yes. I moved in the following day. I couldn't believe my luck. The flat had been freshly decorated, new carpets on the floor, new wallpapers, brand-new curtains – it must have been the only place recently done up in the whole district. Only weeks later, did I hear that a frightful murder had been committed in that flat, the body had been discovered under the floorboards, the victim had torn the curtains to shreds in a death struggle, the walls splashed with blood . . .'

'No wonder it had to be redecorated,' she said.

'The case had been spread over the headlines for weeks. Only foreigners, like myself, who never read the papers, knew nothing about it.'

'Was there a ghost in the flat?'

'If there was, I never saw it.'

'Have you ever seen a ghost? An apparition you couldn't explain? A bad spirit? Or a good spirit?'

'I don't believe in spirits.'

'I do! You must have seen a good spirit some time.'

'Only once.' He seemed to comb his memory, either to recall the event, or for words to explain it. 'It happened when I left Germany.'

She leant forward, her elbows on the table, her head propped up on her two palms, in expectation.

'Why did you leave Germany? You never told me.'

'I had been illustrating an article in a Berlin magazine – I told you I was a photographer – some political piece about the rise of Hitler, how-he-came-to-power-sort-of-thing. For this, they were looking for me. Somebody tipped me off. The same night I took the train to Aachen on the Belgian border. I knew an editor in Cologne. He got me an exit permit to do a job for him in Bruges. I was to meet his reporter there. Probably nobody wanted to take the risk of leaving in my company. I never thought he'd get an exit permit for me, but he did. If there was already a warrant for my arrest, it hadn't arrived yet at the border. I chose the night train to cross the border – one thinks that it's easier to hide at night. Passport control took place before boarding the train, but they had another go *in* the train. An officer – leather belt, shining boots, tight-fitting uniform, sharp eyes, words like whips – came in; his two henchmen waited in the corridor. Every seat was occupied. I sat on the second seat from the window, facing the engine. For no apparent reason, the officer singled me out. He kept on turning the pages of my passport. Those two minutes were the longest spell of time in my whole life. I knew my hands were trembling. I didn't dare to move them for fear of drawing his attention to them. At that moment, a young woman – she sat next to me but I hadn't noticed her before – threw her coat into my lap to mind while she rummaged in her handbag for some documents no one had asked for. It couldn't be clearer: she did it to help me to hide my trembling hands. The officer handed my passport back, saluted and left. The train started to move, first slowly, then it accelerated and we were in Belgium.'

'And?' She inhaled deeply, like those people at the concert who held their breath till the end of a movement in the music. 'You opened your eyes and she had disappeared! Yes?'

'Nothing of the sort. She turned out to be the woman reporter of my editor-friend in Cologne. We travelled together to Bruges. We had quite a good time there, actually.'

'You would!'

A young man came towards them, lifted a great pile of coats from the rack and, when he saw the gathering storm in her eyes, apologized for swinging his mac against her hair.

'You owe me half a crown!' she commanded.

'You're joking,' the youth objected.

'For siphoning the gravy from my plate,' she challenged him.

The young man produced a wad of bills.

'Got change for a fiver?'

'Certainly.'

She opened her bag and tore open her pay envelope. To the man's surprise, she counted the correct change into his hand and pocketed his five-pound note.

2

Lilian grew impatient with him about his attitude towards the lodging she had got for him.

'You must do something about it, Karl! You really must!'

'I know, Lilian,' he agreed, with a guilty smile. If he had produced an excuse for his behaviour, she would have attacked it.

'She's no ordinary landlady, I told you. You'll be more like an independent member of the family, than just a lodger.'

'Yes, Lilian,' he concurred.

Only now did she come to the point.

'Happily, she'll be at the Grummets' on the 24th.'

'I'm afraid, Lilian, the 24th is quite impossible for me.'

'Now, really, Karl. You can't have anything more important than that. There's no better way to meet her than socially. I well remember I asked you to the Grummets' last year and you refused then, too. You said you couldn't manage it at such short notice. I've got a very good memory, Karl. I'm giving you a whole week's notice now. You can rearrange whatever appointments you have. You haven't got anything against the Grummets, have you? You have never set eyes on them. She went to school with my mother. They give this one party every year on their wedding anniversary.'

He remained adamant.

'Sorry, Lillian. I can't.'

The tiny sparks in his brain were busy trying to find an answer to the question that was sure to follow. It did.

'What is this earth-shaking activity you can't postpone from the 24th?'

'Dr Schreiber is coming from Paris. The solicitor who handles my restitution claim.'

'*What* claim?'

'People who suffered a loss of earnings, or loss of property due to the Nazis, can claim compensation from Germany. It will amount, in my case, to a substantial sum of money. Several thousand pounds, in fact.'

She suddenly saw herself telling her mother in Windermere: All right, mother dear, we'll do it then on Karl's money. He's coming in to a considerable fortune any day now. I thought you wished to help, but we can do without. Sorry to have mentioned it.

'That's different, of course. But can't your solicitor . . .' Lilian made this last feeble effort. But he now got quite fluent in telling his story.

'I'm afraid not, Lilian. You see, he's a very busy man in Paris, has only a handful of clients in London. Whenever he comes to London, every hour of his time is allocated weeks in advance.'

In previous years he had been able to deal effortlessly with his problem of the 24th of July. He had only casual acquaintances then who were satisfied with such excuses as an indefinable indisposition from which he could recover the next day. Even listening to a special radio programme, or to finish reading a library book, satisfied them. More often than not, he had no problem at all. He just stayed at home alone, did nothing, allowed the dull pain to flood his mind and let the few memories of Ilse and the baby float in it. The memories were like flimsy paper boats; the passing years made more and more of them founder and sink into oblivion. Still, while only a single one remained afloat, true to training and tradition, the good skipper, Karl Braun, would persevere with his efforts to salvage them.

Once, years ago, on the 24th July, when the sea of his memory still resembled a regatta, he called at the newspaper library in Colindale. He felt a compulsion to read what the British Press had to say on the subject. They did report it, at great length and, he thought, with a certain unholy joy in the headlines. 'Concentrated Bombing of Hamburg. Last Night More Than a Thousand Aircraft of Bomber Command Delivered a Concentrated Retaliatory Attack on the City of Hamburg. Eleven of Our Aircraft Failed to Return.' The gloating had been due, no doubt, to Göring's boast predicting complete immunity from air attacks on the Fatherland. Braun couldn't help wondering about the eleven bombers that had perished over Hamburg, curious whether the one that caused the death of his wife and child happened to be among them.

3

'Daphne and Tom Hollywell are in town on Saturday,' she said, thus making it unnecessary for him to invent a lie as he had had to for Lilian, in order to be left alone on the twenty-second anniversary of that fatal air raid on Hamburg. 'Tell me about Paris!' she demanded.

'The future or the past?'

She looked puzzled. 'What do you mean? You know, Karl, sometimes I can't understand you at all. Probably it's your lack of English.'

'Shall I tell you what you and I would be doing in Paris, or what *I* have done there?'

'Both.'

It was the first time that she gave the slightest indication of not minding going with him. Not actually falling in with the idea, but letting it lapse by default.

'Did you tell the Bagshots?'

'What have the Bagshots got to do with it?' she flared up, but she added a moment later, 'Do you think I might run into trouble? Because of Eve? I can't afford to get a bad name. I told you about the judge.'

'Nobody will spy on you in Paris.'

She sighed.

'I suppose not. They need their spies for more important delinquents. Anyway, Daphne doesn't mind.' She realized the inconsistency of this information and hastened to explain: 'I *had* to tell her when to expect me. But I must pay my own expenses.'

'No.'

'Let me pay for my room. You pay all the rest, but let me pay for my room.'

Now he understood. She was trying to establish that she expected to have a room of her own.

'No, I've got the money and I'll pay for everything: your room and my room and the rest.'

'How can you save anything with me costing you so much?'

'I saved it before I knew you. And I'm coming into a fortune soon.' For a second, he played with the idea of telling her the same story he had told Lilian, but he decided to differentiate between them, even in the lies he told them. 'Someone who owed me money for a long time, wants to pay it back.'

'Did you lend it to him in Germany?' He nodded. 'I thought so,' she said. 'You couldn't have saved much here, could you?'

They were driving through Hyde Park after Covent Garden. He often insisted on escorting her home, although the fact that they were travelling in *her* car scaled down somewhat his self-esteem and his continental chivalry. Having left her, he took a bus, or walked all the way home. He never made use of the Underground. They drove over the bridge that spans the Serpentine. She slowed down.

'Have you ever been locked in Hyde Park?'

'Never.'

She shuddered and stopped at the little roundabout leading to North Gate.

'It was ghastly. I found this gate closed. I drove to the next – closed, too. You imagine there's a sex-maniac behind every bush. The same feeling as when you're passing over a level crossing and the gates begin to close just when you are crossing the tracks. The train can be on top of you before you know it.'

'With all those sex-maniacs on it.'

She ignored this entirely.

'Aren't you curious how I got out? I stopped right here, where we are now, got out hoping to climb over, leaving the car behind – nobody could steal it with all the gates closed – would you believe it, it wasn't locked at all. Just pushed to. I opened it and drove through, just like that!' She tried to snap her fingers but she didn't know how. 'That's another thing I must learn.' In the same breath, she continued: 'I left their blooming gate wide open. I think they deserved it, don't you?' She saw him looking at his watch. 'Are you afraid to be locked in with me?' Her eyes laughed like two devils.

'You can't frighten me,' he said. 'I know the gates are only pushed to. Never locked.'

'All right. Let's see what happens.'

There was not a soul in sight except the traffic in Bayswater Road, but that moved outside the rails, beyond the bushes, in another world. She kept on straining her eyes for a policeman, or for a park warden. Or she just wished to avoid looking into his face.

'You know why I am going to Paris with you? Because you are the only man who didn't try to kiss me.'

'I know you wouldn't like me to.'

'I must be very careful,' she said, staring through the windscreen as if she wanted to make a confession, but doubted that the man behind the screen was a priest.

Now, quite unexpectedly, a chap on a bicycle arrived from outside the park, with an oil-lamp dangling in his free hand. He jumped off, unhooked one wing of the gate when he spotted the car.

'Hey! You! Want to be locked in for the night?'

She started the engine and very, very leisurely, drove towards the exit.

'Come on! Come on! Don't you know the regulation?'

She stopped right in front of him and leaned out.

'Still three minutes to go,' she laughed.

'Not on my watch,' the man replied, showing his large timepiece.

'My car can't go any faster,' she shrugged her shoulders.

'Is that a car?' the man asked.

'It's a hearse, really,' she said. 'The gentleman and I are both dead. We're looking for the graveyard. Can you direct us?'

'Get on with you!' He wanted to give the car a shove but,

she slipped into gear, her car leapt forward, and they were in Bayswater Road.

As always she halted at the corner and he had to get out. She never let herself be seen with him close to her place and she had never asked him up to her home. As if she suspected her legendary judge to be lurking in one of the dark doorways, spying on her.

Now that she had acquired the habit of offering her cheek to be kissed, she quickly scanned the street for danger. 'I have to think of my reputation.'

He kissed her cheek and asked:

'How does it feel?'

'Oh – I don't know.'

'Let me do it again. And watch it now.'

She held out her other cheek, he kissed that too. She pursed her lips as if sampling it. Finally, she said:

'Unusual. But not bad.'

She ran up the stairs. He waited until she closed the door behind her and started his long walk home.

Would she go to Paris with him? – he thought. And if she did, would she go because she trusted him or because she had not considered him as a reasonable risk?

Whatever her motive, to be with her for two whole days and all alone, held something enchanting. Sex didn't come into it at all.

At home he pulled down the blind, sat on his bed and, by the light of his bedside lamp, he wrote: 'B. Karl'. And again: 'B. Karl'. And again and again, until his hand got stiff. He scribbled two pages full of it, two pages on both sides. Until he felt confident that he could do it with a steady pulse. The little flourish at the end of it seemed to have just the right curve. He awarded himself silent praise. Not only for his skill, but also for the intelligence of his younger self for having suggested to Hein in Zürich:

'We deposit the money in the bank. The signatures on the deposit-card must be such that we shall remember them even if we don't touch this money for years. The name on my passport says: Karl Braun. I'll sign myself as "B. Karl". It's different, but it will be part of my name from now on. I shall never forget to sign it.'

They were sitting in the Bahnhof Restaurant, sad and happy at the same time. Sad because so much had been lost and glad because they had managed to cross the border. He reminded Hein how often he had condemned the Swiss for their country's neutrality during the war.

'The place is swarming with British spies,' Hein used to say. 'We ought to crush them. We could do it in a day. Occupy the whole bloody country. In doing so, we would cut one of the main routes for escaping prisoners of war, too. And couldn't we use Swiss money for our depleted economy! I don't understand why the Führer doesn't do it!' Now Hein had changed his tune. 'You know why our leaders tolerated the Swiss? To preserve a corner they could buzz off to when the war was lost.'

Karl didn't argue with him. They changed their English pounds into Swiss money and deposited the lot in a bank in the little square just off the Bahnhofstrasse, the principal shopping street that ran from the Main Station down to the lake. They were led into a private office, had supplied specimen signatures and got a number for their new account. Either of them could draw from it – they trusted each other implicitly. They stayed together for a whole week, until Hein got confirmation from Buenos Aires about the estancia which had given shelter to many a German-in-need in those terrible times.

He signed 'B. Karl' once more. It wasn't bad at all. If a letter looked slightly different, it didn't matter. Bank clerks knew that every signature would develop to a certain degree in the span of twenty years.

There was just another matter: the number of their account. But he would never forget that in a thousand years. '3121968'.

'Without this number we can never touch the money,' Hein said, anxiously. 'To write it down is dangerous. You, Karl, have done more research in the matter of how memory works than anyone else. Now you show me how I can remember it.'

Karl examined the receipt from the bank. It didn't take him long.

'Anything memorable happen in 1908?'

'I was born then,' Hein said.

'Excellent. You will be sixty in 1968. You'll remember that. Or, if you don't, think of the end of the First World War. It'll have its fiftieth anniversary in 1968. Now think of an absurd date. The 31st February, 1968. February is the second month of the year, right? Now: 31–2–1968. There you have it. Or, if this date is too absurd for you, think of the 3rd December, 1968. Comes to the same thing.' Hein wrote down both dates and chose the more conventional

'3rd December'. But Karl always remembered it as the 31st
February, 1968.

4

Wherever Karl and Helen went – opera, theatre, or concert – he liked to be there early. He made her read the
names of the cast, the blurb about the composer or author
and, in the case of an opera, the story of the libretto. She
had become quite an expert. Not a great expert (for that
you've got to grow hair in your ears), but she knew such
things as 'Tschaikovsky wrote a piece called "1912" (or
was it "1812"?); into it he had woven the French National
Anthem and then he crushed it with that Russian theme:
"Ta-ta-ta-tatatata-ta-tat-taa" to show that the French had
been defeated in that year of . . . well, whatever it was.' She
had in mind to visit, one of these days, Napoleon's statue
in Trafalgar Square (or was it at the end of Lower Regent
Street?) – 'Napoleon's Column' they called it. You only had
to ask a bobby, he'd tell you. Beethoven wrote a symphony
to honour Napoleon but when he found out that Napoleon
was letting him down, he added a funeral march, meaning:
Napoleon, my boy, you're dead and buried as far as I'm
concerned! Knowing such personal matters about a composer, or his work, added much interest to the music, like
knowing lots of private gossip about film stars.

Now she was sitting on the First Balcony with Karl,
reading the story of the 'Rosenkavalier'. He saw her eyes
getting moist with grief.

'It's so terribly sad,' she explained her tears.

'Wait until you hear the music. When this lovely woman – always surrounded by admirers – realizes that she is getting old, and she renounces her young lover to a young girl and, at the same time we know she surrenders also her youth – it is heartbreaking.'

She stared at him in surprise.

'I'm not crying for her!' She seemed quite hurt. 'What about that poor old man?'

'What poor old man?'

'The one who came from the country, probably quite a long way too. There were not even trains in those days, were there?'

'In the eighteenth century? Certainly not.'

'There you are. Why shouldn't he marry a young girl if he wants to? The girl was willing, wasn't she? Until that young fellow with that silver rose barged in. That young chap could have got another girl any time. But for that old gentleman, it won't be so easy, will it, honestly?'

The lights were lowered, her argument had to stop for the time being. The curtain rose. She couldn't believe her eyes.

'Look, Karl! Her young man is a girl!'

'Shhht!' A very thin lady called her to order from the left.

'Later!' Karl whispered back.

'Very interesting,' she observed, almost in her natural voice, forgetting everything else for the moment. This provoked more hostile censure from the people around them.

During the interval, he tried to explain.

'On the stage, especially in an opera, there's much illusion. A young woman plays the part of a young man because Strauss felt, that with a soprano and a mezzo-soprano, he could express more beautifully what he wished to express.'

'Yes, but two women! Now, you wouldn't like two men in their parts, would you?'

'It would be monstrous. Although . . .'

'I should say so. What do you mean "Although . . ."? You're not going to defend it, are you?'

'It's all convention. There were times when men with high, falsetto voices took the parts of women and people accepted them. So many things depend on conventions. We adjust ourselves to them. We got used to drinking beer from a tankard and not from a spoon, and eating soup with a spoon and not drinking it from a tankard. You wear jeans without embarrassment. But if you put a skirt over your jeans and I asked you to lift your skirt, you would be embarrassed. Why?'

'I wouldn't be.'

'You are an exception.'

She loved listening to him arguing, playing with ideas, braiding them into a strong logical cord and tying the opposition into knots with it.

'The only thing I like about men,' she said, 'is the way their minds work.'

She adored 'Rosenkavalier', but she did not change her mind about the old roué, called Baron Ochs. He remained her chosen character, who deserved her pity and sympathy.

'Now, in Paris, they would put up tables and chairs here,' he said. He had little more than their holiday in mind these days. They were eating their golden freshly fried fish out of newspapers, standing on the pavement in front of the

Fish-and-Chips Restaurant in Pimlico Road, enjoying the coolness of the night.

'Tell me about Paris!' she urged him. 'About your love affairs, about everything! What was the weather like when you first arrived?'

It amused him that she thought of the weather, but he knew that when you arrived at a new place, you would always remember, had it been snowing, or had one sat on the terrace of a café, the awning turned down against the blazing sun, or rain had been pelting down and you had no umbrella . . .

'I remember best the queues around the Prefecture, where every foreigner had to report. And I see before me the silly staff-photographer from Berlin, who arrived in Paris a few weeks ahead of me. When we shook hands in the Paris Café, he asked: "How much money did you bring with you?" I told him: About three thousand francs. He shook his head, sadly. "That's not enough to die!" They were full of these expressions. I knew what he meant, but he explained all the same: "You'll have to find an apartment. That'll cost you five hundred. Just the premium! You'll have to pay rent. You'll have to live while you're learning the language. Without that, they'll sell the skin from your back and the flesh from under your skin. The chap who'll help you to get your permit to stay here will want two hundred to begin with. Got anybody to do it?" I told him I had no one. He promised to send somebody who was as good as any, and cheaper. I asked why I couldn't do it on my own. He was full of indignation. "Man! Have you seen the queues at the Prefecture? You'll spend the next fortnight there doing nothing, just standing in that queue. You can't even learn French there for everybody speaks German."

'I stayed in a tiny hotel called the Arc d'Elysée. The owner had two little boys, not more than five or six. Both were magnificent marksmen with the catapult, firing at everybody on sight. They would be thirty-five now. One morning, the chambermaid told me by sign-language that somebody was waiting downstairs to see me. I found no one at all in the hall, but the concierge pointed towards the entrance. In front of it, stood a taxi and in the taxi sat my visitor, a friendly young Frenchman. He explained, once again with gestures, that I should fetch my passport and the money, and he would take me to the Prefecture to get my permit. He seemed very sure of himself and I thought, perhaps he had an uncle working in the Permits Department. The greater was my astonishment when he stopped the cab at the very end of the queue, bade me pay the driver and get out. He, himself, made elaborate preparations to do likewise. Only now did I realize that his army greatcoat, thrown over his lap, hid a pair of crutches and, there where everybody ought to have his right foot, he had nothing but an empty trouser leg, turned up half-way and secured by two large safety-pins. He declined my help, got out on his own, dragged himself with unexpected agility to the very end of the queue, planted himself on the tripod of his one leg and two crutches. I followed him, astonished, my anger growing with every step.

'I was fuming. The money I gave him – which I so sorely needed – the cheery attitude with which he went about cheating me, made me blue with rage. The inability to swear, since I had even less knowledge of the necessary French swear-words than those needed for polite conversation, had almost choked me. I tried to gesture to him that I expected to be taken inside the building for my money, and not to line up outside. He countered with a flow of soothing French words and mollifying gestures, not unlike how grown-ups try to deal with tantrums of children. His pantomime became even more expressive, when he spotted a policeman approaching, pleading with me to shut up. I did not. I wanted to go up to the custodian of the law, to put my grievance before him. He might even speak German, since they had put him on this special duty of keeping order among us German refugees. He came straight to us. He addressed my French friend, patting his crutches in the nonchalant way Frenchmen converse among themselves. My Frenchman thanked him and, almost as an afterthought, he pointed at me. The "agent" eyed me with some suspicion, finally nodded. My French guide took my arm, thanked him again, and pulled me towards the main entrance. Miraculously, I understood the meaning of their conversation. The policeman had been instructed to give preferential treatment to invalids. My Frenchman told him that I came with him, there was an unbreakable bond between the two of us, and so I, too, was allowed to pass. In simple words, my Frenchman carried out a profitable business, based on two assets: his disability and his country's courteous attitude towards the disabled.'

The next day, in his lunch-time, Braun called at the bank and asked for a statement of his account. He had known the clerk at the counter for years. Blond and tall, he had never acknowledged Braun's 'Good morning' with more than a non-committal mumble, and was a staunch member of the Athletic Club of the bank. Hospitals played rugby, teachers preferred cricket, their pupils swimming, executives took up golf, but banks went in for athletics. A junior brought a copy of Braun's account sheet, sealed in a flimsy brown envelope. When Karl tore it open, its flap came unstuck, revealing the hideous slimy, freshly licked stuff on it. He had slightly over £182 to his account, quite a fortune. It had taken him fifteen years to save it. He drew ten pounds and calculated how far the rest would go. He wondered what the blond clerk would say, if after the holidays Braun paid in the round sum of £20,000? Even the manager would be impressed and would have to instruct his staff that, from now on, Mr Karl Braun was entitled to a courteous greeting whenever he called at the bank. Braun had often amused himself with imagining that bank managers held a staff meeting first thing every morning, to hear and memorize clients' current balances, and get instructed as to the manner of treating them properly. The manager would read out: 'Mr Rothschild, balance: three million two hundred thousand and seventy-five pounds – he is entitled to our most courteous greeting, even his secretary is! Next, Mr J. Kolm, balance: three thousand two hundred and seventy-five pounds – the greeting due to him: 'Good morning, Mr Kolm.' Next: Karl Braun, balance twenty thousand one hundred and eighty-two pounds? . . . Are you sure, Miss Leacock? Well, miracles do happen. It should teach you all a lesson and make a mental note: Mr Braun should be greeted 'Hallo, Mr Braun!' . . .

5

When Braun phoned the office, Lilian said: 'I had one emergency booking, Karl, but I sent someone else. I remembered what an important meeting you have tonight.'

'I'm grateful, Lilian.'

'Will you ring me? It doesn't matter how late. I'm anxious to know how it goes?'

'It'll be much too late. If it isn't, I'll call you.'

'Good luck, Karl!'

'Thank you, Lilian.'

Whatever the cost, he had to be alone tonight. Helen was going out with the Bagshots – Kolm had to go to a druggists' lecture, arranged by one of the big combines. Strohmayer never came home before midnight. To be on the safe side, Braun told him he felt off-colour and intended to go to bed early.

On the way home, he went to St Michael's, Chester Square. He sat in the cool church, head buried in his hands, oblivious of time and prayed for them and for himself. If, once in a while, he had doubts about a clear conscience, he never had them on this anniversary. Hadn't his life been spared by the very action on which his fellow men wanted to convict him these days? He had a whole week's leave to spend in Hamburg. On his third day, a priority telegram arrived from Wittau, telling him that 'Case 92' had unexpectedly regained consciousness and was behaving in a most peculiar manner. The patient's memory seemed to be jumbled up, he kept on messing up things that had happened years before with memories of events that occurred only a few minutes ago. It sounded like a real break-through at long last. Ilse pleaded with him to ignore it, but he couldn't miss a chance like that. The risk of the patient dying was much too great, his most promising patient, on whom he had operated three times already and who had been kept alive only by using all the tricks medical science could conjure up. How could he do anything else but return immediately? He did. If he had stayed, he too would have perished the following night. Under the circumstances, his life was spared to carry on his work.

When he left the church, the lights were already burning in the street, dominated by the blue of the B.O.A.C. tower. He walked home, saw Mr and Mrs Mulholland, for a moment, watching the passers-by from their unlit first-floor window. They withdrew as soon as they were spotted by Braun. He heard the phone ringing as he entered the house. It stopped while he climbed the stairs but, the moment he opened the door, it started again. Thinking that it was less annoying to answer it now than let it go on, he picked up the receiver. To his astonishment, he heard Helen's voice.

'Oh, Karl, I thought you would never answer. You must come at once. I feel dreadful.'

'What's happened?'

'I'm lonely and depressed.'

'I thought the Bagshots were taking you out tonight.'

'Tom's got trouble with the car. They're arriving tomorrow. Come and take me out somewhere gay, or I'll go potty.'

He told her he couldn't tonight.

'Why? What's special about tonight?'

'I've got some sinus trouble.'

'Oh, but going out is the best cure for that! You forget all about it.'

'Really, I can't, tonight.'

'Well, it can't be helped.' You could hear how disappointed she was.

'I'll try Ann.' She rang off rather abruptly. It put him in an ugly mood. What on earth made her telephone? Why the stress on *going somewhere gay*? Tonight of all nights. It was always *he* who pursued her to go out with him. She must be wondering why he refused tonight. The pursuers of Eichmann knew the date of his wife's birthday, they observed him taking a bunch of flowers home and that was the final proof of his identity. Perhaps the police know about the raid on Hamburg, and are watching to see what Karl Braun will do when asked to go out tonight.

He dialled her number but couldn't get through.

They knew, in Ludwigsburg, that Dr Reitmüller had been married and they would have marked on his file what happened to his wife and child: killed in a bombing raid on Hamburg on the night of 24th July. 'Look, Mrs Taylor, ask him to take you out on the night of 24th July. Let's see what happens?' He dialled the number again; it was still engaged. 'To a gay place, Mrs Taylor, that's very important. The gayer, the better. You say he'd take you anywhere, any time? Well, we'll see. And don't tell him in advance. Don't give him a chance to find an excuse. Take him by surprise!'

He tried the number again – still without success. She had been talking now for a long time. He went downstairs and stopped a cab. He was so anxious to rectify his blunder, that he got out at Bayswater Tube Station and called her from there. She was still talking. As he tried again, he noticed the station porter staring at him. The man had stopped sweeping the stone floor in the booking hall and gaped at him. Or was he watching the next phone box where two young women had squeezed in and now had some trouble getting out? This was the station where he and Hein boarded the train on that fateful morning.

The porter reverted to his sweeping. He did it very methodically, sprinkling a few drops of water ahead of his broom to reduce the rising dust. Braun left the station, walked past the porter as calmly as he could, turned the corner, hesitated for a moment at her door, and then entered the house. He had never been there before. He found her flat and rang the bell. It had a childish, chiming sound. He heard her make an excuse into the phone and then, without approaching steps, the door flew open. She seemed shocked at the sight of him.

'Nobody has seen me,' he apologized. 'I tried to phone . . .' He looked drawn, she thought, and a little pathetic in his effort to smile. Her shoeless feet ran over the carpet and, without a further word, she replaced the receiver. 'Weren't you talking?' he asked.

'It doesn't matter.' The next second, she regained her composure. 'Are you better?'

'I took a couple of pills, I'm quite all right now. And I'm going to take you out.'

'Let's go then!' Suddenly she seemed in an awful hurry.

'Where are we going to?' He watched her running for

her bag, finding her shoes. The room looked a mess, but the nursery beyond it, was in perfect order, gleaming with polish, full of colour. At this moment, the telephone rang.

'Don't answer it! Let's go! It's Ann. I don't want to talk to her.'

She practically pulled him outside.

The Snake-Charmer turned out to be one of those twist-clubs which had shot up all over London in the last few years. Wherever enterprising people could find an empty basement, an unoccupied attic, plus any old record player, they were sure to find hordes of young persons, anxious to indulge in this their particular tribal dance – particular to their very own tribe: youth. Swinging, sweating, spiralling, twirling, undulating people filled the room. The new-comers found a spot on the bench along the wall, squeezed into it and sat down. In the coloured dimness, generated by the blue, red and yellow bulbs, nobody took any notice of them. Braun felt as though thrown into a dish containing acid in a photographer's dark-room, lit up only by red and yellow safety lights. It also *smelt* like acid.

'I'll teach you the twist!' she shouted into his ear, for in the prevailing cacophony only an assault on the eardrums from the closest quarters guaranteed result.

He shook his head, but she dragged him on to his feet. He could feel compressed human flesh expanding behind them as soon as they got up, leaving no more visible gap than before.

'Come on, Karl!'

'I don't know how,' his lips seemed to say.

'There are no rules! You do what you like! That's the beauty of it!'

He felt sick. Now that his eyes got a little used to the smoky, rainbowed darkness, he was struck by the relentlessness, the silent, grim determination and the sternness of the dancers. They did not speak and did not smile. In a few hours – he thought – a dirty sun will rise outside. They will go on twisting. The sun will set and rise again and again, but they will go on and on twisting, until they will have lost their youth and shrivel away.

He couldn't stand it any longer. He used to think that he had surrounded himself with a strong armour. For years he had toiled to harden this armour, until he believed it to be impregnable. Now, in his ears, the bombs were falling and he realized that no tempered steel and no thickness of reinforced concrete would withstand direct hits. The jukebox screamed, the women screamed, the babies screamed, and he passed out.

6

The hospital waiting-room was lit by a huge white globe. Helen had a lurking fear of hospitals, of their silence, their secretiveness and their whiteness. The nurses wore white, the furniture, the walls, the beds, the doors, even the faces of the patients were white.

Opposite her sat an old lady, her face carefully plated with layers of warpaint – a welcome relief from all that whiteness. Her lips resembled two lengths of wide red tape spread over rough ground, forbidden territory, trespassers will be prosecuted. Why doesn't anybody tell her how pathetic she looks? Now she opened her bag, took out a cigarette, lit it, and shifted her chair so that the 'No Smoking, Please' sign moved behind her back. She saw Helen's glance towards the sign. 'You mustn't mind that, dear. If they ask me to put it out, I'll do so. I'll even apologize. But by then I shall have had a puff and that's all I need. They provide ash-trays, don't they? They expect some people to smoke.' She picked up an ash-tray from the table to prove her point. 'I'm not the only one. Are you an accident? You must be, or they wouldn't let you wait here. They are very strict about visiting hours, very strict. Is it somebody you were with? Or did you cause it, dear?'

Luckily a nurse came in and said:

'You mustn't smoke here, Mrs Marcus, you know that.'

The old lady stamped out her cigarette on the floor, disregarding the ash-tray.

'I only want your key, Jean. I must have left mine on the table and slammed the door. I walked from Wigmore Street to Gower Street and no key. So I walked from Gower Street here. Let me have your key, Jean, or I'll have to spend the night in this hospital.'

The nurse called Jean, handed over her key.

'Why does it always have to be me, Mrs Marcus? You've got three lodgers. Why do you always come here?'

'That's not true, Jean. You mustn't be unfair. I borrowed Mary's key yesterday, and Marion's last week. I do it strictly in rotation.' She lit another cigarette in the door. 'It'll be under the mat. 'Bye, dear.'

She collided with a young doctor, in the door, who asked her, gallantly:

'Are you the young lady waiting for Mr Braun?' She swept past him. Helen stood up.

'How is he, doctor?'

'Very angry. Otherwise, fine. He'll be down in a minute. He'll meet you at the desk. Nurse will show you the way.'

'Why is he angry?'

'I gather he didn't want to strip.'

She found Karl pale and embarrassed.

'I'll get a cab. I'll take you straight home,' she announced.

'What about your car? Let's walk to your car. A little fresh air will do me good.'

She protested, but got nowhere. When they crossed Dean Street, he said:

'Now we can go back to your club and finish your dancing lesson.'

'No fear.'

Some jokester had chalked on her car: 'Drinka Pinta Milka!' This reminded her that she hadn't eaten since lunch-time and made her, suddenly, ravenously hungry, but she didn't dare to mention it for fear that he would insist on going somewhere to dine when he should really be resting. Instead, she asked him why he got angry about stripping in hospital.

'Who told you I got angry?'

'The doctor. You should know they always strip you in hospitals.'

'Why should *I* know?'

'Everybody does.'

'There was no necessity for it.'

'How do *you* know?'

'I have been in hospitals before.'

'Where? What was the matter with you?'

'Nothing. General check-up.'

'And they didn't strip you?'

'They did. They do it for a check-up.'

'Perhaps they wanted to check up on you.'

'Did he say anything else?'

'He said you were in good shape. But you need a tranquillizer.'

'The doctor said that?'

'No. I say it. You are too excitable tonight.'

He laughed.

'I need a holiday.'

'How many more days?' she asked.

'Six.'

He went upstairs. The flat, the house, the street, were silent. Strohmayer hadn't come in yet. Usually, he could hear Kolm breathing, the creaking of his bed. Tonight, not the slightest sound came from him. Perhaps Kolm was the informer after all. It would be logical to get one of the lodgers to do it. They wouldn't trust Strohmayer. But probably they wouldn't trust Kolm the Jew either. The best bet was still that they had hired an outsider for the job. Step by step, his thoughts returned to his favourite brain-creation, the young Englishman whom they had recruited to investigate him, who had been told all that was known about Dr Reitmüller and who must be going great guns by now. In his mind's eye, he saw again the tall, sunburnt, handsome young man: Johnny, he called him – easy-going, always smiling, always polite, well brought up, always a bit apologetic – Johnny would never accuse anybody without a 'Sorry, old man', except of course a girl, and then he would say: 'Sorry, my dear.' Johnny must have met Helen by now. It was Johnny who suggested the New Forest for a holiday and who else but Johnny could possibly be behind the invitation to that 'gay place' tonight? 'Helen, my girl, you talk him into taking you to a gay place tonight. Never you mind why tonight of all nights. I'll tell you afterwards.' 'But that's easy, Johnny,' she would argue, 'Karl would take me anywhere, anytime.' 'You do what I tell you. It must be a gay place, mind you. The gayer, the better.' It must have been a great surprise to her when Karl behaved exactly as Johnny predicted and did refuse to take her out. She must have been on the phone for hours to Johnny about it. Johnny told her: 'He won't go anywhere tonight, he's sitting in his room, full of gloom, and I'm going to take you out instead. Doll yourself up and I'm going to call for you in ten minutes.' That's why she wanted to get out of the flat in such a hurry. When Johnny arrived and found her gone, without leaving a message on the door-knob, he knew that Karl must have turned up. She must have mentioned the Snake-Charmer, the gayest place she knew, and Johnny went there to check, saw Karl being loaded into an ambulance, phoned the hospital and asked the doctor to look for a tattoo-mark in the patient's armpit.

The 'patient' sat in the dark, wondering what Johnny would make of what had happened tonight? He would be a bit shaken, to say the least. The suspect had behaved differently from what he had expected. Against Johnny's prediction, Karl Braun did go out with Helen after all, and he had no tattoo-marks anywhere. The two conspirators were discussing what to do next, probably at this very moment. Karl couldn't resist the temptation. He tiptoed from his room, straining his ears for any sound coming from the direction where he thought Kolm to be. Dialling a number didn't make much noise and no word would be spoken, no coin inserted into the slot. He dialled the number and heard, not the engaged signal, but the normal ringing tone. He replaced the receiver, almost regretfully and went back into his room.

One had to be careful about the deductive powers of a fertile brain. Once trained for critical examination and to present the fullest picture of possible dangers to its master, the brain tended to overdo things when not watched closely. It kept on conducting its scrutiny like a sorcerer's apprentice, piling up conclusions, until they had drowned the man instead of saving him. How he needed a holiday! He'd know next Saturday for certain. They wouldn't allow him to leave the country if they suspected him. They would question him about Hein, about the camp, about the time he left Germany, the places where he had lived since. He would answer their questions to the best of his ability, without indignation, but with polite tolerance, showing the willingness of a citizen who knew that the police had to do their job, had to check on people – sometimes on innocents. He had answers ready to every conceivable question. He had a perfect story. They were welcome to check it as much as they liked.

Tomorrow he would call at the B.E.A. office in Regent Street and buy the tickets. He would have to buy a guidebook of Paris and study it a bit. He might even buy a map of Argentina. Suddenly he felt a longing for friends. If he got the money in Zürich, he could do anything he liked. He could fly to Buenos Aires. He would be a doctor once more, he could play the violin again, and he wouldn't have to face Lilian about that lodging she had got for him.

In the silence of the night, he heard steps on the pavement below. If he decided to go to Argentina, he would never see Helen again. But what future had this whole business with her, anyway? He could hear feet climbing the stairs. When they had passed the first-floor landing, he knew it would be Strohmayer, in company with someone, probably one of his undistinguished young ladies, for there was whispering in the hall. Braun distinctly heard Strohmayer saying:

'He's asleep.'

And another male voice, answering:

'We better do the same.'

It was Kolm. It struck Braun as rather odd that the two came in together. Perhaps they met by chance coming home. Or Kolm called at the bar where the co-founder of International Press and TV Service reigned supreme behind the counter.

Karl undressed in the dark and prayed that he would be allowed to leave the country, that she should spend a few days in his company, that he should get the money in Zürich. Here he paused, making the Heavenly Computer wait. What else? – he asked himself. What else could he do with all that money? Well, he hadn't got it yet. He might not draw all of it; just enough for a few days. It would depend on how things were shaping. Of course, if he decided to go to Argentina, he would have to draw everything. The Brotherhood needed money, Hein said so.

He raised his head from the pillow and – with one finger – he scratched on the pillowcase: B. Karl. He smoothed it out with the back of his hand, as if it could leave a trace to betray him.

A few minutes later, he fell asleep.

7

The next morning he overslept. He woke up with a start when the newspaper was slipped through the letterbox. He had no time to investigate why his alarm-clock failed to ring. He made a quick calculation, decided not to call at the office but go straight to the first job of the day. Kolm's legitimate allocation of time in the bathroom commenced at eight o'clock, consequently he couldn't do any better than to have breakfast now and *follow* Kolm. He fetched his paper, lit the gas in the kitchen and waited for the kettle to boil. On page four of the morning paper, an item caught his eye. Similar to the tabulator-like device which regulated the muscles of the human face, there existed another. Its function was to catch sight of familiar formations of letters, picking them out from a sheet full of words. The paragraph ran:

WITTAU TRIAL STARTS IN FRANKFURT TODAY
From Our Own Correspondent

Bonn, July 24.

The trial of eleven S.S. men from one of the worst Nazi Concentration Camps – the one in Wittau – and of four members of the medical staff of the Experimental Hospital attached to the camp, has opened in Frankfurt today.

A medical orderly, Hermann Schmiede, had admitted in court under cross-examination, that he had many times selected victims for experiments in the hospital. He always did this on the specific orders of Dr Otto Reitmüller who needed inmates of comparatively good physical condition and above-the-average intelligence. He described the notorious Dr Reitmüller as a vain, ruthless, ambitious, self-centred person, anxious to show results, for there was a constant pressure from above to close his establishment if no quick and spectacular results were forthcoming. Consequently, Dr Reitmüller had to operate again and again, giving his patients no time for sufficient recovery from previous surgeries. Schmiede gave grisly accounts of how the experiments were carried out . . .

He stared at it for a long time. If Kolm had come in, he couldn't have helped noticing that something extraordinary had happened to his fellow-lodger, Braun. At last he folded the paper, turned off the gas and went back to the sanctuary of his room. There he reread it and, knowing that he would have to examine it, analyse it, again and again, he carefully tore out that part of the column which contained the item. Only after he had done it did he realize the foolishness of his deed. How could he now part with it? And if he kept it, wouldn't the mere fact make Strohmayer suspicious? He stood there, in front of the damage he had done, cold sweat covering his body, as if waiting for a miracle to make the torn page whole again. He had to do something quickly. He put the newspaper and the torn-out bit into his tool-box, dressed as fast as he could and tiptoed from the flat to get another paper.

His legs took him automatically to Mr Mulholland's shop. He checked them just in time, before he made another mistake. The newsboy would remember that he had delivered the paper; why would Mr Braun want another? Only people who find something of particular interest in a newspaper, want to buy another copy. He knew no other newsagent in the district. He hurried along the street, aimlessly, knowing that time was running out. Stuck under front doors, he saw the morning papers, some of them his own brand. But he dared not touch them. Suddenly he saw a paperboy, free-wheeling from the far end of the street towards him, turning off at the next traffic lights. From the corner, Braun could see him dismount only a few houses away in front of a tobacco shop. But, although the shop distributed newspapers not a single one was left of the one he wished to buy. The man offered him others and thought him rude for being so curt and running out of the shop without a word.

He hailed a cab and drove to Victoria Station. There, at last, they had plenty of his morning paper, great stacks of it. He could have bought fifty, not just one. He dropped his own into the litter basket. He managed to get a bus. A few minutes later, he was in his room again. He could hear Kolm messing about in the kitchen and waited for him to fetch his tray. The satisfaction of a job well done flowed through his limbs as he sat in the tub. He had to be careful. Perhaps a little more careful than before.

He arrived exactly on time for his first job of the day. He avoided calling the factory in order to put off the inevitable reckoning with Lilian. But she knew his working schedule and it was easy for her to seek him out.

'Oh, Mrs Merriman,' she cooed into the telephone, 'this is London Pianos. Is our man with you? I wonder if you would be so kind as to let me talk to him for a moment?' 'Our man' came presently. 'Oh, Karl, how did it go?'

'What, Lilian?' He had already forgotten what he told her about his preoccupation the previous night.

'Your solicitor from Paris! What news?'

'Oh, yes. Everything is going according to plan.'

'I had a lovely party. I talked to your future landlady. I made an appointment for you with her for tomorrow. She's sweet. You'll like her.'

'I'm afraid I can't make tomorrow.' Here we go, he thought. He heard her gasp, and added quickly: 'I've got something very important tomorrow.'

'What can be more important . . .' she began, but he cut her short.

'You'd be surprised, Lilian.'

'Well,' she snapped, 'if that's the way you feel about it . . .'

Braun didn't worry unduly. He was sure he would find a way to pacify her. More than anything, he wished to be alone.

In spitting rain, he took the bus for Victoria to carry out the next job on his list. He climbed up to the upper deck and there settled down to sort out the fears which crawled like ants all over his mind.

(He remembered Hermann Schmiede – barber by profession, a little rat by character, who looked like a rat, omnivorous and always famished by an insatiable greed. He met Schmiede first as a very young doctor in a Hamburg barber's shop. Schmiede sold him a bottle of expensive hair-tonic, cut his hair, shaved his face, and sold him a bottle of after-shave lotion, too, making the client vow to avoid the fellow in the future. But when he revisited the shop, Schmiede took possession of him as of an old customer. Six months later, Schmiede began to talk of moving to Berlin, asked his customers for letters of introduction, which they willingly gave him in the hope of getting rid of him. The young doctor sniffed the breeze of freedom among the smells of shampoos, creams and lotions. But when he returned for another hair-cut, another barber made a claim upon his hair. This time the customer dug in his toes, only to learn that Hermann Schmiede had made a deal with the highest bidder and transferred his clients for the price of twenty marks per head. Understandably, the purchaser now claimed those heads and all that grew on them.)

Even today, a quarter of a century after, Braun flew into a temper at the thought of Schmiede while his bus inched along the Edgware Road towards Marble Arch, engulfed by two opposing floods of vehicles. From his perch, he watched the people walking along the pavement, taking advantage of every awning for protection from the drizzle.

(It was early 1940 when he heard of Hermann Schmiede again. Ilse had her baby in a Hamburg nursing home. In her first letter after the baby's birth, she wrote that she had some lovely flowers from an old friend of his, by the name of

Hermann Schmiede. The man had joined an ambulance unit and asked to be transferred to the Experimental Hospital in Wittau, where he knew the doctor was doing a tremendous job for humanity, the Führer and the Fatherland. On his arrival at Wittau, he greeted the doctor as a long lost brother . . .)

Long before the bus stopped, Braun noticed a group of lads fooling about under the canvas canopy of the kitchenware store by the bus stop. Passers-by described wide circles around them, stepping into the rain rather than brush against them, avoiding their leer as if the mere meeting of those furtive eyes would mean courting disaster.

(What made Schmiede say that Dr Reitmüller was brutal and sadistic? Or were those not the words the newspaper quoted from the trial? He remembered now: 'ruthless and self-centred' said Schmiede. Why 'self-centred'? He wasn't preoccupied with his own person as a self-centred person was supposed to be! On the contrary: he was preoccupied with something vital for the good of Mankind with a capital 'M'. He certainly wasn't 'ruthless', but unbiased, just and unimpeachable. He would never do anything to serve only his own purpose unless it served the common purpose as well. He would go to any length to help others, disregarding his own interest. He loved his work; he was a good family-man; adored his wife and his child; he was religious, prayed to God and respected His laws. He was a romantic and romantics were the salt of this earth. This is my case, Your Lordship. I plead not guilty. Members of the Jury, have you reached your verdict? We have, My Lord: Not guilty! . . .)

The appearance of the five lads broke the thread of his thoughts. The pack came storming up the stairs like pirates boarding a ship, two of them advancing to the front, the remaining three taking possession of the rear, and immediately they commenced to lob obscenities across the no-man's-land between them. Two elderly ladies withdrew at once to the comparative sanctuary of the lower deck, braving the hail of jeers.

'You've annoyed the ladies, Bert!' jibed the taller of the two hooligans from the front.

'Who, me?' asked Bert with indignation, then changed his voice to a high soprano. 'Let's get out of here, Elsie, dear!' He proceeded to mime the two old ladies' inglorious retreat, making the most of their awkward balancing act as they tried to compensate for the drunken oscillation of the bus. To make his buffoonery more authentic, he pulled his ruddy-faced chum to his feet and, arm-in-arm, the two staggered from front to back and then in the reverse direction. When their fun wore thin, Bert deliberately bumped against one of the four remaining passengers, a pipe-smoking, bowler-hatted gentleman who, up to then, had followed their antics with a condoning smile of approval, firmly convinced that this would provide a non-aggression pact with the scoundrels. It did not. He lost his pipe as the result of the jolt and when he stooped down to retrieve it, another hoodlum gave his bowler a push, and it slipped right off his balding skull. Still hoping against hope that his latest misfortune was pure accident, he glanced up only to realize from the general merriment that his one-sided truce had been rudely broken. He collected his pipe and bowler, consulted his watch – by which action he meant to establish an alibi for his sudden departure – and at Marble Arch, left the bus, leaving only Braun and a young couple on the almost deserted battlefield.

Braun felt disgusted but not afraid. He hoped to God to avoid a brawl, with the inevitable police statements, the witness-box in court, an over-zealous counsel defending these thugs who just to discredit a hostile witness would do his best to take him to pieces.

The girl beside her very young and very tall escort was neither afraid nor concerned about the situation. She gripped her pastel-blue umbrella tighter and went on talking to her cigarette-smoking friend, glancing up only occasionally. Her young man nodded from time to time listening, seemingly with absorbed attention, but always conscious of the need to face an impending emergency manfully, his face flushed, his fist clenched, his muscles so tense that it hurt.

'Come here, Mac!' Bert called, and an open-shirted youth, with black fingernails, rose to join him close behind the girl and her escort. Bert pointed at the couple and announced: 'Conversation!'

The others roared with laughter. Mac now produced a magnifying glass from his trouser pocket, held it close to the girl's well-groomed *coiffure*, scrutinizing it with great attention to detail. The other thugs surrounded him, awaiting the final result of this meticulous examination. The girl stopped talking. Her boy-friend stamped out his cigarette. Mac reported:

'Hair!'

The boy friend turned slowly as if he wished to put it off as long as he possibly could.

Braun repeated to himself: No brawling! You can't afford to be mixed up in a fight!

At this moment of truth, a cheerful voice called from the stairs:

'Fares, please!'

A vermilion smile on a shining black face appeared from below. A well-padded chest, covered by a London Transport tunic, followed; on it dangled a compact little ticket printing machine. Next, a leather belt emerged which held up a pair of pants almost as wide as long, the lower ends falling over a pair of non-regulation sandals. She croaked again in her friendly Caribbean accent:

'Fares, please!'

The five thugs gaped, awe-struck. Mac advanced towards her as if he could not believe his eyes. The girl with the blue umbrella rose and, followed by her towering friend, passed through the enemy ranks and descended the stairs. Mac stretched out a hand to touch the ticket printing tool over the conductress's ample bosom, whereupon she cranked the handle, making the contrivance click and gurgle. Mac withdrew his fingers like a shot.

'Black bitch!' he sneered.

'Where are you going?' the little conductress inquired.

'Victoria,' said Bert meekly.

The black lady made her ticket printer gurgle and click five times. She said politely each time, 'Eightpence, please, thank you.' She collected the money, handed back the correct change, rang the bell to halt the bus at the request stop to let Braun get off at Hobart Place and, in no time at all, her non-regulation sandals, her large bottom, the London

Transport tunic and the vermilion smile had dropped under the horizon. Braun followed her, unmolested, convinced that once again his guardian angel had averted an acute danger.

Suddenly it flashed through his mind: Hein's ticket! Hein had no ticket in his pocket! Wouldn't the police find it strange that the dead man had no ticket on him? What if the police wished to find out where the man had boarded the train? One of those smart-alecs from Scotland Yard would reason: it couldn't have been lost, we have looked – the carriage was empty and clean. There was one simple explanation. When two friends travel together, more often than not, one of them buys both tickets and keeps them till they reach their destination. Who could that friend be? What made them take such an early train? Was it because at 5.40 in the morning you can have a carriage to yourself, no one would watch you, no one could overhear your conversation; you could board at different stations and leave separately. We know that Colonel von Stampel had little to hide. But what about the other person? What did *he* have to hide? So, Johnny got to work . . .

8

When Braun joined them in the kitchen, Kolm and Strohmayer were already engaged in a lively discussion. Strohmayer said:

'It's always the little man who gets caught. Never the big fish.'

Kolm wiped his glasses, smiled in a rather superior way, and snorted:

'Aren't you making a mistake? Fishermen say: "That big fish is clever. Never gets caught." But, in fact, it's the other way round. By some fluke it never got caught and this enabled him to grow big.'

'What is it about?' Braun wanted to know.

They were talking of the Wittau trial. Strohmayer had brought home a German newspaper – somebody left it in Anthony's Bar – it was full of sordid details about the case. He was reading it aloud to Kolm when Braun walked in. He explained to the new-comer:

'They caught a medical orderly by the name of Hermann Schmiede. He's supposed to have taken bribes from the inmates of the camp.'

Braun opened the refrigerator pretending to look for something. He heard Kolm answer:

'That's bunkum to begin with.'

'Why should that be bunkum?' Strohmayer sounded quite indignant.

'What is it you're looking for?' Kolm inquired.

'Milk.'

Kolm came over to see.

'Have some of mine.' He waited for Braun to straighten up before he tackled Strohmayer. 'I say, it's bunkum because the inmates of concentration camps had nothing to bribe with.'

Strohmayer waved his German paper in triumph.

'Yes, they had! It's all here. First, gold teeth. Gold fillings. And later, Jews who expected to be sent to the camps invented all sorts of tricks. Those who had money, bought precious stones: diamonds, rubies . . .'

'Where would they hide them?' A still sceptical Kolm scoffed. But Strohmayer had all the answers.

'In their teeth. It's all in this paper. Some Jews, before they were loaded into cattle-trucks, managed to find a dentist they trusted, let their teeth be pulled by him and replaced them by artificial dentures. Not made of gold, for they knew that gold teeth were confiscated in the camps, but teeth made of a bony substance that looked like the real thing. The dentist made a cavity in their dentures in which they could hide a fair-sized diamond. Can't you see?'

Kolm couldn't.

'What would Medical Orderly Schmiede offer in exchange for a fair-sized diamond?'

'He could select the donor to be transferred to the Experimental Compound.'

'Don't be silly, Leslie. To hand over a diamond – his only earthly possession – for what? To be carted over to Dr Reitmüller's hospital, where they cut open his head, chopped up his brain, made it heal, then cut it open again and again—' He turned to Braun for help and reason. 'Tell him, Karl! It's sheer nonsense.'

'It isn't,' Strohmayer insisted. 'A prisoner in the camp was starved, full of lice and sure to die. When selected for the Experimental Ward, they cleaned him up, fed him, he was put to bed between clean sheets and most of all: he was given time. Three months, four months. In that time the war could end, Hitler could perish, a miracle could happen. What was a lousy diamond worth if not the only possible chance? Now, Braun, tell him that I'm right!'

Braun looked from one to the other. He had to say something.

'Did Schmiede accept bribes?' he asked with unsteady voice.

'Of course he did. He's admitted that much already. But his defence is that he actually *saved* those he had selected for experiments. And he did. For a *while* he did! Later, of course, these tooth-cavities were discovered, a report was sent to the proper authorities and circulated to all camps.'

This set off a new train of thought in Kolm's mind.

'Göring might have got the idea from it.'

'Quite likely,' Strohmayer agreed. 'That capsule of poison hidden in Göring's teeth was exactly the same sort of trick.'

'There was a clever bastard who cheated his judges all right,' Kolm concurred. 'He must have been laughing to himself while all those high-and-mighty prosecutors were reading the lesson to him.'

'Lecturing him on crime and punishment,' Strohmayer chimed in. He couldn't hide his admiration. 'Do you think *that* made him so cocky?' He said this straight into Braun's face. 'What a coward!'

Kolm disagreed.

'Göring wasn't a coward. To commit premeditated suicide you need to be brave.'

'I agree with Kolm,' Braun said, glad to steer the conversation into another direction. 'In human behaviour, it had always been an achievement when Man managed to control his basic instincts. Our society would be unthinkable without it. Now, there is no stronger basic instinct than preserving life. And if you have the strength to take it, if you are brave enough to destroy it, you've really achieved something.'

An uneasy silence followed. Strohmayer broke it.

'You want to hear some more of Hermann Schmiede's trial?'

'Let's have some coffee,' Braun said.

'My brother-in-law,' spoke Kolm as he filled up the electric coffee-mill with coffee-beans, 'by the name of Vaclav Krumpholz, he is in the camp of Wittau . . .'

'*Had been*,' corrected Strohmayer. But Kolm shook his head.

'He has never left. Consequently he must be there still.' He took a paper filter from a box, folded the edges to give it added strength, fitted it into the porcelain funnel and laid both on top of the pot. 'He was a huge man – 182 kilos. A chest like a beer-barrel. He and a few others were commandeered to dig in the kitchen garden for the officers' mess. Four months later, he was a skeleton. They had no more use for him. He was sent into the gas-chambers.'

'If he had a couple of little diamonds hidden in his teeth, Hermann Schmiede might have saved him,' Strohmayer said. 'How do you know all this? You haven't been there.'

'That's another strange story,' Kolm sighed. He plugged in the coffee-mill, but waited with his finger on the switch. 'As soon as the war was over, I wrote to Moravska-Vary where he used to live. I addressed it to the burgomaster; he passed it on to a Mrs Lisa Marek. The only person from the town who survived Wittau. She did some cleaning for the camp-commander; she was a very good needlewoman, too. She managed to get through the whole grisly experience, was repatriated and lived in Moravska-Vary another fifteen years.' He switched on the grinder. It made an ear-splitting noise that grew more high-pitched as the beans broke up.

Strohmayer had put on the kettle and Braun fetched the cups and saucers.

'You want to smell?' Kolm asked. 'Nothing smells like freshly ground coffee.' He took off the perspex top and held up the contents to sniff.

'Look!' Strohmayer pointed.

In the dark-brown powder there was a whole unmangled bean.

'Mrs Lisa Marek,' said Kolm and snorted happily.

CHAPTER FIVE

1

BRAUN HAD SUCCESSFULLY avoided Lilian for two whole days. On the third something happened that brought things to a head.

The evening started harmlessly enough. He and Helen were driving to the Festival Hall, to their last concert before the holiday. She was gay and reckless. He felt the sadness of the final stage of something he could not quite define. Things were building up to the inevitable cessation of an important period of his life. It seemed he was travelling towards a terminal where he had to get out, find another station, and take another train. Befittingly, the programme at the concert included Mozart's G-minor symphony, his favourite composer's favourite orchestral work.

'I had a letter from Eve,' she announced. With one hand on the wheel, she opened her bag with the other and dropped a letter into his lap. 'Isn't she clever?'

The letter contained nothing but cut-outs of photographs showing an important day of Eve's life in Sweden. Leaving her daddy's house by car (waving frantically into the camera), arriving at a village, on the edge of the forest (more waving), changing to a pony, riding through the forest, playing with a tame fawn, watching some wild fowl, picnicking on the shore of a lake, and then, most of the action in reverse. The pictures were carefully trimmed, so that no offending outside person would appear on them. Karl remarked on this. She nodded.

'She's having a grand old time. It makes me feel less guilty about my own holiday.' Suddenly, she remembered something. 'Did you know that Mozart lived in London?'

'Who told you that?'

'Nobody. I found out for myself. Ain't I clever?'

He agreed about her cleverness, but thought there must be some mistake. Mozart might have visited London while touring the capitals of Europe, but he had not lived here.

'You never believe me, do you?'

'I always believe you. Hey! What are you doing?'

They were approaching Westminster Bridge, when she changed direction, turned right to go round the square.

'I'm going to prove it to you. He did live in London. I know the house and if he were still alive, I'd see him once or twice every week, because the house is just round the corner to Thomas Harrower's. I could get him a more suitable house with my general knowledge of properties. And you should be ashamed of yourself since *you* happen to live practically next door to him.'

She made a perilous U-turn where Pimlico Road branches into Ebury Street, taking no notice of a taxi which had to mount the pavement to avoid her. She jammed on the brake, killing her own engine, and with a dramatic gesture revealed a tablet embossed in the wall.

'I had no idea,' Braun admitted, watching the cab backing menacingly towards them.

'And you call yourself a music-lover!' Now she, too, saw the taxi. 'What do you think you are doing?' she yelled, and hooted furiously, as it came to a halt inches in front of her own car. The driver got out, a fat, bald-headed fellow.

'A woman! I should have known. Lady, why don't you push a perambulator?'

'Did you know that Mozart lived here?' she addressed the cabby. 'I thought you didn't! Go to evening classes, my man, and find out about the secrets of the Universe. Did *you* know that Mozart lived in this very house?' she now asked the taxi's passenger, who had emerged from the cab out of sheer curiosity.

'No, I never knew,' the middle-aged man admitted, obviously quite impressed.

'Well, he did. And if you hadn't got yourself such a splendid taxi-driver, you'd never have found out. I'd gladly raise my glass to you in that pub over there to celebrate the day when *my* friend and' – here she touched the cabby's arm – 'and *your* friend had learnt where Mozart lived, but we've got to hurry to a place where he lives now.'

The passenger eyed the pretty girl.

'Perhaps we can have that drink another time?'

'Tomorrow week, Thursday, 7 p.m.,' she said, without batting an eyelid, and started the engine. The cabby climbed back on his seat, and started his.

'I'll be there,' said his fare, and pulled out his diary to note the date.

'I'm not sure I can manage,' mumbled the driver, moving off, to let Mozart's Public Relations Officer get on her way. Everybody was waving to everybody.

'You're not serious about Thursday week, are you?' Karl asked, as they drove towards Westminster Bridge.

'No,' she laughed. 'How can I? I'm starting my holiday this week-end.'

They were late and just missed the doors being closed for the duration of the first part of the concert. The members of the orchestra had already assembled on the platform. Helen and Karl were half-way down their row when the conductor appeared.

'Look, Lilian!' said Millicent Turner, applauding the conductor wildly. 'Isn't that fellow one of our tuners?'

Lilian disliked Millicent Turner on account of the airs she put on (being the Senior Partner's secretary). At this particular moment, she hated her guts. They were sitting beyond the orchestra platform, on the dais, called the 'choir'. She saw them all right – how could anybody miss them, Braun and that beatnik-type creature, disturbing the peace of the now hushed hall and the peace of one Lilian Hall in particular. She tried desperately to penetrate the curtain of light spread over the orchestra, and watch those two absurd people worming their way into the third row of the stalls where, according to their status, they had no right to be. It spoilt her whole evening. When the lights went up and she watched them again, this time submerged in deep conversation, she felt waves of injustice swelling in her bony breast. What in Heaven's name could he talk about to this little slut? Perhaps she was a foreigner, like he was – she did look a bit continental – and they were talking in their foreign tongues. Lilian always suspected that Karl had never quite understood her choicest expressions. Foreigners never did.

EMERIC PRESSBURGER

2

Late afternoon, on Thursday, two swans landed on the tiny island overlooked by the windows of the piano factory. Nobody took much notice of them except three swans already nesting there, and Lilian Hall.

'Mr Parsons!' she gasped, when she brought in the outgoing mail to be signed. 'They are not our swans! They are strangers!'

The junior boss signed the first letter in the folder.

'They must have heard of our own Swanhilda's easy virtue and come to try their luck.'

'I don't see why these foreigners should disturb the peace on our little island!' she declared passionately, while she turned the blotting-paper over. 'I'll call the League! Just look, Mr Parsons, how our own swans are defending their nests! It's a disgrace!'

The junior boss signed his name once more and refused to look.

'While we're getting fat orders from the Continent, I won't have any loose talk about foreigners,' he said.

'Well, I don't like them,' she announced defiantly, and turned another page.

Mr Parsons had heard something from his father's secretary about rumours of Lilian's crush on Braun, the tuner and repairer. Once or twice in the past, she had dropped complimentary remarks on Braun's ability and his above-the-average intelligence. So, that's how the wind blows, he thought, but he did not pause and only when he had finished with another batch of letters, did he add:

'Perhaps they are naturalized British swans, Miss Hall.'

'Makes no difference,' she hissed. Back in her own office, she went to great trouble to find the 'League' in the telephone directory. She described the intruders to a gentleman on the other end of the line, was put through to another gentleman, repeated her minutest details: 'They have *pale* bills, not the orange ones our British swans have, and *pale* legs, not black ones.'

'They are Polish swans!' exclaimed the man with a very strong Slav accent. 'How very interesting! Where are they? I'll pop over myself. Don't let anything happen to them, lady!'

When the man arrived, she refused to see him and persuaded Jack Cartwright to deal with him. She waited for Karl to call at the office at the end of the day, a procedure introduced by herself some years ago, to discuss which urgent requests from the customers would have to be dealt with before the 'close-down', and which could be safely put off till work was resumed after the holiday. He was caught completely unawares by her icy remarks which she had kept all last night, and the best part of today, in the coldest compartment of her refrigerated mind.

'We saw you at the concert last night,' she began. 'How can you afford those expensive seats, Herr Braun?'

'I get them at a cut price, Miss Hall.'

'Does this apply also to the partners you take along?'

'You should know, Miss Hall. You have been my partner.'

'Don't be impertinent, Mr Braun, or you will force me to complain to Mr Parsons.'

'Go right ahead.'

She did not complain for she knew that young Parsons would only laugh, make some silly remark, and do nothing. She had a bitter experience in the past when her pot-shots, aimed at another piano-tuner, misfired in a most alarming fashion. He was Braun's predecessor, a clever young fellow, an Englishman, rather good at his job but very insolent. She decided to teach him a lesson, changed his schedule, gave him instead of the plum jobs only those in lower-middle-class homes as far away as possible from his lodgings. Unfortunately, piano-owners in the poorer districts tended to express their appreciation of a job well done more freely than more prosperous citizens. Letters started to pour in praising the young man's work. Lilian intercepted these letters, until one of the writers complained of not having received an acknowledgement. When Mr Parsons, Junior, heard about this from the senior partner, he started a thorough investigation, not only because he prided himself for answering every single letter by return of post but also because quoting such letters looked pretty marvellous in the firm's catalogue.

For twenty-four hours Lilian allowed Karl a stay of execution. She hoped that he would telephone, or call at the office to talk things over, to give an explanation. For such eventuality, she kept a few sharp words, to be followed by some tears and a piece of information known to no single person south of the Lake District, but to herself: at her mother's boarding-house in Windermere, a room was kept for an unnamed friend of hers who, though a foreigner, was a perfect gentleman and with whom she intended to go into partnership in more senses than one. But as Karl did not telephone and did not come, she decided to show him the weight of her absolute power.

Karl happened to be working in Eaton Place, not far from his own lodging. He intended to finish early, go home to change to be ready when Helen called for him at seven. They were going to the Chinese Restaurant to talk about their impending adventure, deciding the last dubious points like where to meet on Saturday morning and at what time. He had bought a thick volume, called *Cook's Continental Time-table*, which contained even the most insignificant movements of continental trains, including those between Zürich and Paris, and Paris and Millau. He intended to work out a schedule for her, explain it to her tonight, suggest alternatives and make plans with her, knowing that making plans was almost as exciting as carrying them out. He worked fast, whistling softly to himself – a thing he hadn't done for years – and which the red-headed lady on the balcony, lying in a deck-chair enjoying the sun, could not hear. Shortly before five o'clock, the telephone rang, bringing the lady from the balcony into the room.

'It's for you,' she said, slightly resenting being disturbed.

'This is Miss Hall,' the caller announced as soon as Braun took the receiver. 'Mr Parsons wishes you to go to the Albert Hall, not later than six tonight. They are rehearsing there now.'

'But, Miss Hall, we never do the Albert Hall . . .' He began worrying about his date.

'The people who tune the Albert Hall are closed down for their annual holiday, Mr Braun.' She understood from his tone that it didn't fit in with his plans, and this made her enjoy it more. 'It's no use arguing, Mr Braun . . .'

'I'm afraid I can't make it. I've got a ticket for the theatre,' he lied.

'I told Mr Parsons that you would probably be busy, but he insisted on your going.'

'Put me through to Mr Parsons, please.'

'Mr Parsons has gone already. Goodbye, Mr Braun.'

She put down the receiver rather gleefully, he thought. She must have waited to convey the message until her victim had no alternative left. The red-headed lady stood in the balcony door, listening, somewhat alarmed, to the piano-tuner's part of the conversation, and also a little surprised that piano-tuners should have such extravagant habits as going to the theatre, a pastime she indulged in only on the rarest occasions.

'I hope this doesn't mean that you'll be doing a rush job on my piano?' she asked.

'Only that I'll have to work faster, that's all.'

'No need to be ill-mannered,' the lady said from the deck-chair. 'You don't want me to complain to your employer, do you?'

'You please yourself, my lady,' he smiled. Nothing could ruin his good-humour today.

He finished the job and went home to change. He didn't wish to offend Parsons, whose humour and whose manners he rather liked. He guessed that the firm welcomed the chance to trespass, by invitation, on territory otherwise forbidden by ethical considerations. The job couldn't be a big job. Some tiny flaw sustained during transportation. He called Helen at the office and asked her to meet him at the Albert Hall; it was on her way and didn't make the slightest difference to her.

'You know what the temperature is in Paris?' she asked. 'Eighty-five!'

'How do you know?'

'Don't you read the paper, Karl? It's in the paper every day. You want to know how hot it is in Gibraltar? Or in Madrid? Yes, sir. Very well, sir. I'll make a note of it, sir. Good afternoon, sir.'

He might not have been in the picture as far as the temperatures in Europe were concerned, but he knew that Mr Valentine must have walked into her office.

He pushed up the blind and opened his window as wide as he could, laid out a fresh shirt and the blue suit, and went to the bathroom to have a shave. He was just about halfway through when he heard the hall door being opened. It struck him as most unusual. Kolm never finished before 6.15 and Strohmayer used to spend what he called 'the cocktail hour' at Anthony's bar. The 'boardroom' he called it. Braun listened from the bath. The visitor's steps were neither those of Kolm, nor of Strohmayer – it was a woman. They paused for a moment. He heard energetic knocking on the door and realized that the strange woman was knocking on his own door. For a moment, it made his blood run cold. When he opened the bathroom door, the visitor turned. It was Mrs Felton, his landlady. His appearance from an unexpected direction frightened her no less than her lodger, but she collected herself quickly.

'Mr Braun!' she charged him, 'what is the meaning of this?'

She had opened the door to Braun's room and pointed an accusing finger at the furniture. Now he understood.

'Good afternoon, Mrs Felton,' he said. His politeness seemed to confuse her.

'Good afternoon,' she acknowledged. 'Is this how you take care of my furniture, Mr Braun?'

'The fact is, Mrs Felton, that I treat your furniture with so much respect . . .' He had intended to finish his sentence with: . . . that I hate to cover it up with rags, but she gave him no chance.

'It seems to me a plot, Mr Braun. I don't blame you. I blame that artful dodger to whom I pay a weekly sum to look after my furniture. You are given notice, Mr Braun, as from next Saturday. I felt in my bones that it couldn't be mere chance that your blind is left exactly half-way down, obstructing my view, preventing me keeping an eye on my own furniture. As far as your accomplice is concerned, I'll deal with him myself.'

She swept across the hall and was gone.

Under normal circumstances, it would have worried him. But not now. He caught himself whistling again, while finishing shaving. He wrote a note for Strohmayer to warn him of imminent danger. When he had finished the note, he wrote on another piece of paper, several times: 'B. Karl', tore it up and put the pieces into his pocket. His watch showed a quarter to six. It was too late to rely on public transport. He decided to take a cab and call in at Anthony's Bar to have a word with Strohmayer. He kept the cab waiting and went inside. He had never been there before and it surprised him to see how distinguished the place looked, with its heavy furniture, smoky wood-panellings and the smell of good cigars. It was pretty full, but he saw Strohmayer, as soon as he entered, sitting at a small table with another gentleman, munching assorted salted nuts. There were no drinks on their table. Strohmayer stood up and came to meet him.

'Welcome to my boardroom,' he greeted the visitor. 'Come and have a drink!' He kept on shoving Braun gently towards the counter, like a collie drives sheep towards the sheep-dip, with the single difference, that here the dog happened to be bigger than the sheep. He wouldn't take any notice of Braun's lament about time and his cab waiting outside. 'Anthony, my boy!' he called to the barman, who took two tumblers from the rack. 'Anthony, this is the most illustrious Karl Braun I told you about.'

The barman, well-trained in the part, smiled as only barmen can – a dash of loftiness mixed into a gill of servility – asked:

'How's the Foreign Press, Mr Strohmayer, sir?'

Strohmayer roared with laughter.

'Anthony, this is my room-mate, Braun!'

The barman stopped pouring whisky into his partner's glass.

'Hallo, Karl! What's it going to be?' He shook hands with the new-comer and, seeing that the two were anxious to be left alone, turned to another customer. At long last, the time had come for Braun to pass on his information. Strohmayer took it calmly.

'Did she see the stuff on top of the wardrobe?' he inquired, after a moment's intensive brooding.

'I don't think so. In fact I'm pretty sure she didn't. What difference does it make?'

'Think very hard. It's very important.'

'I'm certain. She stood in the door. She couldn't have seen.'

'Good. It'll cost us something. I'm willing to go fifty-fifty. Although you benefit more from it and should really pay two-thirds. But, no. It wouldn't be fair. You pay one-third and I pay one-third. We'll send her loose covers to the cleaners! I'll tell her that I know someone at the cleaners who, during the last week in July – and only then – cleans at half the usual price. She'll be delighted. Perhaps you and I should only pay 25 per cent each . . .'

'Who pays the rest?' Braun asked.

'Mrs Felton, of course. She will want to send more stuff to my cleaners. But – as I said, they clean cheaply for this week only! Thanks for letting me know.' He waved to his accomplice as the cab drove off.

The stage door-keeper knew of Braun's arrival. Braun told him that he was expecting a young lady to call for him. An attendant led him inside.

There is always something romantic about an auditorium just before its doors are opened and the audience begins to pour in. An embalmed corpse just before it gets resurrected – still cold, still silent, but an air of expectancy trembles about it. The heart had not started to beat yet, only the suspense of anticipation is there. On a much lower level, one had the impression of peeping into the private life of somebody very lofty, of something very secluded.

Only the lights above the platform were burning. It was obviously some sort of a late rehearsal, called a

couple of hours before the performance. The members of
the orchestra had been allowed a few minutes' rest, the din
of their chatter could be heard from the rest-rooms. The
piano stood in its proper place, its lid still down. Braun had
to open it to get at the strings. The attendant had gone to
tell his superiors that the piano-tuner had arrived. Only
now did Braun realize that he had to attend to something
before opening the instrument. On top of the piano lay a
violin, left there by one of the fiddlers. For a moment he
hesitated. Then he lifted it from the piano, gently, gingerly.
It felt like a bottle of brandy in the hands of a reformed
dipsomaniac who hadn't touched hard liquor for years. His
fingers were twitching, his hands shaking to such an extent
that he almost dropped it. He peered into the darkened hall.
If somebody *was* watching him, the snooper was invisible
to him. First, he had focused all his senses through the eyes
to penetrate the gloom. Now, he switched them over to his
ears. And suddenly he heard a whisper. It seemed to come
from one of the front rows. First he couldn't understand the
word. Then he realized that somebody was calling him. Not
by 'Karl', nor by 'Braun'. The voice said: 'Herr Doctor!'
He advanced to the very edge of the platform. Whoever it
was, the eavesdropper was scurrying now towards the exit.
At the same time, he heard steps from the far end of the
stage and when he turned, he saw a middle-aged man, in his
shirt-sleeves, coming towards him.

'You play the violin?' the man asked. He spoke with a
Slav accent and Braun recognized the famous pianist whose
pictures were plastered all over the bill-boards outside the
Albert Hall. 'You hold the violin like one who plays it,'

the pianist explained. Braun mumbled something, placing the violin on a chair, while the pianist played a few chords to demonstrate the trouble. 'This!' he shouted, banging away at the offending key. 'This! Can you hear? Is this a concert piano? This is a muck!' He went on punishing it, then he tore open the beautifully polished mahogany lid and watched Braun like an omnivorous beast, ready to devour not only the piano-tuner but the piano as well. It took Braun only a few seconds to remedy the fault. He played a chord and stepped aside. The pianist tried it, and his face lit up. Now he was in love with the keyboard, the makers of the instrument, the piano-tuner and the whole British nation. His chubby fingers glided over the keys and the keys responded as to magic. He held out his right hand while his left, reluctant to leave caressing his newly won love, went on romping over the ivories. 'Thank you, my friend! Thank you! Will you stay for my concert, my friend? You can't? Can you come on Sunday?'

'Very kind, but I'm starting my holiday tonight.'

'Holiday?' the great man asked. 'Where do you go for your holiday?'

'The Continent,' Braun said vaguely.

'I play all over Europa after London. You're welcome, anywhere I play, my friend. Look, Mr Turner!' he discovered a young assistant manager below the platform, crossing the gangway with a young woman in tow who, when they reached the edge of the light, turned out to be Helen. 'This gentleman must be let in freely to any concert of mine!' He held the piano-tuner's hand tight in eternal friendship. 'What is your name, my friend?'

'Braun.'

'His name is Braun, Mr Turner!' the pianist repeated, endorsing it. 'Mr Braun must be let in freely, no matter whether sold out or not sold out!'

'You wish me to fetch Mr Turner, sir?' the young man asked.

'No. You tell him what I said. And have a fine holiday on the Continent, my friend!' At last he let Braun's hand go and, allowing his right hand to join the left, returned his full attention to the keyboard. The members of the orchestra were trickling back on to the platform. Braun jumped down to join Helen below.

'Are they going to play?' she asked in a whisper. 'Can we stay for a moment?'

Karl looked at the young man who said:

'The place is yours.'

'You stay – I'll be back in a second,' Karl told her. The conductor rapped his baton for silence.

'Third movement, Letter B, ladies and gentlemen!' – Karl heard him calling as he hurried along the half-lit corridor.

'Has anybody been looking for me?' he asked the doorman at the artists' entrance.

'Hasn't he found you?'

'No. Who was he?'

'I don't know. He asked for the man from London Pianos and I told him that you were up on the platform. I can't leave this door. He came out a moment later. I thought he must have found you.'

'What did he look like?'

'Oldish. Little fellow. Glasses, bushy eyebrows, foreign accent. Why don't you ask the cabby?'

'He took a cab?'

'Yes.'

'And you know the driver?'

'I ought to. He's always at this entrance every afternoon – for the last twenty years.'

'Got his number?'

'What would I do with his number? He's always here.'

'He's not here now.'

'He'll be back.'

'Would you do me a favour?' Braun took a pound note from his pocket and pressed it into the doorman's hand. 'Get his phone number. I want to find out where he took the man. It would give me an indication who he might be. I'll try to phone you later.' The doorman promised to do his best and Braun returned to fetch Helen. In the cool, curving corridor, he paused. Before he spoke to the doorman, he could have persuaded himself that he had suffered from a psychopathic condition, sort of paranoia, which resulted in delusions of persecution, vivid enough to hear non-existent voices. But somebody real enough had been talking to the doorman, somebody who knew about the factory, who had been watching him holding the violin. Even that fool of a pianist remarked about the way he handled that violin. Perhaps the whole plot of sending him here was nothing but a trap, as was the calling him 'Doctor', to see whether he understood it, reacted to it.

He rewound the film of the last ten minutes' happenings and let it run through his mind again and again, watching for clues. The voice called 'Herr Doctor'. The owner of the voice seemed to advance towards the platform, when somebody – the pianist most likely – made him leave in a hurry. The man couldn't be from the police. Certainly not from the British police. He spoke with a foreign accent – the doorman said. Whoever he was, he wished to be certain about his quarry's identity before he did whatever he planned to do. Did he go to Scotland Yard from here? The driver of the cab would know. But was it likely that a foreign investigator would contact Scotland Yard on a Friday evening, when every office would be running only half-staffed? If the man knew of Braun's intention to leave the country tomorrow, he would call in Scotland Yard. If he had been at London Pianos, he would know of the holiday. Did he know about Paris? Did he know of Helen? Would they watch the airport tomorrow? Have they told Interpol already in case Braun managed to slip through the controls at the airport? He had to get to Zürich as soon as possible, draw the money, leave Switzerland, preferably for Madrid or for Lisbon, and from there get a plane for South America. Perhaps he would be safer without Helen. He could turn, right now, walk out, take a cab to the Air Terminal and within ninety minutes he could be in the air. What would Helen do? She would surely report it. That young man, who wasn't Mr Turner, would help her to get in touch with the police . . . PIANO-TUNER DISAPPEARS MYSTERIOUSLY. Suddenly Braun was struck by another idea. It came to him clearly and forcefully and he felt positive that this time he was on the right track. The man couldn't be an agent of War Criminals Investigating Bureau. The whole thing would be too amateurish for words. He was sent from the factory to check whether Braun did turn up at the Albert Hall. Braun never agreed to do the job when Lilian spoke to him. Lilian got worried – she said that Mr Parsons attached great importance to the job being done. To make sure, she got in touch with another piano firm – they were helping each other in an emergency, like doctors. She asked them to send somebody to do the job in case 'our tuner, Mr Braun, didn't turn up, though most probably he would'. That's why the man's description didn't fit anybody at London Pianos. The man came, saw Braun working, and left. He hailed a cab, for he had been told: 'Get a taxi, London Pianos will pay for it.' As for whispering 'Herr Doctor' . . . when a man's nerves are stretched to breaking point, he would hear anything. There was the case of the Oberleutenant Schulmann . . . Here Braun smiled to himself and shook his head: there I go again. He wondered: who had the better chance with such complicated machinery as the brain: someone who knew the extent of its intricacy, the brittle-ness of the wheels within the wheels; or someone who knew nothing, who did not worry about the smallest disorders, and did not constantly strain his ears to discover whether the minutest parts were turning and ticking over smoothly. Would a snooper call the suspect by his clandestine title? Of course not. A snooper would wish to remain concealed. He could snoop far better if he remained unknown. With this in mind, Braun went inside.

Helen stood alone by the door. She turned when he came in, smiled, and indicated that she wished to stay a little longer. But a moment later, the conductor stopped the orchestra and said:

'That's it ladies and gentlemen. Thank you.'

3

At such an early hour – only just past seven – it was easy to find a table in the Chinese Restaurant. The manager came to greet them and to pass round the latest bulletin on Papi's state of health. He seemed to be enjoying himself at the seaside, doing a survey for the firm on the possibility of opening a Chinese Restaurant there for the summer months. When the manager had gone and they had ordered their dinner, Karl said:

'I've got a surprise for you.'

Her eyes widened into two sprawling question-marks.

'What? Come on, Karl! What is it?'

'We are taking the first plane in the morning. I'll call for you at 6.30.'

'You are joking.'

'I'm not. We are booked for the 8 a.m. plane. I couldn't get us on any flight later. They're booked solid.'

'Heavens! When am I going to pack? You are not serious!'

It took some time for him to convince her that he meant it, that she had plenty of time to do her packing when she got home tonight.

He felt confident and reckless – no doubt a repercussion to his pessimism of late. Everything would be all right. He would be in Paris tomorrow and in Zürich on Monday. The bank would pay him his money without the slightest difficulty. He would spend two lovely days with her, and then he would decide what to do? He might come back to

London. Or he might fly to Buenos Aires and live on the estancia for ever and ever, amen.

She, always starved, started to wolf down her food, but stopped suddenly, freezing her chopsticks in mid-air.

'You don't seem to be excited at all!'

'Why should I be excited?'

'Going back to Paris after all these years! Will you phone your old flames?'

'No fear!'

'You must phone *one*, Karl! You must have had one who meant more to you than the rest! What was her name?'

'Michelle.'

'That's a boy's name. Don't tell me, you . . .' She giggled and he had to explain the difference between Michelle and Michel. She wanted to know more. She wanted to know everything.

First, he spoke of his favourite café, the Brasserie Lorraine, then of his apartment in the Rue Quentin-Bochart, the parties he gave there, the girls – gay, lovely creatures – he and his friends used to invite.

'You gave them those phony oysters,' she remembered.

'The oysters were genuine. The little green ones called "Portuguese" which look so ugly and taste so good. Frank could open them just like a professional. He used to stand for hours in front of restaurants, watching the man with the leather apron opening oysters all day, and Frank learned the trick, bought the proper little knife specially made for the job, and set to work.'

'Who got the idea of those glass pearls?' she interrupted.

'I did.'

'You *are* cruel, Karl. It's inhuman to do a thing like that.'

The expression 'inhuman' made him wince.

'What's inhuman about a harmless little joke like that?'

'Harmless, indeed! How would you like some jokester to put a fair-sized rock into your bed next to your naked body?'

'I don't see the connection. Who said anything about putting rocks into peoples' beds?'

'Do you think that a poor little oyster doesn't feel pain? Haven't you learned in school that pearls are formed because you irritate the flesh of an oyster? You *are* very ignorant, Karl, really.'

'But oysters are not alive when they come out of a barrel,' he tried to argue.

'That's not true. Dan has shown it to me. You just squeeze a little lemon on them and you can see how they twist in pain.' She demonstrated what she meant by screwing up her face.

'Nothing of the sort. It's the reaction of citric acid on any fibrous substance. If you'd learn cooking . . .'

'I *know* how to cook, if you please!'

'Then you know that even boiling water makes the fibres of meat contract.'

'Karl!' she announced, like a teacher to a hopeless pupil, 'you might know a lot about music, but your knowledge of the flesh and blood of living things is next to nothing.' She piled another mountain of assorted Chinese food on his plate, but took nothing for herself. 'I must be careful. I don't know how my tummy will take to flying. Now, tell me about Michelle. Was she pretty? Tall? Short? Blonde? Brunette? What did she do with her pearl?'

'She never had a pearl. She never came to my parties. She was married to a very jealous husband, she had to be care-ful. She had a wonderful figure. I would have been jealous, too, if I had been her husband.'

'Where did you meet her?'

'On the balcony of my apartment.'

'You just said she never came to your apartment.'

'I didn't. I said she never came to our parties. None of my friends knew that we'd met. She was my next-door neighbour.'

She gasped.

'Go on, Karl! Let's have it!'

'There was a balcony running across the whole front of the house on every floor. You know those Parisian houses and their balconies, the french windows opening on to them in every flat. They are divided only by token barriers . . .'

'How did you meet her?'

'I watched her waving to her husband every afternoon, when he left for work . . .'

'Didn't he work in the morning?' she asked incredulously.

'He managed a night-club. He left at 6 p.m. and returned at dawn. She used to be absolutely terrified of him. She said he would kill her and kill me, if ever he found out about us. She had never been unfaithful to him . . .'

'You believe that?'

'I do. You see, coming to me, was foolproof. She could come over whenever she felt like coming; the door of her flat was next to mine. Even if her husband did return, unexpectedly, we could hear him ringing for the concierge and we could hear the concierge opening up for him. In a great emergency, I could help her over the balcony. If he had phoned her during the night, she could hear the phone ringing from my flat, and she could slip over.'

'And he never found out?'

'Never. We had some sticky moments, though.'

'Tell me.'

'I suppose we came closest to disaster one night, when we went to have a drink at a bar in the Place Victor Hugo.'

Helen looked in utter disbelief.

'How did you dare?'

'In time we got bolder. She had thought up little tricks in case he called while we were out. She could have gone for a packet of cigarettes to the bistro around the corner – we never stayed away for long – she would telephone him in his club and she knew he wouldn't call her for an hour or so. It was the devil in her, just to show off, just to prove to herself that she couldn't be kept locked up like a slave. We would take a cab, drive to that bar – not more than five minutes' drive – we would have a quick drink, get another cab, and I would return her to her prison without the warder noticing her absence. It made things spicier, I suppose. One night – it must have been a few minutes after midnight – she didn't feel like going back so soon and decided to phone him at the club and so establish an alibi. For a minute or so, she couldn't get through. It had never happened before. When she did get him on the phone, her husband said: "I'm coming home. There was a shooting incident in the club, the police have closed the premises for the night." I watched her growing pale. "We must hurry!" she cried. A moment later we were standing on the street, trying to get a cab. None came. You can imagine her panic.'

'And yours,' said Helen.

'And mine. And you can imagine our horror when the commissionaire told us that no taxis were running that night. He had heard it on the radio. There was a dispute about taxi-fares and the cabs were called out to strike as from midnight.'

'What did you do?' Helen asked in breathless terror, sharing the thirty-year-old predicament of a woman called Michelle.

'It's hard to believe now, but I must have spent the hardest ten minutes of my life on that corner. Worse than anything I can remember. Worse than the few minutes in the train when I left Germany.'

'What happened?' she urged him on.

'We stopped a private car. Michelle told the man about her jealous husband and the man – a true Parisian – understood. He must have covered the distance in record time.'

'And her husband? Was he there?'

'No. As it turned out, he couldn't get a cab either. He had to take a bus and then walk the rest of the way.'

'God! You were lucky, Karl!'

He sighed and agreed.

4

Helen parked her car in the nearby square where it would while away the time for the next fortnight and where – according to her – it would be safer than in front of the house. He helped her to squeeze into a tiny space, watched her putting the engine into gear, pulling the handbrake as tight as she could, locking both doors, and then she stuck one arm through the gap between the frame and the ill-fitting soft top. She observed that in spite of her precautionary measures, her most effective safeguard against theft was that nobody would think it was worthwhile to steal it. He followed her back to the house, keeping at a reasonable distance all the time, saw her fumbling for her key. She held it up triumphantly as soon as she had unearthed it from her bag, forgetting in her excitement that her mythical judge might be watching from one of the windows. When the door closed behind her, he hailed a taxi. Money had no meaning any more. Ten minutes later, the cab passed under the B.O.A.C. tower. The azure hands across the clock's azure face showed exactly ten o'clock.

Stuck under his door, he found two messages. The first said: 'Don't worry about Mrs F's draperies. I have collected them and have spoken to her. Everything is O.K. If I don't see you – have a nice holiday – Leslie Strohmayer.'

The second message – a letter really, but without a stamp – read: 'Please ring tonight or tomorrow morning the Regent Palace Hotel, Room 299.' No name, or any other indication of the sender.

For some obscure reason, as soon as he read it, he associated it with the man in the dark auditorium. He had quite forgotten about him. The whole incident, the snooper, the doorman at the Albert Hall, and the taxi driver, had evaporated from his mind. Once again, his very own sorcerer's apprentice had set to work piling up evidence, suspicion, reasoning and counter-argument. He made a superhuman effort to sift them, to put them into logical order, so that he could deal with them. It might be just an innocent inquiry – somebody needed a piano-tuner, or repairer, somebody who lived in the country, came to town, stayed at a hotel for the night, heard from Lilian or Parsons, or Cartwright, that a Mr Braun might do the job during his holiday . . . Or Mrs Felton had already spoken to someone about the room, somebody anxious to move in, somebody who wanted to ask whether Mr Braun would be kind enough to leave sooner than the customary one week's notice . . .

While he thus argued the case, another part of his brain urged him to look up and dial the number of the Albert Hall. He asked for the stage-door and was connected with it; the doorman remembered him at once.

'I spoke to Fred,' he reported. 'He came back here just as I said. His fare was a short fellow, fiftyish, glasses, bushy eyebrows, little moustache, foreign accent, just as I told you. Does it make sense to you?'

'Where did Fred drop him?' Braun asked, making an effort to sound casual.

'Somewhere in Pimlico Road. He can't remember the number. The gentleman asked him to wait, came back a minute later, and Fred drove him to the Regent Palace Hotel. All right?'

'Yes. Thank you.'

It was far from being all right. In the general gloom he could discover only one single glimmer of hope. He went to his room and reread the note. 'Please ring tonight or tomorrow morning . . .' The man, whoever he was, had no knowledge of Braun's intention of going abroad in the morning. For a moment, he thought he would call him at his hotel, talk to him, make an appointment with him for tomorrow afternoon or tomorrow evening – the later the better – but the next moment, he rejected it. He needed only a few more hours' grace. The fellow would wait till late morning. Only when no call came during the morning, would he start something new. He would have to report to his Embassy, they would get in touch with Scotland Yard – but not immediately. There was something very much in Braun's favour: this wonderfully holy English week-end. Tomorrow, Saturday, no one of consequence would be working at the Embassy, and very few at Scotland Yard. Those who came in would be assigned already to a case, far more urgent than the case of Karl Braun. Again, for a second only, he thought of leaving Helen behind. But if he did, there was no way of telling what she might do. It was lucky that, if it had to happen, it had happened in holiday time. They wouldn't find anybody, except the watchman, at the factory. It would take some time to figure out where Lilian had gone and Parsons and the rest. Perhaps nowadays they treated such cases as routine. The war, the Nazis, the camps, War Criminals were old hat. To everybody under thirty, the whole period must appear as mythical as the Boer War. Scotland Yard might not be interested at all. The position of Interpol hadn't been clarified either.

He pushed up the blind and for a few seconds stood by the open window. For the first time, since this whole mess started, he felt an extraordinary sense of strength. The sort of vigour a policeman imagines a hiding criminal would have, a sort of toughness one would never experience one-self, but one believes an adversary has. To be sure, the police force was infinitely mightier than one single fugitive. But their collective purpose was infinitely weaker. The driving forces behind *their* efforts were a sense of Duty or Bravado, a Desire for Advancement. The compulsion that drove a fugitive, derived from the motive of self-preservation. How did Kolm put it? 'Only when you have given up every hope, are you lost. All those Jews who perished, they had all given up hope . . .' He pulled his smallest suitcase from under the bed, opened it, and placed it on the bed. He stooped once more; he had to crawl half under the bed to reach the large trunk. When he touched the old eiderdown, it felt cool and a bit rigid. Just like a hibernating animal. He found the small brown box, opened it, parted the cotton wool and touched the spare set of false teeth. My God, wasn't that strange, the other night, in the kitchen! Talking about Field-Marshal Göring! . . .

He closed the box and shoved it carefully in an oilcloth-lined recess of his suitcase. Should he take the portable radio? It wasn't worth it, he had had it for years, the tuning mechanism was faulty, it couldn't be turned beyond the Third Programme. He would have liked to take the eiderdown though, but that, alas, couldn't be done. Like a flash, a word sparked into his mind: Aestivate! That was it: the word he could never remember, the correct term for spending the *summer* in a state of torpor – the variant to *hibernation*. He said it aloud: 'Aestivate.' As if he wanted the eiderdown to hear it, to compensate him for interrupting his slumber. Who knows what will happen to you – he thought. Mrs Felton will sell you to recover a week's rent, or Strohmayer will pinch you before *she* does and will lie under you with his various undistinguished ladies . . .

He began packing in the dark, wondering how long it would take before they found out that he would not return. He selected six of his best shirts: he could tell them easily apart from the rest, they had buttons on the cuffs instead of holes for cuff-links. (It was amazing, this keeping a tag on everybody without imposing any compulsion, simply by the curiosity of friends, workmates and relatives. Lilian would be very angry when he did not turn up on Monday morning after the holiday.) Only one suit – the blue one – he would be travelling in the grey. (He would buy a few things in Zürich and he would buy something very nice for Helen, too, and send it to London. It depended on how much money was paid out to him in Zürich. The 31st of February, 1968. There was the whole difference between Hein and himself. Hein preferred to remember the number as the 3rd of December.) All ten pairs of socks, two pyjamas, three underpants, three neckties, one pair of shoes and the raincoat. With his index finger, he scratched on top of the uppermost pyjamas: B. Karl. He smoothed it out immediately.

On the opposite side of the street, a light went on in the dark girl's bathroom. She opened the window and drew the curtain aside. It would be warm in her flat, the sun had been on it the whole afternoon. He had not seen her since the day he moved in – the first day and, now, the last.

He closed both suitcases and pushed the large one under the bed. What made him remember the word 'aestivate'? He had tried for years and had never succeeded. Somehow, he must have touched a tiny cell in his brain that fired another. Suddenly he knew: the radio! He heard the word for the first time on the radio. He could recall it, exactly; it was a word-game on the radio, two teams were given unfamiliar words; they had to interpret their meanings. He had never succeeded in recalling the word in connection with the eiderdown, it never occurred to him in connection with the radio either. But 'eiderdown *and* radio' together, did the trick. Perhaps memory-cells resembled the flabby sub-divisions of an umbrella. With each new experience, a tiny umbrella is created. Etched on its floppy sub-divisions were: name, appearance, smell, sound, colour, and so on. A spark on any of these sub-divisions could open the umbrella. If not used regularly, the spokes would get rusty – one tiny spark wouldn't be enough to open the whole umbrella, several segments would remain hanging limp, or open only partly. (We would remember the length of the word, guess that the word contained several 'r's, that it had a Latin sound, etc.) But *two* sparks *could* supply enough power to open the whole umbrella. This would explain why people tried to associate a word they wished to remember with another word. With the right sort of sensitive instrument, one should be able to measure the electric current trans-mitted to a certain memory cell, first from one source, and then from several additional sources . . .

Braun woke up very early. The July sun rose even earlier. It had climbed level with the horizon of roof-tops and, for a moment, it sprayed sparks and jets of blinding light over them.

He tiptoed to the bathroom, shaved and had a quick bath. He dressed, wrote two notes, one for Kolm, another for Strohmayer, ending both with 'au revoir'. He opened his door and found himself face to face with Kolm. He held a small hip-flask of whisky in his hand.

'It's for you,' he smiled. 'Whisky for the road, as the English say,' he snorted, rather pleased with himself. They shook hands. 'Have a wonderful time in Paris and good news from your solicitor about your restitution. That's why you're going to Paris, right? To see your solicitor?' Braun nodded and the old Jew said: 'I knew it.' As if the only reason to go to Paris was to see one's solicitor about one's restitution.

'And *you* have a wonderful time in Prague, Jaro. I hope you'll find it as you remember it.'

'How could that be, Karl? How could Prague be the same without Jaroslav Kohn, I ask you?'

Braun phoned for a cab and when he stepped into the street, the cab was already there. A very polite driver opened the cab door, took Braun's small bag and stowed it away beside the driver's seat. Braun looked up and saw Kolm and Strohmayer, both in their pyjamas, waving from the window. Kolm made a gesture which seemed to concern the cab and meant: What magnificence! Braun acknowledged it with a flourish. They were still waving when the cab drove off.

Helen stood in the window, surveying the street, keeping a look-out for the judge and his informers. She flew down the stairs, anxious to get away before one of them spotted her.

'Good morning,' she greeted the cabby. 'Good morning, Karl. What a day to go to Paris!'

At the terminal they checked in their luggage and took the B.E.A. bus.

In spite of the early hour, there were a great number of cars on the M4, people starting their week-ends early to avoid the main exodus. London Airport, like the road, was chock-full.

When the bus entered the tunnel, Braun's confidence deserted him. He began to perspire profusely, his hands were shaking like that fellow's who crossed the German border into Belgium and whose story he had told her not so long ago. If he could only take a few deep breaths without drawing her attention to his jumpiness! He hoped desperately that they would let him pass and, if not, he hoped that they wouldn't arrest him in her presence. He would ask to be taken into an office, tell them he wished to disclose something very confidential. To her he would say that he would be back in a moment. Once alone with them, he would promise to be as helpful as he could if only he didn't have to face her again.

As they drove out of the tunnel, he felt faint, and certain that he could not go through with it. He could pretend some sudden indisposition – he knew the symptoms so well that he could fool any doctor. They would take him to the sick-bay, release him later, and he would be free to go anywhere he liked. But where would he go? Back to Pimlico Road, or back to the Continental Departure?

'I'm so excited!' she said. 'Look, my hands are shaking!' She held out her hands and he took them firmly into his.

'Breathe in and out several times,' he commanded. 'Like this.' He demonstrated and she followed his example. 'Better?'

'Much better.'

The bus stopped in front of No. 1 Building, called Europa.

Inside the building, they took the moving staircase to the first floor.

'Karl! Why don't you answer? What's the matter?' She had to repeat her question. 'What can I bring back for Eve? Can I buy a watch in Paris? A cheap one?'

They crossed the Emigration Hall to the gate marked 'British Subjects'. The Emigration Officer was a singularly efficient man, who compared passengers with their photographs. Had he been instructed to make a very special check this morning? He glanced at Helen's passport and then at her. Then he took Braun's passport, opened it, said 'Thank you' and Braun joined her on the other side of the barrier.

CHAPTER SIX

1

THEY WERE FLYING very high, surrounded by a green haze below and a blue haze from every other direction. The tall, pretty stewardess made her little speech through the speakers, welcoming passengers on board in the name of Captain Masterton and his crew, promising that the flight would take fifty-five minutes. She then appeared in a tight-fitting white overall at the far end of the gangway, busying herself with a number of jugs and many trays, helped by another dark girl with thin lips and a very fine nose. The steward, not to be outdone by the weaker sex, distributed newspapers and little cards to be completed before arrival for the French Immigration. Then Captain Masterton spoke. He told his passengers the exact height they were flying at, the geographical points where they were to cross the Channel and, the welcome information, that at Le Bourget the sun was shining. A moment later, breakfast-trays began to arrive; the steward poured steaming coffee and, as if all this hadn't been sufficient, the passengers were given further preoccupations: passing from person to person a large sheet of paper which gave a summary of both the Captain's and the Stewardess's speeches with such additional information as the speed of their aircraft on the ground, the speed in the air, and the surprising fact that the Captain's first name was Cyril and his aircraft had been knighted and called 'Sir Michael Kinnerton'. It was remarkable how Captain Masterton and his crew managed to transfer their passengers not only from London to Paris, but also from a rather drab existence into a colourful never-never-land.

Conscientiously, Helen completed her immigration card before she tucked into her breakfast, made sure that no one saw, and passed it to Karl for examination. She had answered every question correctly, but to the query 'Sex' she put 'Yes'. Before he could comment on it, she snatched it away and corrected it to 'Female', making use of the existing letters. It reminded him of Kolm who had carried out a life-saving surgery on his name. And Braun marvelled how distant Kolm, Pimlico Road, London Pianos, and the rest seemed to him now.

He experienced another fleeting panic when they passed the French Immigration Officer, who fumbled under the shelf beyond the opening of his cubicle, but it turned out to be only for a packet of cigarettes which he broke open with one hand, while his other hand continued handling the passengers' passports.

The bus carried them through busy streets, full of shop-pers among the crowded stalls of the Saturday morning markets. She took in everything: the horse-butchers' plaster horse's heads over their doors, the names of the bistros, the little red-painted stumps of the tobacco shops, the fly-overs of every intersection with the boulevard leading into the centre of the town. Suddenly she exclaimed:

'Your café! Isn't that your café?'

He followed her pointing finger – it was. 'Brasserie Lorraine' it said in bold letters on the dark-red awning which stretched above the huge terrace that spilt over from the Place des Ternes into the Rue du Faubourg St Honoré. He quickly recovered.

'Here's the Metro,' he pointed out the entrance to the station in the square. 'Did I tell you about the robbery?' She shook her head. 'I sat there on the terrace, one morning, when a car parked close to the entrance. Two masked men jumped out and ran past me inside. A third accomplice stayed in the car and kept the engine running. A moment later – it couldn't have been better timed if it had been rehearsed for days – a delivery van drove up and parked in front of it, reversing so close that the other car couldn't move an inch. The delivery man's only reaction to the getaway car's desperate hooting was a rude gesture as he started to unload barrels of oysters from his van. When the raiders reappeared, carrying their loot, there was utter confusion. Their own vehicle hemmed in, they tried to move the van, but it refused to start. They resorted to the pedestrian way of pushing, fired several blanks at the driver who dived behind his barrels. They raced to another car, but couldn't force its doors. Finally, they plunged into that underground station. The police caught them there.'

While he spoke, the bus had skirted the Place des Ternes, mounted the Avenue de Wagram, and was passing the Arc de Triomphe. It turned into the Avenue Marceau towards the place d'Alma and the Seine. He remembered his extensive study of the map of Paris.

'The Rue Quentin-Bochart's on the left.'

'Where?'

'Here,' he pointed it out.

If she had not been so excited herself by seeing the sites of Karl's exploits, she would have been surprised by the curiosity written all over his face.

The cab found the Hôtel Arc d'Elysée in the Rue Bassano, but it was full.

'Ask him about the little rascals,' she whispered. The concierge, who spoke a little English, raised his eyebrows. Karl had to explain.

'Mademoiselle means that when I stayed here first, the patron had two little boys, they must have been five and six, they used to take pot-shots at everybody with their catapults. You know "catapult"?'

'Ah!' chanted the concierge. 'Do I remember, *voyons!* Catapult – *une fronde!* Monsieur, I am one of those boys! My brother, Armand, has died in Algérie. The Arc d'Elysée had been sold when my father moved to Algérie, the new patron made me concierge. I see to it that you do get the rooms. Must it be two rooms?' he asked smiling, with the best intention to help a friend from the past who used to be such a splendid target for his and his brother's catapults. 'Bernard!' he roared, and added, without anybody appearing, 'Clear 118 and 120!'

A voice grunted from the luggage room under the stairs and it was agreed that Mr Braun and Mademoiselle would go out, sightseeing, returning around lunch-time when the rooms would be ready for their use.

Helen left for the ladies' room. Karl asked the concierge for a taxi.

'Where do you want to go?'

'Arc de Triomphe.'

'It's only one minute from here,' the concierge protested. 'This street is the Rue Bassano. Right?'

'Right.'

'You go up the Rue Bassano that way, right?'

'Right.'

'No!' the concierge said, springing the trap. 'Left! You turn left. Two hundred metres. You can see the Arc de Triomphe. *Voilà!*'

Following the concierge's advice, they walked.

'Is it far?' she asked.

'Two hundred metres.'

'Couldn't we just sit in the sun and have a drink?'

He hailed a cab and said, grandly:

'Place des Ternes!'

The driver said nothing and set out for a sightseeing tour of Paris. They passed the Gare St Lazare, their bad-tempered driver cursing every other car on the road. Ten minutes later, they crossed the Place de Clichy, climbed for a few minutes, skirted a cemetery and Karl knew that the driver had misunderstood him, and that he had to find an explanation why he, Karl Braun – for years a resident in Paris – didn't realize it before. When she got nervous, and reminded him that the square with the Brasserie Lorraine could not possibly be that far from the hotel, he smiled wistfully. Finally, the cab stopped and she read the street sign: Place du Tertre.

'Why didn't you stop him before, Karl?' she complained.

'Do you know, Helen, I've experienced a strange coincidence. Thirty years ago, I took a taxi to keep an appointment in the Lorraine. The driver misunderstood me and brought me here. It just shows you my accent hasn't improved.'

They paid their cab, hailed another and this time, he said: 'Place des Ternes, Brasserie Lorraine.'

It took another half an hour, but this time, it was the right place. They sat in the sun and drank beer. You could order a small glass of draught beer, called a 'bock', or a large one in a tall glass, a 'double', or an enormous size, in a very large glass tankard which was called 'formidable'. She wrote them down in her small diary for future reference.

'Wait till Bagshot hears about this.'

They walked up to the Arc de Triomphe. She marvelled at the simplicity of its eternal flame.

'Dan wanted to show it to me when we drove through Paris, but he caught sight of a double feature in a cinema in the Champs-Elysées – he said he had missed them both in London, and he took me to the flicks instead.' She giggled and he guessed that she fancied Dan to be a splendidly dissident non-conformist for such eccentric behaviour.

She sighed and he felt jealous. Not so much jealous of the bond between them, but because he could afford to offer her so little now.

'Come with me to Zürich,' he said, out of the blue.

'Are you mad? You know Daphne's expecting me. I didn't know you were going to Zürich.'

'We'll send her a telegram. Do you remember that friend of mine I spoke to you about?'

'Who learnt how to force open those poor oysters?'

'No. The friend who owes me money.'

'Is he in Zürich?'

'Yes. He wants to – he might pay back his debt. We could fly over tomorrow and come back on Monday.'

'Couldn't we go tonight and come back tomorrow?'

'I'm afraid not. He's usually away over the week-end.'

'I can't let Daphne down. She's expecting me. Is he rich, your friend?'

'Very.'

'He must be a very honest friend. Can I meet him? Perhaps we'll visit him in Zürich one day.'

'I haven't seen him for a very long time. He may be a little embarrassed at owing me money all these years.'

'Tell him I owe money to lots of people. That'll ease his mind. I owe Ann, I owe Bagshot, I owe my bank manager . . .'

'You mean, the bank.'

'No. I mean the manager, Mr Pound.'

'Your bank manager is called Mr Pound?'

'Herbert Pound. He said the bank couldn't afford to take unreasonable risks, but he can.'

'How much did you touch him for?'

'Ten quid.'

'Did he ask what for?'

'He did. And I told him the honest truth: travellers' cheques. And he gave it to me. Just like that!' She tried to snap her fingers, but she couldn't. Undaunted, she went on: 'Anyway, the money he gave me has never left his bank. He gave it to me and I paid it in straightaway. That made all the difference, I suppose.' Suddenly she remembered Karl's rich and honest friend. 'Tell him . . . what's his name . . .?'

'Hermann.'

'Tell Hermann that I owed money even to my baby daughter. I took it from her piggy-bank. Fifteen bob. I took it on her birthday of all days. I had to give her a party and I was bankrupt. But I have put it back since. Only three more weeks to go! Twenty-one days and four hours.' She smiled at him, remembering that he had taught her to count the time.

'Where do we go to lunch?'

'What's wrong with your *brasserie*? You would enjoy eating there after so many years.'

They walked back and went inside. The *gérant* came, dressed in a stuffy dinner-jacket, stiff collar and the rest, to take their order. Another individual, in a faded blue over-all, wanted to know what they wished to drink. A waiter, in a white jacket, brought stiffly ironed napkins, a plate and some cutlery. They were sitting by the window, wide open now, sniffing evil smells that rose from the basement. Facing them, there was another row of tables and beyond them a slightly raised part of the restaurant, somewhat more elegant than the rest, with a glass door to the Rue du Faubourg St Honoré where, on a mock carpet of green turf, stood barrels of oysters. A man with a leather apron and a sturdy little knife, split them open and placed them on plates, filled to the brim with cracked ice.

'You want some?' the *gérant* asked, sensing her interest.

'No fear,' she said, and the *gérant* – proud of his English – wondered whether it meant yes or no. He recommended the *gigot de pré-salé* and explained to Helen that this was a speciality, a leg of mutton, from sheep grazing on meadows close to the sea-shore where occasional high tides made the grass salty. Before the *gérant* withdrew, Karl asked him about a predecessor of his, a Pole, whom Karl used to know back in the thirties, but the *gérant* shook his head.

'It was before my time. The employees here come and go.' They saw him talking to the lady behind the cash register who, in turn, called below and up came a wizened old man – a kitchen-hand probably – who came over and told them that he, indeed, remembered Monsieur Pizecky, the *gérant* from Poland, who joined the *maquis* when the Germans occupied Paris and nobody had ever heard of him since.

'What makes you remember him?' Helen asked as soon as the old man descended the stairs.

'He first taught me what *pré-salé* meant. I was sitting at one of these tables, ogling a very pretty girl opposite—'

'I knew there was a pretty girl in it somewhere,' she teased him.

'Anyway, this Polish manager tried to explain to me the meaning of *pré-salé* . . .'

'What was *she* doing?'

'Nothing. Waiting for her lunch and reading her paper. She gave me not a single glance.'

'What a shame!'

'When the waiter brought her order, my friend the Pole stopped him and brought her meal over to me to have a look. You see she, too, had ordered *pré-salé*. I nodded and he went on serving it to her. The whole thing must have looked as if her meal had to be presented to me for approval before she got it.'

'And did you meet her?'

'I did.'

'You would.'

'I had to explain to her what it was all about.'

2

Their rooms were tiny, with a thin wall and a flimsy door between them. The floorboards creaked, the hot-water tap produced the hammering of a carpenter gone crazy, while the cold tap whined and sobbed alternately. You could tell precisely what your neighbour was doing at any given moment of day or night.

Helen stretched her tired limbs and immediately fell asleep. He could hear her steady breathing in the next room, although she had closed the connecting door. He was sitting by the window, a map of Paris spread over his lap, studying it in view of the immediate future and contemplating the present. He wasn't doing too badly. The mistake of pronouncing Place des Ternes wrongly was stupid but, in the end, he had risen to the occasion and straightened it out quite successfully. He should have noticed, though, that the driver was going the wrong way. It coldn't be helped now. In every other respect, he had pulled it off. He had not put a foot wrong. The concierge here, at the hotel, turned out to be trumps. He almost wished she would be more critical. She could so easily be duped. He itched for closer scrutiny, so that he could present some of his really great guns. For he had first-class evidence – documentary evidence – of the years he had spent in Paris. There *had* been a lightning strike of cab-drivers in Paris in 1934. If one took the trouble to look it up in the newspapers of the day – there must be a newspaper library in Paris similar to the one at Colindale in London – it could be readily confirmed. Or take the house in the Rue Quentin-Bochart. There *had* been a murder there in 1933, and a German refugee photographer *did* live there and he *did* have somebody called Michelle living next door, married to a man who worked at a night-club, and there *had* been a shooting incident in that club, the very night when the cabbies went on strike. The whole thing was absolutely foolproof. An impostor could find out about a cab strike in Paris, but not that on the same night a chap happened to shoot his girl-friend in a night-club whose manager lived in the Rue Quentin-Bochart . . .

He wondered what urged him to prove his case when nobody seemed to have doubts about it? Was it a sort of bravado? Like a tennis player who, after five sets of gruelling play, jumps over the net to show off his remaining strength – unnecessary but spectacular.

He counted his money, jotted down all future expenses he could think of, added twenty pounds for 'unforeseens' and established that he had enough. Enough for what? Certainly enough for expenses in Paris, for a return ticket to Zürich for spending a day there, and he still had about thirty pounds over. Helen had her own ticket, she was all right. He, himself, had the return part of his ticket from Paris to London, just in case . . . He had never thought of this eventuality, seriously. What happened if he couldn't get the money in Zürich? He had nothing to sell, no one to borrow from. If he couldn't draw the money, he could never get to Argentina. Just as well – he thought. They only wanted him at the Brotherhood because of his money. The Brothers were going through thin times at the present, Hein said so. They wouldn't want another mouth to feed under the circumstances. On the other hand, it might be true that they wanted a doctor. It stood to reason. The Brothers must be getting on in years, most of them would now be well over sixty. He shuddered at the thought of spending the rest of his life among disgruntled sexagenarians who had one single purpose in life: to become octogenarians. Still there might be others like himself, interested in the sort of life he was, who loved books and music – he would buy a violin; perhaps one of the Brothers played the piano. On Sundays, they could make music, take long walks, the air would be clean and sharp . . . Suddenly he knew that all he was yearning for was peace. Rest, after twenty years of running. That man at the Regent Palace Hotel seemed to him now completely harmless. He almost pitied him. That chap had to run, too; the only difference was that the fellow was running *after* somebody and not *before* him. What an existence! How upset he must have been when he learnt that Karl Braun had gone. He wouldn't dare to report it to his superiors for some time. He would interview Strohmayer and he would also interview Kolm. He would check at the offices of international airlines, at the airports, and when finally he had established that Braun had flown to Paris, he would do the same and stand in front of the Air Terminal in Paris, wondering what to do next. For whom did he work?

He had no standing with Scotland Yard, otherwise they would have helped him by now. If he had worked for War Criminals Investigating Bureau in Ludwigsburg, he would have had some contact with British authorities.

He could be an amateur of course. Somebody who read about the reward in the papers, who had a clue, who had worked on some sort of a theory, a crackpot . . . No – the man had a foreign accent. Crackpots in Britain were British crackpots. And what made him come to the Albert Hall? And if he did, why didn't he wait?

Zürich on Monday. The day after: Buenos Aires. He'd never hear any more about that man with his bushy eyebrows, glasses, and foreign accent. It hit Braun like a thunderbolt: Eichmann! The logical process in his brain was exactly the same as when he remembered the word: aestivation. The line of approach to find an answer as to the identity of his pursuer needed another. 'Buenos Aires' had supplied it. Eichmann had been kidnapped in Buenos Aires and then carried off to Israel. Would they try it again? It certainly would explain why they couldn't call in the police.

He had to pull himself together. Terrorists had great dis-advantages to contend with. They, too, were on the wrong side of the law; they had probably limited resources . . . True, they did succeed in the case of Eichmann. But Eichmann was alone. If he had belonged to the Brotherhood, no terror-ist could have harmed him. They trailed Eichmann for weeks, checked his movements, watched his habits – they even knew the date of his wife's birthday . . . How must he have felt when they descended upon him! Did he call for help? How he must have hoped that something went wrong with their plan, that a customs officer might discover him at the airport before they had shanghaied him into that plane, waiting to abduct him. A rat in a trap couldn't be in such terror, for a rat would not know what to expect. Did they beat him up? . . .

Helen stirred in the next room. But she went on sleeping, quite unaware that her stir had whisked her friend from a state of terror into reality. He was in Paris, in a small hotel. Nobody knew about his whereabouts. The hotel registration form lay on the table not yet completed. Hotels were slack in France, the authorities had tolerated it. Even the police had no knowledge, as yet, that Karl Braun was staying in a hotel in the Rue Bassano. He decided to delay completing the registration form as long as he could. He stepped to the window and surveyed the street. Except for a young couple, there was not a soul as far as the eye could see. The young man was pushing a pram, his wife had her arm in his. They ambled along aimlessly. They stopped in front of the shop at the corner, read the notice on the shutters: 'Fermeture Annuelle' and walked on.

Zürich on Monday! Everything will be all right – most things were. Nothing was given free, but he had paid the price with bank-notes of sleepless nights, the silver of ghastly hours and coppers of anxious minutes. The reputation of Swiss banks got established by their service to clients on a 'strictly business' basis and 'no questions asked'. If a depositor could say: I deposited my money twenty years ago and then I just gave the number of my account, signed my name and – hey presto – I got the lot – it would be better advertisement than the most elaborate and most expensive publicity.

He scribbled on the dusty window-sill: B. Karl. He wiped it off and held his hand under the tap. The crazy carpenter started knocking immediately and he knew it was the hot-water tap. He heard the creaking of Helen's bed and her child-like squeal as she woke up. He went to the door.

'My name is Karl Braun, you are in Paris, France, and perfectly safe.'

A moment of silence followed and then an uncertain, plaintive wail, more human than the first, as she laboured to collect her wits and, finally, the mournful inquiry:

'What time is it?'

'Five-twenty.'

She took half an hour to get ready. By six, they were walking the short distance to the Avenue Marceau, turned left and left again, until he announced:

'*Voilà!* This is it. The house where I used to live.'

They stood on the opposite side of the street, overlooking the building, not unlike the other buildings in the street, with their shuttered windows and parallel lines of balconies. She stood in wonder and speechless, as always, when confronted with momentous manifestations. At long last, she said:

'Do you think she lives here still?'

'She doesn't.'

'How do you know?'

'I wrote to her. My letter came back.'

Her gaze swept the front of the house.

'Which floor?'

'Second.'

'Left or right?'

'Right.'

'Did she ever have to climb over the partition?'

He shook his head. Behind the ground-floor window, the suspicious face of a buxom woman appeared.

'It isn't her?' she asked.

'What an idea!'

'Why? How old would she be now?'

'Fifty-five.'

'You're right then,' she giggled. 'This lady couldn't be more than forty-five. But she is watching us. Are you sure?'

'Must be the concierge. They watch everybody. They know everything. They make first-class informers for the police.'

'Let's ask her. Perhaps she knows where Michelle moved to.'

It was no use arguing with her and he succumbed. The concierge eyed them with mistrust. The fact that Karl spoke a miserable French and had to translate every word to his companion, didn't make things any better. After several *'Non, monsieur'*-s, she produced a somewhat more verbose answer.

'What does she say?' Helen asked eagerly.

'She remembers that a letter came for her some time ago. The postman had been asking for her.'

'Your letter, I suppose.' When he nodded, she went on: 'Ask her whether we could see the flat?'

'How can I?' he resisted.

'Excusez, madame . . .' she began, and he had no choice but to ask the question for her. He succeeded in explaining that he used to live here, three decades ago, but the woman showed no interest until he pressed five francs into her hand.

'*Mais non, monsieur!*' she protested, kept the money, and explaining that the tenants were on holiday in Pourville, she consented to take them upstairs. While the concierge unlocked the flat and opened the shutters, he watched Helen, with face flushed, wide-eyed, similar to a child who sees for the first time something mysterious and taboo, doubting the propriety of watching it, but too curious to turn away.

'Here we stood in the dark,' he told her, still on the landing, 'only our two doors witnessing us, never whispering a single word . . .'

'Ssssht!' she stopped him, but her eyes were encouraging him to go on talking.

The drawing-room was long and narrow; it widened in front of the windows. Parallel to it, ran the bathroom and a tiny bedroom. The kitchen opened from the minute entrance hall. The concierge went into the bathroom, either to turn off a dripping tap, or just to let them be on their own for a time worth five francs – not more, not less. He sat down on the shabby armchair by the window and pointed on to the balcony.

'This is where I used to watch her before I knew her. You see, you can just catch a glimpse of someone beyond the partition, if she cared to be seen.' He opened the balcony door and they stepped outside. 'She could hand me her telephone before she came over, so that she could answer it from here when it rang.' He smiled to himself. It was exactly as he had told her in London.

The concierge came to join them and watched them curiously, hoping to catch the meaning of their talk.

'Ask her about the murder in the flat,' she begged him,

but when he obliged, the woman shook her head vigorously and burst into a lengthy monologue. He translated:

'She only joined the honourable profession of a concierge after the war.' By the time they said goodbye to her at the bottom of the stairs, she had become a sort of friend. 'What five francs can do!' he commented.

'How much are five francs?'

'About eight shillings.'

They went to a travel bureau in the Champs-Elysées and he bought his ticket to Zürich, checked the time of her train to Millau. He had not given one single glance to the colourful folders which advertised flights to South America.

She insisted on returning to the Brasserie Lorraine to dine. She felt over-awed in strange surroundings, but the Lorraine, with its few familiar faces, the smells by the window, the stories Karl had told her from its past, seemed almost 'home' to her. The *gérant* recognized them. She ordered a '*formidable*', couldn't cope with half of it. Outside, the terrace began to fill up, the street lamps were switched on, a newspaper vendor came in, followed by an Algerian who peddled rugs, and another man who sold roasted peanuts. She watched them and the people who didn't seem to take any notice of the pedlars.

'If you get your money in Zürich, Karl, you must buy a rug from this Algerian.'

'What would I do with a rug?'

'It would look nice in front of your bed at Mrs Felton's place. Nobody buys anything from that poor man.'

The pedlar appeared to be very unhappy indeed. As if it were not enough that nobody bought his merchandise, people also got impatient with him, told him the French equivalent of 'beat it' and a party of youngsters saw fit to make fun of him. There were about half a dozen young people in the party, the girls pretty, full of contained fun, the boys loud and uninhibited. One of them told the pedlar to display his wares, and he obliged with great fervour and expectation, explaining the unique qualities of each individual rug as he laid them out on the backs of the chairs, smoothing them down, rubbing them with his palm, focusing his whole love and care on a single one as soon as one of his customers got interested or merely glanced at a particular rug. But hardly had he done so, when another of the party would notice a different rug and the pedlar would shift his whole attention to this new one, giving it preferential treatment only to realize that there was a third person who fancied a third of his carpets. In no time, all chairs around them were covered with rugs, every would-be customer was asking questions about his, or her, special selection, the pedlar twisting, patting half a dozen rugs in turn, like a juggler who had too many objects in the air, anxious not to miss any of them. To add to his torment, now the waiter of the section appeared to demand that he remove forthwith his display from the back of the chairs so that business might proceed as usual. The waiter indicated, with a wink of his eye, that he understood the fun and volunteered to play a part in it. The pedlar saw his chance of doing business rapidly fading and made a desperate effort to persuade the waiter to tolerate his exhibition just a little longer. But, to his horror, the customers' interest had now completely disappeared, leaving him no alternative but to collect the range of his goods and depart.

'You! Come here, please!' the pedlar heard from an unexpected quarter and in a foreign language.

There was nothing Karl could do to persuade her that pedlars in France were used to such treatment, nor that travelling with an Algerian rug all the way to Millau and from there to England, was impractical to say the least of it.

'Will he take a traveller's cheque?' was all she said, and when Karl shook his head, she asked him to lend her the money till tomorrow. She selected, with one glance, a white rug with a blue design, heard the price, nodded several times, and took possession of it. The party of young people on the terrace applauded, the *gérant* came, took a look at it, pronounced it 'a real Algerian handicraft made in Yokohama' and called on the pedlar to depart without opening a new exhibition for the sake of these noble, immensely wealthy and rather foolish foreigners.

3

On the way back to the hotel, she suddenly stopped.

'Now I've had it,' she said. 'It always happens when I get excited.'

'You have had what?' For a moment he had no idea what she meant.

'We'd better find a chemist. There must be one open all night.'

Now he understood. They found a chemist which sold practically everything, like American drug-stores. First she refused to go inside but when he entered the store, she followed, keeping a safe distance to demonstrate that she had nothing to do with that man who, in his awkward French, asked for a packet of those unmentionables. She saw from the corner of her eyes that they directed him to another counter while she busied herself with selecting enormous picture postcards which had a little tune stamped on them, like real gramophone records. Eve would scream with joy, unless Dan had already bought one for her in Sweden. She remembered that she had no French money in her pocket, so she had to wait for Karl at the cash desk. She looked anxiously about her, but nobody seemed to have noticed that they knew each other, after all, nor that she had just picked up that man in front of the cash desk.

They found the communicating door between their two rooms wide open. She searched for the key and swore that she had seen it in the lock before they went out.

'You haven't got it, Karl?' She tried to make him confess to it, but he swore he had never set eyes on it. Before she closed the door, she made a little gesture which meant: 'Sorry, not my fault,' and said, '*C'est la vie.*' He heard her fumbling and pushing something heavy against her side of the door. The rest was silence.

He undressed in the dark, stood in front of the open window and sent up, to the Great Computer, words of gratitude for favours received during the day. All his prayers had been granted, except the money in Zürich, and he sensed now that would be all right, too. He would always remember this day as long as he lived. To make sure, he retraced every little scene in his memory, to carve their records in his brain just that much deeper: her happy face in the flat in the Rue Quentin-Bochart, her indignation at the sight of the rug-pedlar's plight and her ridiculous embarrassment in the drug-store a short while ago. He would recall these moments often and for many years under the starlit Argentinean sky. The moment he first saw her at Thos Harrower, the Estate Agents. How he met her against all odds in the yard of that mews – met her, kissed her, had taken her to Paris and for one single night had slept only inches away from her. Only a flimsy door, some easily movable furniture, those 'unmentionables' and his conscience between them. He had never tried to make love to her and she could sleep, undisturbed, at any time and in any place. She was too exquisite to be treated irreverently. He remembered the Führer's private train, beautifully equipped. When people heard that the Führer had put it at the disposal of danger-listed casualties, who had to be moved before the advancing Russian Army, they warned against it. Everybody thought it foolish. They had forecast that wardens and soldiers would carve their initials on the fine wood panels, foul the priceless carpets – only to find that the perfection of the fittings, the beauty of the setting, had challenged the men to show unexpected consideration. Nothing had been harmed, and he couldn't harm her or offend her either.

Outside a wind was blowing up. He fastened the shutters and wondered whether hers had been fastened too. He woke up later to a tremendous thunderstorm, shutters banging, lightning flashing. He jumped from his bed and knocked on her door.

'Helen! Are you all right?'

A whimpering voice answered but he couldn't make out what it said. He turned the door handle and, with due caution, pushed it open. The easy chair, destined to barricade the entrance, slid back on its wheels. He found her completely submerged under the sheets.

'Why didn't you call?' he asked her. But she just shook her head under the sheets and refused to surface. He fastened the shutters and stroked the blanket over her hair. Then he mopped up the rivulets under the window which resembled the estuary of the Amazon, with the Atlantic Ocean under her bed. She sat up to scold him.

'You are hopeless, Karl. Look, what you've done!'

Only now did he realize that, in his hurry to grab the first thing suitable to sponge up the soaking floor, he had seized her Algerian rug splendidly spread in front of her bed. She switched on her bedside lamp and focused it on him as he spread the soaking wet carpet over the radiator. On the radiator, he saw the cellophane packet he had obtained for her in the drug-store on the way home. It was unopened and intact. She knew that he had found out her little deception and giggled. He laughed too.

'You *are* a cheat.' He sat on her bed. She dived once more under the blanket. He couldn't tell whether the shaking of her thin body meant that she was sobbing or giggling. 'Don't you trust me?'

'No,' came from under the blanket. 'All men are beasts.' Later, when her head bobbed up, she startled him by confiding: 'Shall I tell you something? When I first met you, I could have sworn that you were spying on me.'

He couldn't believe his ears.

'I?'

'Spying on behalf of Dan,' she explained. 'To take Eve away from me. You were a foreigner – you could have been one of his friends. You could have come on a business trip to England and he could have asked you to find out about me.'

'You are crazy. I wouldn't do a thing like that.'

'I don't know. You've got a cruel streak in you.'

'What makes you say that?'

'You're pig-headed.'

'Would you say I'm ruthless?'

'You're obstinate when you want to gain your end. I can imagine when you were still a press-photographer, you always got the pictures you were after. No matter whether it embarrassed your victim or not. You didn't care a damn about the suffering of your victims. Am I right?'

'What on earth are you talking about?'

'I know what I'm talking about. Don't press-photographers invade the privacy of people?'

'It's the duty of a press-photographer to photograph the news. It is his job. The readers expect nothing less from him.'

'Alcoholics expect alcohol. Drug-addicts expect drugs. Sex-maniacs expect to rape little girls. I hate people to say that they do things because it's expected from them. It depends on you alone whether you do things, or you don't. When a reporter puts in his paper that Mr Valentine's real name is Mr Briggs: that he murdered his wife forty years ago, spent thirty-five years in the clink and for the last five years has managed Thos Harrower & Co. under the name of Valentine . . . Oh, I've lost the thread of it – what am I trying to say, Karl?'

'That Mr Valentine murdered his wife. It doesn't surprise me at all.'

'I know what I'm trying to explain to you, you block-head. What's the use of making his secret public when he has already paid for it, settled down again . . . whose interest could it be to ruin his whole life? He'd never get another job . . .'

'If one reporter doesn't do it, another will.'

'Let him. The first reporter could say "I haven't done it and I'm proud of it".'

'Who told you all this nonsense? It's not your own, is it?'

'Daphne,' she admitted. 'But I agree.'

'There are things you do,' he explained, 'because they have to be done. They might seem cruel at the time but without – what was the word you used? – "obstinacy"? Without obstinacy, perhaps even without cruelty, there is no progress.'

'Then I would rather not progress but stay put.'

'What about me?' he asked. 'Can I stay put?'

'No. You will now progress into your own room.'

He kissed her on the cheek. She let him do it. But she said firmly:

'Good night.' She showed him to the door with the spot-light of her bedside lamp. 'Do you snore?'

'I don't.'

'Then you can leave the door open.'

4

The train which carried through-coaches to Millau left shortly before 9 p.m. from the Gare d'Austerlitz. He intended to put her safely on it, take another cab for the

Gare de l'Est and catch the Zürich train due to leave almost an hour later.

They both had a hectic day in Paris. In a way, he felt relieved to be going to Zürich where he did not have to memorize the lay-out of the streets, but could permit himself the luxury of being a stranger in a strange city.

He watched her silently as she dug into her bag and unearthed an old photograph, gone yellow. The acquisition of this faded photograph marked the end of their week-end in Paris.

They began the day by taking the Metro to the Place de la Concorde. She thought the Metro smelt, was dirty, and the passengers in it were much more solemn and irritable than on the London Underground. But the square she found 'super'. They walked over to the Madeleine; it had been cleaned and it looked beautiful.

'When you see an ancient story on the flicks,' she said, 'the streets and the buildings always look so oldy-worldly. Have they never been new?' She remembered she had seen it before with Dan who had tried to find the best delicatessen shop in France ('that's what he called it anyway'). Dan knew nothing more about the address except that it could be found somewhere behind the Madeleine. 'You must know the shop, Karl, you lived in Paris.'

But he didn't know anything about the shop.

'I never had the money to shop in the best delicatessen in France.'

'What did you feed your guests on at your orgies? Apart from those oysters and pearls? You know where we haven't been yet? That pub in the Place Victor-Something! You know! You took Michelle there when the taxi-cabs went on strike!'

'Place Victor Hugo.'

'That's it. We'll go there, shall we?'

But first they walked to a wonderful spot called the Place Vendôme, then crossed the Tuileries and went for an hour into the Louvre. He had to race her from room to room. She hated to miss anything.

'We must come back,' she decided. 'Why don't we stop here for another day?'

'What about your Bagshots? You've sent Mrs Bagshot a telegram. She'll be fetching you at Millau Station tomorrow morning.' He thought of his depleted finances and didn't dare to encourage her to stay.

'Bagshots be blowed! How are we for money? You know I still have my travellers' cheques. Am I making you bankrupt?'

'Who cares?'

'But if you don't get your money from Hermann, what then? You don't want to go back to London after only two days' holiday. What would people say?'

'I'll tell you when I see you in London.'

'Would your bank manager give you an overdraft?'

'I shouldn't think so.' The subject embarrassed him and he hastened to change it. 'You know, once I did diddle a bank, and I never knew I did it.'

'How?' Her eyes widened in admiration. 'Banks never make a mistake. I always hoped they would and that I'd find I'd got a thousand quid more than I really had. You know: one thousand and twelve pounds, instead of twelve.

But I don't think you'd get a job in a bank unless you were first-class at doing sums.'

They were crossing the Seine, towards Nôtre Dame, both very tired on their feet, but both determined to keep going and include this last sight on their list before resting.

'I used to send money to my friend in Germany. As much as I could afford. Even from Paris.'

'Hermann,' she nodded knowingly.

'He had a family. A wife who was sick,' he elaborated his lie.

'Can I meet her too?'

'She's dead, I'm afraid. Anyway, whenever I made a little money, I sent them some of it.'

'For whom were you working?'

'An agency. The boss was a man called Monsieur Ramponneau.'

'Funny name. Go on.'

'This Monsieur Ramponneau never paid us photo-graphers . . .'

'Karl!' she interrupted him. 'Why haven't you got a camera? You could make super pictures of me in front of the Madeleine, on the bridge, sitting in your Brasserie Lorraine . . . Sorry for interrupting. If he never paid, how could you live and send money to Hermann?'

'Fellow-photographers told us that the boss had a much greater stake in horse-racing than in his photo agency. He owned several racehorses, he followed them to all the races. We had to watch for his horses in the papers. If they happened to win, we had to be on the spot. If we were, he would sink his large hands in his pockets, pull out a wad of bank-notes and distribute large sums among us. He had with him a little fellow, an accountant, who made a note of the payments, so that the books would always be up to date.'

'What about your diddling the bank?'

'I'm coming to that. In those days little banks kept on cropping up every day. They were no more than money-changers, dabbling also in transferring sums to other countries. For their lack of reputation, they made up by offering a more attractive rate of exchange. When one of us discovered that a bank paid a few francs more, it spread over the whole refugee colony like wildfire. One day I heard about such a bank. It had offices in the Rue de la Paix, on the second floor of a house not far from the Opera . . .'

'Oh, Karl! Can we go to the Opera?' She remembered that there was no time for it. 'Perhaps we can come over again. Wouldn't it be grand to tell Daphne that we went to the Opera in Paris? She's never been, I bet.'

He told her that the Opera would be closed at this time of year and hoped he was right.

'Sorry,' she excused herself again. 'Go on!'

'Well, I found the bank. They said they would transfer my money to Germany and they did offer a considerably higher rate than other banks. A fortnight later, Hermann wrote: no money had arrived. I went to the bank. They swore they had transferred it. Another week passed and Hermann still had not received it. I got very frightened. These little banks popped up, withered, and died with great regularity. They had no capital and no staying power. The gentlest draught nipped them in the bud. As soon as

I entered their premises, I knew that something was very wrong. In the whole narrow room with its half a dozen desks, there was only a single clerk working. I told him that my money had not arrived and now I wanted it back – or else. He called his chief – the president himself – the president swore that the money had been transferred and begged me to wait another week. But I couldn't trust him any more. I threatened him with the police. Either they paid my money now, or I would go straightaway to the police. He took my receipt and returned with the money.

'You are very cruel. I told you before.'

'Wait a minute. The very next day, I received a letter from Hermann, thanking me for the amount I had sent. The bank *did* send the money after all.' Helen gasped. He went on: 'The following morning I went to apologize. There was no bank any more. A policeman stood at the door. He asked me if I happened to be another victim? The president and vice-president had both fled, and if I cared, I could add my name and address to the endless list of creditors, although, in his private opinion it wasn't worth the effort or the ink.'

'So they didn't embezzle your money after all?'

'No. But they needed another day. They were afraid of the police and thought that the whole swindle might be discovered sooner if I went to the police. To gain another day, they reimbursed me just to avoid an investigation. They had probably another, much bigger, banditry in the making and it was worth buying another day of time.'

As always, she sided with the underdogs.

'You *made* them run away. Can you imagine how you must have frightened that poor president? Given time, he might have settled everything. This is Nôtre Dame! I recognize it. Ain't I clever? I've only seen it in films before. With Quasimodo, the hunchback, playing the principal part. He was wonderful.'

They went inside. There were quite a number of tourists in large parties, swarming around guides who were lecturing to them in different languages. When they stopped for a moment near the largest of the parties, the American guide spotted them immediately, and motioned to them to move on.

'Fancy being so mean,' she commented. 'And in a church of all places.'

They took a cab. It drove along the river, almost up to the Eiffel Tower, then crossed to the other side. The Place Victor Hugo turned out to be a quiet sort of place, outside the main tourist haunts, with cafés under red awnings. When he paid the driver, she said:

'If there hadn't been a strike that night, you might have got this very cab, you and Michelle.' The cabby looked old enough to have been around in the thirties, and so did his taxi. 'Have you ever seen a cab driver smile in Paris?' She surveyed the cafés. 'Now, which one is it?' He pointed out one at random. She took a deep breath. 'And you and Michelle stood on that corner waiting to get a cab?' He said 'Yes' and her involvement grew accordingly. 'Now I really feel that I know you. The reason why I never got to know Dan was because he'd never shown me the places he went to, never introduced me to people he cared for before he met me. Now, I'm almost part of your life. I have sat with you in cafés where you used to sit, you've told me things that happened to you and they would have sounded to me just like a million other stories, had I not been there myself – although years later – but still I have been there. You follow?' They sat on the terrace of one of *their* cafés. She ordered Pernod and hated it. 'I'm not very good at expressing myself, but you know what I'm trying to say. The best thing is to be with someone and go through things together. The next best thing is to listen to a story and go to the places where it happened. Even if it is thirty years after. It's easier to recapture everything, don't you agree?'

'I haven't been to any of the places where *you* have been.'

'Would you like to go with me to Bandol? I'd show you the beach where I got my sunstroke.'

'Your heat-stroke,' he corrected her. 'What about your friends, the Bagshots?'

'Not this time. There will be other holidays.'

'Perhaps you'll get married again. It's just possible.'

'I? Married again? Never.' In the same breath, she grabbed his arm. 'Oh, Karl! Ask him if we could buy his catapult!' She had discovered a little boy firing paper missiles at sunning cats.

'What for?' he wondered, but beckoned to the boy who came over, full of mistrust, his weapon at the ready.

'You'll see,' was the only explanation she gave. A moment later he reported on his negotiations.

'He's willing to part with it for one franc. One and six in English money.'

'Will he take English money?'

When Karl translated, the boy shook his head.

'Cash in French currency or no deal,' the boy insisted in French.

'Will he take a travellers' cheque?'

He wouldn't, and Karl advanced another franc against her travellers' cheques which never got changed. She refused to tell the purpose of the purchase. Only when she said goodbye to the concierge in their hotel, did she reveal it. She handed the catapult to him with much flourish.

'Souvenir for old time's sake,' she reminded him of his childhood. The concierge – otherwise a tourist-hardened Parisian bloodsucker – took it with moist eyes and for a moment was lost for an answer. Then he asked them to delay their departure for a second, dashed into the locker room below the stairs, and returned with a faded photograph. He handed it to her as a token of eternal friendship. It showed him and his brother as infants, with basque berets on their heads, in short pants, holding their catapults in their hands.

Now they were sitting in a taxi that drove them to Austerlitz Station. She dug into her bag and pulled out the faded photograph, turned it over and examined its back.

'You know what I'm looking for?' she asked, absorbed in her search. 'I'm looking for your name.'

'My name?'

'It's obvious: you were a photographer, short of money – the owner of the hotel wanted his kids photographed, why shouldn't *you* have done it?'

But she couldn't find any name. The cab jerked to a halt and she forgot all about it.

They called a porter – more to find the train than to carry the light-weight luggage. He bought her some magazines, a London paper, a cup of tea from a trolley on the platform, all the time sadly conscious that he would never see her again. Out of the blue, she startled him by saying:

'I wish I could stay with you.' He almost said: 'Why don't you?' He checked himself just in time. It would only drag out the inevitable. She said: 'I'm glad you picked me up in Delman Mews. And I'm looking forward to seeing you again. The concerts, the opera, our meals, even our little quarrels – I enjoyed them very much. Don't laugh. After a quarrel, people know more about each other than after tenderness. You know what I mean? We'll talk about it in London.'

The porter indicated the coach to her; in the door she turned and slightly raised her Algerian rug in place of waving, and was gone.

He turned several times, hoping that she would reappear in the window. But she never did.

CHAPTER SEVEN

1

BRAUN'S TRAIN FLASHED across the half-lit landscape, gathering speed, pulsating gently. It had a beautiful name: the Arlberg Express. If he could stay in it, instead of getting off in Zürich, he could watch, from the window, the mountains he and Hein had trudged over after the war was lost, exactly twenty years ago.

He had not glanced at his fellow-passengers ever since he had taken his seat. As soon as this all-night journey began, he closed his eyes to be alone. The second-class compartment seemed to be full of first-class people. He took to everyone immediately. They were self-contained, single individuals, except for the handsome, very young couple by the window. There was no conversation barring those two and what they had to tell each other had to be spoken in whispers.

He said a silent prayer and marvelled how easy it was to string the words together in the mind and then switch them off on the threshold of speech. You could pray aloud, or you could let the signals travel just far enough to allow your tongue and your lips to *form* the words without a sound resulting, or you could produce and arrest the words simply in your mind.

He should have goaded himself to sleep, for tomorrow he had to have his wits about him. Still, if he felt tired in the morning, he could always take a room in a cheap hotel before calling at the bank.

Wasn't it usual to give well-behaved prisoners a remission? Why had they clapped on him another five years? Twenty-five years running concurrently. Had he been caught right at the beginning, they would have given him ten or fifteen. He would be a free man now. But he knew he could never have stuck it out in prison. His strong sense of justice would have reared up against petty persecutions by his warders. He would have flown into a temper, blown his top, antagonized fellow-prisoners and authorities alike.

But he wasn't 'ruthless', or 'vain', or 'self-centred' as that idiot Schmiede had called him. We'll see how Hermann Schmiede will take to jail. Let's hope they'll give him a few years. Although Braun doubted if prison was the right sentence for Schmiede. He would, very likely, organize some nice, profit-making enterprise in jail, make money, bribe his warders and have a tolerable life. Just as Strohmayer would, too. But Braun preferred Strohmayer, who had an endearing inefficiency about him, was a lazy bungler really, while Schmiede was a vicious, unpleasant practitioner. Strohmayer did everything with an apologetic smile, hardly believing his own luck. Schmiede, on the other hand, had expected to get away with it, life owed it to him.

A male voice in the compartment asked, in French, if anyone objected to the light being turned out? It sounded like the old gentleman by the door who was reading a French paperback on the Napoleonic wars. Braun thought:

They hated Napoleon, too – especially after he had lost. Still the French had not changed the names of their streets and squares called after the heroes of his glorious campaigns. They still had an Avenue de la Grande Armée in Paris. Braun doubted if there ever would be another Hermann Göringstrasse, a Göbbels Platz, a Rommel Allee, or a Himmler Brücke, in Berlin? No one will remember Dr Otto Reitmüller either, who did all the spade-work to discover how memory was stored in the brain, who carried out his unique experiments using his advanced technique of surgery on the living human brain.

He could see the lights go out beyond his tightly closed eyelids. Now he could open his eyes: the compartment was dark. Through the half-open window he could feel the coolness of the night. Occasionally, unexpected flashes of coloured signals on the track, or beams from illuminated stations whipped across his face. He caught sight of the girl by the window staring at him. Her boy-friend had fallen asleep and was gently snoring. She, for one, will remember this journey through the night just as Braun will. The night when she went on her honeymoon in Switzerland. The night when she found out that her newly-wed husband snored.

Helen would be fast asleep, dreaming of her child in Sweden, or of her Algerian rug, possibly even of Karl Braun. She would be puzzled about what had happened to him and then forget all about him. One day, perhaps – it could be in four years and ten months time from now – he would write to her. He might even come over to England and look her up. He would call himself Dr Karl Braun in the Brotherhood. He should have listened to Hein when he insisted on writing down the address of the estancia. Once in Buenos Aires, he could easily trace them. It would be strange to get used to them, such a large community, after so much loneliness. The presence of Hein would have made it easier. He wondered if they had anybody else from Wittau? Probably not. Hein would have mentioned it if they had. Didn't Hein look ghastly just before he died? Nothing could be done about him. No doctor could have saved him. Hermann Schmiede is talking rubbish. 'Ruthless', 'ambitious', 'selfish', indeed! Since when is being ambitious a crime? Why 'ruthless'? Schmiede is confusing ruthlessness with determination. And why 'selfish'? What good would have come of it if Hein had died in Karl Braun's arms instead of dying on his own? Hein would be the last person to expect it, for Hein happened to be a realist . . .

He wondered if Hein's sudden appearance started those nightmares again? Probably Hein had nothing to do with it. They started as a consequence of the disappointment over extending the date he regarded as his salvation. Extending it by another five years, unexpectedly, cruelly. They were the result of the dejection that got hold of him. The earthquake which shattered his world, his life, his hopes, his belief in freedom almost attained and then, suddenly, snatched from his grasp . . .

He watched the cars racing the train, gaining on it; but in the long run the train overtook them and left them behind. In theory, some cars were faster than any express. But with slower cars hindering them, road repairs, sharp bends, level crossings – they had no earthly chance against this one-track-minded monster.

2

In Bâle the train had crossed into Switzerland. A lot of people got out, including the young couple. The girl gave Braun a curious look as if she had remembered him staring at the invisible landscape during the night.

Not once did it occur to him that he might still be in danger. Only two instances bothered him: getting the money and what to do if, for some unforeseen reason, the bank wouldn't pay? The formalities at the bank seemed so simple, that he began to fear he might have forgotten part of them. Just to know the number of his account and produce the right signature – was that all? What if they ask: can you tell us exactly how much is in your account? They might want an answer just for checking. Banks always check. Even if you want to change currency, they ask for your passport. He made a thorough calculation, trying to recall every single factor. They had crossed the border from Austria, their rucksacks heavy with things they had treasured most, and did not want to leave behind. Hein carried three of his favourite pipes and a large box of cut-throat razors, seven of them for every day of the week, each marked with gilt letters: Monday, Tuesday, and so on. He, himself, had in his pack a copy of the diary of his research but, on Hein's advice, he burnt it in the first mountain hut they had stopped at on Swiss soil. In the linings of their coats, each had 150,000 Swiss francs, in 1,000 franc bank-notes. In the soles of their boots they had one hundred English £10 notes which they had bought in

Salzburg on the black market. That made about 170,000 Swiss francs each, 340,000 altogether. More than £28,000 at the present rate. So, if they ask, the answer would be: 340,000 francs.

B. Karl – the 31st February, 1968, and 340,000 francs. He went through the motion of signing his name. The Frenchman who sat by the door gave him a curious glance from behind his paperback on the life of Napoleon. There were people who could see through considerably more than a 180° angle. Others couldn't. The Frenchman would have opened his eyes even wider, had he realized that he watched a signature worth £28,000.

The entrance to the bank – he remembered – was from the little square where the famous sweetshop stood. You could get chocolate-coated cherries there in 1945 – in spite of six years of war. He and Hein were led into a director's office – the director had a bristling black moustache – they told him that they wished to deposit their money and he suggested a 'number-account' as the safest way to do it. Either of them could draw from it. They exchanged the English pounds into Swiss money. Braun remembered these pound-notes gave him a scare several years later, when he read in the papers that many of those beautiful white bank-notes were forgeries, printed on the Führer's order, perfect in every detail, but counterfeits all the same. The purpose was to weaken the pound. Only the Bank of England could tell them apart. If those bank-notes were counterfeit, the Swiss bank might have traced them back to depositors who had exchanged them, back in 1945. Would they prosecute after twenty years? If the bank couldn't tell that they were

EMERIC PRESSBURGER

counterfeit, how could one expect ordinary citizens to do so?
In the worst case, they could deduct the equivalent of these
pounds and pay out the rest . . .

The second eventuality worried Braun far more. If he
couldn't get the money, he couldn't pay for his passage to
Argentina either. He couldn't have done so even before he
spent his savings in Paris. Anyway, he would never regret
that he was reckless in Paris. Perhaps he could have found
a cargo-ship for the money he had. The plain truth was that
he had spent it and nothing more could be done about it.

He could try to get a permit to stay in Switzerland. There
was a shortage of labour everywhere. Or he could return to
Paris – people in France were more liberal (or more slack)
about these things. There were always jobs to be had which
nobody else wanted. The authorities allowed a limited
number of foreigners to do domestic work; they did it even
in England. Nursing was another free occupation. Street-
cleaners were in demand, station men on the underground
railway. He had a British passport, he could get a working
permit in France, only for a few months, till he could save
enough for the fare to South America. His passport was
valid for another four years.

3

To his surprise, the station in Zürich was small, not at all the
busy terminal he remembered. The Arlberg Express didn't
think much of it either and departed without the slightest
delay. His apparent bewilderment attracted the notice of a
railway official, who indicated that the station-name read

'Zürich (Enge)' and was a small stopping place for the use of important trains with no time to linger.

Braun had lots of time on his hands. Though Swiss banks opened earlier than the banks in England, he made up his mind that to be one of the first customers was no less ill-advised than to be one of the last. First thing in the morning, there would be too few people in the bank, clerks would have too much time to spend with each customer. The afternoon he regarded as unsatisfactory, since then the employees were tired and – in the course of the day – had developed a certain resentment towards the clients. Ten-thirty to eleven o'clock seemed a happy medium. And so he crossed the square, selected from among the blue trams one which passed the main station and clambered aboard. The tram crossed the Bellevue Bridge, where Kolm threw away his passport, turned towards the East and prayed. The bridge swarmed with people going to work. If Kolm had arrived in Zürich at eight o'clock on a Monday morning, he would have experienced some difficulty in praying on this bridge.

Of course, if you wished to, you could pray anywhere and at any time. To demonstrate this, Braun closed his eyes and thanked the Great Computer for past help and asked for more. He wondered if it mattered that whenever he prayed, he always asked for something. On the other hand – he thought – he never reminded *it* of his good deeds either. He took it for granted that they got chalked up automatically. But if they were, why weren't his wishes known as well? Perhaps God was simply one's own conscience. Take for example, the case of Karl Braun. *He* always knew the balance sheet of his own accounts and felt accordingly. He could be contented regardless of material, or physical comforts. And he could be unhappy in spite of them, even in spite of spiritual affluence. You achieved something – right or wrong – and like a flash it appeared entered on your account. And not only entered, but changed into your very own individual currency. The exchange rate was what really mattered. You could be a man for whom ten thousand pounds embezzled showed up as a lesser figure than a thousand won on a bet, or a hundred earned by honest work. A week's drudgery might count less than an hour to write a poem. You could hurt somebody out of spite, or you could inflict upon him the same suffering in the cause of advancing human knowledge and the two would appear in your books as quite different aggregates. You were always aware of the exact state of your account-sheet, you knew when you were solvent and when in the red and you felt always according to your solvency.

The tram turned away from the lake into the long straight avenue, lined on both sides by elegant shops and called the Bahnhofstrasse. Then it skirted the little square where the famous sweetshop stood and where the bank used to be. But the old, distinguished building he remembered was not there any more. In its place now stood a modern edifice. Suddenly, he panicked. What if his bank had gone bust? He twisted his head to catch sight of an inscription that would put his mind at rest, but either he looked at the wrong places or the architect disapproved such a lapse of taste as to put the name on the façade. He turned to a fellow-passenger.

'Wasn't there a bank here some time ago?'

The man nodded gravely.

'Still there. That new piece of architecture, that's it. Banks never die.' He spoke as an Englishman would speak of the Rock of Gibraltar, an American of their dollars, or a Russian of the memory of Lenin.

At the railway terminal he deposited his suitcase and then ambled among hurrying crowds of people. This station did look as a big, important station should. In Britain and in France, railway stations were time-worn, grimy and gloomy. In Switzerland and in Germany they were contemporary, all chromium and stainless steel. The fact that this 'Hauptbahnof' embraced the Zürich Air Terminal proved its importance: an adult sheltering a mere baby.

He changed ten pounds into Swiss money, ordered breakfast in the station restaurant (II Class) and wrote on his paper napkin: '31 February, 1968 – B. Karl'. He folded it and put it into his pocket. The waitress brought him another napkin.

Perhaps it would be wiser, after all, to take a room in a cheap hotel, have a few hours' rest and go to the bank refreshed . . . He tried to assess the sharpness of his mental powers and found it satisfactory. I'm not going to postpone it – he said to himself. This is *my day*. I leave for the bank in exactly an hour from now. I'll get that money. *Then* I'll take a room. And it won't be in a cheap hotel, but at the best place in town . . . He worked up a healthy defiance against his irresolution, even against caution. He had been cautious enough for twenty years . . .

He would take a room, then go to a travel bureau and book his passage for Buenos Aires. Suddenly it occurred to him that probably he would need a visa for South American countries. He would go to the Argentinean Embassy and get it. He might buy an air ticket to Rome, or to Athens in the name of Braun and another to Madrid in a fictitious name. They check passports and tickets at airports, but never the two together. He would check in for the Rome plane, otherwise they would page his name, but fly to Madrid instead. That would throw them off any scent they might still have in their nostrils. In Madrid he could get a plane to any South American country. Perhaps it would be safer to get his visa in Madrid, too. Once in Buenos Aires he would find the Brotherhood.

He wouldn't hand over all his money to the Brothers. If they don't like it, they can lump it. Anyway, they won't know the exact amount. If Hein had told them, Hein made a mistake as far as the exact amount was concerned.

He walked down the Bahnhofstrasse towards the lake, stopping in front of shop-windows, making plans as if he had the money already in his pocket. He would buy a violin. They had a better choice of violins in Europe than in South America. He might buy it in Madrid though, it would be cheaper. But he would certainly buy books. Of course, there were plenty of book-shops in Buenos Aires, too, but they might not have the very latest editions and certainly not the more specialized works he could now afford to purchase. Not so fast, not so fast! You can always get catalogues sent and you can order books from there. He mustn't forget the medical journals, they were even more important than books. He thought again of the Brothers, the discipline among them and their depleted resources. They would have a sort of business manager who would be holding the reins, to whom the Brothers were expected to apply for every penny. He couldn't be a great economic wizard if he let their finances run down the way Hein said he had. It would be wise to leave part of the money in the bank. First he thought of leaving perhaps two to three thousand pounds' worth but as he stood and watched the clocks advancing minute by minute simultaneously in perfect unison towards 10.30, he raised the size of his nest-egg several times.

He entered the bank with pounding heart. A uniformed man asked him his business. Braun said, as quietly as he could:

'Deposit account. Numbered account.'

'Please write here your name and the number of your account.'

He did so and said:

'Can I wait anywhere more private?'

'Follow me, please.'

He was led along the corridor and into a small room, with a desk, a telephone, writing-pad and paper on the desk, two chairs, a reading-lamp, stacks of beautifully printed folders giving details of some building project in Bolivia, huge figures of loan-issues, percentages – all figures with many 'noughts'. Helen and Eve would call them 'hugs'. The thought made him smile. He was a bit nervous. Outside the window, chromium bars intensified the cell-like character of the bare little office.

The longer he waited, the more nervous he became. He took the pad from the desk and scribbled on it: 'B. Karl'. Or he thought he did. When he tore it off to hide it in his pocket, something made him look closer. He had written 'Karel' instead of 'Karl'. Suddenly he fell into a panic. If he could only open the window and take a deep breath. But he didn't dare. He had the impression that in this ultra-modern office somewhere, hidden, there was a device to watch clients. Now the telephone started to ring and rang urgently, but in a subdued voice, like a person calling who, for some reason, had to restrain his tongue. At the very instant the door opened, the ringing ceased.

The big man who entered brought a file with him. He held out a fleshy hand and sat on the opposite side of the desk.

'Mr Karl,' he began, after glancing at his papers, 'we haven't had the pleasure of seeing you for a long time.' Braun nodded. 'Forgive my curiosity, Mr Karl – what does the initial "B" stand for?'

'Bruno!'

'Of course,' the man agreed happily. 'I was racking my brain but couldn't think of a Christian name beginning with a "B". There must be very few. Not in our country that is. In England there are several, I know: Barney, Barnaby, Barry, Bert . . .'

'Bruce,' Braun added and he felt much more at ease.

'How much would you like to draw, Mr Karl?'

'How much exactly is in the account?'

'Three hundred and eighteen thousand four hundred and twenty francs and eighty rappen.'

'Could I have half of it? Say: a hundred and fifty thousand?'

'It's your money, Mr Karl. How will you have it?'

'Large notes, please. Some change for a thousand, perhaps.'

The man nodded, apologized for leaving Mr Karl alone to fetch the money, and departed.

Was his ordeal over now? Or was still more to come? Was this the time for the experts to scrutinize his signature? The man didn't even mention the name of Hein. Of course, if he kept strictly to his instructions, he had no need to. It would be marked clearly in the files. The man had no business to mention it. The money could be drawn by either of the depositors, at any time. What did the man say? Three hundred and eighteen thousand francs. That came to almost £25,000! The man will bring him half of it any moment. First: the hotel. Then some shopping. Then he would choose the right airline. He would study the time-tables during his lunch, somewhere on the lake. He mustn't forget the visa . . . Perhaps a hundred thousand francs could be left on some sort of savings-account which brought interest. With 4 per cent interest, in eighteen years, it would double itself. In eighteen years, he would be seventy-one. So what?

The door opened once more, the man with the file returned. This time he did not sit down, but opened his file. In addition to the documents, it contained also a number of large bank-notes and a receipt.

'Will you sign here, Mr Karl.'

The man hardly looked at the signature, but recounted the sheaf of 1,000 franc notes and handed them to the client to check the number once more. When that was done, he asked, casually:

'Are you expecting anyone, Mr Karl?' Braun must have looked astonished, for the man explained: 'Two people are waiting for you in the hall. The reception clerk rang through before. We are very careful in the bank, with all these currency restrictions in different countries. Some treasuries employ their own spies here. Did you know that?'

'What do they look like?'

The other dialled a code-number on the phone, put several questions, and reported:

'They came this morning as soon as the bank opened. When they saw you arriving, one of them approached the reception clerk and asked for your name. Naturally we don't give any information.'

'What do they look like?' Braun asked once more.

'One: rather short, moustache, glasses, bushy eyebrows, he spoke German. The other much taller, sunburnt, he wears a light brown gaberdine suit like Americans do. Would you care to leave by the back door? I'll be glad to direct you, Mr Karl.'

They walked fast. The brightly lit corridor seemed endless.

'You go down the stairs, Mr Karl. Turn right, through the double door and you are on the street.'

A few seconds later, loaded with a sheaf of new Swiss bank-notes, and a stack of fresh troubles, Braun stepped outside into the narrow street. He couldn't see anybody waiting for him.

He was more annoyed than afraid. The fact that he had about twelve thousand pounds' worth of Swiss francs in his pocket, made all the difference. With money one could do anything. He could move faster than before, he could buy a gun, he could even hire a bodyguard if he felt like it. Perhaps he could walk into the Hôtel Baur-au-Lac, at the far end of the street and ask the porter for a cab. He could see the top of the enormous pine tree in the garden of the hotel. As he hurried towards it, he changed his plan slightly. It was better to enter the hotel through the side entrance, cross the restaurant into the lobby. He was almost level now with the restaurant.

He crossed over, saw the doorman open the door for him when a cab stopped by the door and a lady got out. It took her ages to pay the fare, she twice counted the change and three times the coins for a tip. All this time Braun sat in the cab and waited. At last she went through the door and Braun said:

'Hauptbahnhof!'

The taxi – a big American car – moved off. Just in the nick of time, Braun stopped it from turning into the Bahnhofstrasse – the most direct road to the station – the street which ran past the bank.

'Cross the Bellevue Bridge. Drive along the other side of the lake!'

'Limmat Quai,' the cabman said, and did as told.

How did they know about the bank? Braun couldn't figure it out. Were they so efficient? For a single moment he thought of asking the police for help. But that would be really stupid. He had a fair chance of outwitting a handful of trouble-makers. But to rouse the police with their countless snoopers, access to passport controls, hotel registrations, extradition laws – it would be a fatal mistake. He had to keep clear of the police, but so had his enemies. And he was far from being alone. Dozens of powerful friends in the shape of large, handsome Swiss bank-notes were at his disposal to protect him, only waiting for their master's command.

4

It was 11.15 when he reclaimed his suitcase, all the time thinking hard how to outwit those two waiting for him at the bank. They must have got suspicious by now. On his way to the indicator board of departures, his eyes were caught by a sign clipped to one of the gates leading to the platforms:

Berne – Lausanne – Geneva

Exp. 11.30

Just what the doctor ordered, he thought. He bought a first-class ticket to Geneva. He stopped at the bookstall, purchased a Swiss timetable and several newspapers. He felt safe, almost contemptuous. He knew already: he would cross from Geneva into France, double back to Paris, or travel by train to Madrid, or Barcelona, or Lisbon – anywhere. The whole world was at his feet. He found it just a little disappointing that the first-class compartments were as crowded as the others, but he found a seat and a few minutes later the train departed with an elegant, lilting movement, synchronized with a reassuring whispering sound. Travelling by air, there was always that little nervous hurry, dashing from one country to another; even the food they served had to be gulped down in full gallop. They brought the trays and as soon as the last person to be served got his, they began collecting them from the first. And trains had other, far greater, advantages. You didn't have to announce your name when you bought your ticket, just to mention one.

He studied the timetable and found that he could get a train in Berne for Paris, or he could change at Lausanne, or travel to Geneva, cross into France and go to Lyon. He had a train from Lyon to Barcelona tonight, called the Hispania Express. It carried sleepers – he would sleep like a log.

In Berne he went into the dining-car, took his newspapers, ordered lunch and a bottle of their best wine. He had no chance to read, since in the crowded train the dining-car had to serve lunch in two sessions and he was expected to vacate his seat for the second. It didn't matter. In a packed dining-car you couldn't read a newspaper, anyway. You were bound to annoy people when you turned the pages, brushing against them or against their food, which was even worse. When he took his seat again, he opened his Swiss newspaper and settled down to browse in it. He read the political news, but his exhausted brain couldn't cope with it. As he turned the pages, a headline arrested his attention: a full report on the progress of the Hermann Schmiede trial. Braun had almost forgotten about Schmiede. Good Heavens, were they still at it? Obviously they were. He plunged right into the middle of the prosecutor's interrogation.

'I was told to select two or three people,' Schmiede was answering a question.

'Told by whom?'

'Dr Reitmüller.'

('Oh – Oh!' – Braun thought, leaning back against the luxurious cushions of his seat.)

'What were the requirements you were told to look for?'

'Healthy people who could survive several surgical operations . . . Well, comparatively healthy. And people with some intelligence. Most of them were in a sort of stupor when they arrived at Wittau. They'd been pushed around for weeks . . .'

'What exactly was the procedure?'

'When we were getting low in patients a note was sent from the medical compound to the camp commander requesting half a dozen people. He sent it back with his initials on it and I went over with it and selected them.'

'How was the selection done?'

'I did it by looking at them first. You could tell from just looking at them who were in a very low condition. Then I checked some basic things . . .'

'Like what?'

'Temperature, blood-pressure . . .'

'Have you any qualification for this?'

'What qualification do you need for checking temperature?'

'*I*'m asking the questions. What were you in peace-time? What was your profession?'

'Barber. But I was trained by Dr Reitmüller.'

'How did you become a medical orderly?'

'I knew Dr Reitmüller intimately. I knew his wife. I was what you would call a friend of the family. Dr Reitmüller trusted me.'

'What happened to the patients after they had arrived in the medical compound?'

'They were cleaned up, put to bed. The morning after, Dr Reitmüller, himself, checked them over. First, a physical check-up, then he talked to them. He was looking for people with strong incidents in their lives.'

'I suppose he had not much difficulty in finding such people.'

'No.' (Laughter from Schmiede, but he checks himself.) 'I know what you mean.'

'What happened then?'

'The doctor selected two or three.'

'What about the rest?'

'They got sent back.'

'Didn't those chosen protest?'

'Oh, no! They were happy. The *others*, those who were returned, protested. We had quite a lot of trouble with them, as a matter of fact. Hysterics and the rest. Some refused to go back.'

'How were the experiments carried out?'

'The patients were fed and rested for several days. Then Dr Reitmüller told them to write down some vivid memories from their lives. Funny ones and sad ones, at random. The next day he told them to describe the same episodes by spoken word. They were not allowed to look at the stuff they'd written previously. If they'd missed out something, Dr Reitmüller reminded them of it. It was to make them carve their memories deeper, the doctor said. Then he put them under hypnosis and ordered them to repeat what they said. All they were telling us got recorded. Then he operated on their brains. He cut out a few microscopic cells, closed up the wound . . . I'm not a surgeon, I can't find the right expressions to describe it. Anyway, they were kept in bed. It took them six or seven weeks to recover. Then they were hypnotized again and ordered to describe the same events as before. To note discrepancies if any. Then the doctor operated once more. Another bit of their brain was snipped off. Again we waited for them to get the colour back in their cheeks and once again they were made to tell their stories and the doctor noted any departure from the original. And so on . . .'

'How often?'

'Three times the most. We had only one who survived four.'

'Does the figure 92 mean anything to you?'

'No.'

'Doesn't it remind you of anything? Think hard.'

'It's 8 less than 100 . . .'

'Nothing else? Were the patients known by their names?'

'No. They had numbers. You mean *Patient 92*?'

'Precisely.'

'Oh, yes. I do remember. One of our best patients.'

'How many times was he operated upon?'

'Three times. No other patient had survived three operations before him. Later, of course . . .'

'This patient, Number 92, might have survived even a fourth operation but for you!'

'What did I do?'

'In Dr Reitmüller's absence, you tried to make him talk,

put him under hypnosis . . .'

'I had to. Dr Reitmüller was on holiday. Visiting his wife.
I was told by Dr Reitmüller to do my best . . .'

'How could he tell you if he was on leave?'

'He phoned.'

'Where was he on leave?'

'Hamburg. His family was in Hamburg.'

'And in his absence you went on with his experiments? A
totally unskilled medical orderly?'

'I knew what this Number 92 meant to him. He gave me
strict orders to let him know should something unexpected
happen. When the man regained consciousness and got
weaker by the hour, I got worried . . .'

'That he might die?'

'That he might die in the doctor's absence.'

'So you telephoned Dr Reitmüller in Hamburg?'

'I sent him a telegram.'

'Why not telephone?'

'I wouldn't have had a chance of getting through by
phone . . . In 1943! With all those army priorities . . .'

'You were unable to get through from the camp in
Wittau, an important experimental station, recognized in
the highest places . . . and you want us to believe that Dr
Reitmüller managed to get through to you from Hamburg?
On a night when Hamburg had been severely bombed? I
suggest that you sent that telegram and then put the patient
under hypnosis yourself, or tried to . . .'

'I didn't.'

'Were you afraid of Dr Reitmüller?'

'I was. He had a foul temper.'

'You said he was quite considerate.'

'When he kept his temper he was. But not in an emergency like this! Not when it concerned something that didn't suit his book! I once saw him hit a man – they were playing chamber music – the man played repeatedly a false note . . . He had a terrible temper . . . was determined to show results. The Ministry threatened to close his establishment. It had cost too much and employed too many skilled medical people needed in other places . . .'

'I ask the court for leave to proceed with other witnesses and I will continue with Hermann Schmiede tomorrow. The prosecution will put in as evidence a volume of case-histories, a diary kept by Dr Reitmüller . . .'

The only other person in the compartment, a middle-aged lady, was engrossed in reading a colourful magazine. The rest had gone into the dining-car. Braun blessed this magazine for its absorbing appeal. Otherwise she couldn't have helped noticing how her fellow-passenger's face changed colour from white as a sheet to a feverish crimson. With all the ingenious devices nature had endowed man for self-defence, why was he unable to hide his feelings?

They had his diary! He thought he had burnt all copies in existence. He destroyed even his own, on Hein's advice, as soon as they had crossed the border. It hadn't been easy to do it – it contained details of four years' scientific research! He read and reread every bit of it, to remember every single item, again and again, before he burnt it page by page. They must have discovered the only other copy, the one he sent to the Ministry! As he thought of it, a number of further horrors descended upon his mind. Foremost among them was the fact that he had told Helen certain parts of it. Passages of the diary might be read out at Schmiede's trial, printed in the papers and noticed by anybody who had heard of them before.

He had told himself that Helen never read newspapers and certainly not the accounts of war criminal trials held in Germany. She spoke no other tongue but English and English papers wouldn't report the trial in detail. But she might have told about it to others. She was bound to tell the Bagshots about her adventures in Paris. About the concierge at the hotel where they stayed . . . She even had a photograph of the concierge . . .

So what? – his rational self argued. I'm out of their reach. In twenty-four hours I'll be out of France, out of Europe. I'm covering up my steps right this very moment. I've shaken them off, there wasn't any doubt about that. Yet, the other half of his reasoning cautioned him: If Helen, and through her other people, connected him with Schmiede's trial, they were bound to tell the police. The police would track him from country to country. The newspapers would print the progress of their search. Everybody would read it. Hotel porters, airline officials, booking clerks, customs officers – everybody. Those kidnappers would read it!

But even if he could call on Helen, what would he tell her? Surely, he could find a way to caution her. She was a simple-minded creature, she would believe anything. He reached for his timetable, found the Paris–Béziers trains – she took one of them last night. Heavens, she had only arrived in Millau six hours ago, travelling the whole night, she couldn't have told anything to anybody yet. She had probably been fast asleep ever since she got to her hotel. He had her address, she wrote it down with her own hand: Le Rozier, Hôtel du Rozier at Muse. He would think of something to tell her.

He studied the map of railway lines on the cover of his timetable. From Geneva he had to get to Lyon. From there he could travel south, change at Tarascon or, better, at Arles and again at Béziers. Or he could go from Lyon to Vichy, take a cab to St Germain and catch the same train Helen took last night. He would be in Millau tomorrow morning, exactly twenty-four hours after her. This would give him four hours in Vichy, and some rest he needed. He decided to follow the latter course.

He had only ten minutes to wait in Geneva. By a quarter to six he was in Lyon. The Vichy train left an hour later. All the way to Lyon he had been thinking what to tell her, but for all his pains he had nothing to show. Perhaps he *was* too tired. Perhaps when talking to her he would think of something. This gave him an idea. He changed some Swiss francs into French, walked out of the station and on to the square, found a hotel and asked the concierge to put through a personal call to her. Ten francs tip conveyed the necessary urgency to the man and a few minutes later he heard a tiny, far-away voice at the other end of the line. It sounded more as if it came from the other end of the world and it wasn't Helen's. The distant voice said: Madame and Mademoiselle had gone to Montpellier but would be back for dinner.

'Montpellier?' Braun asked in utter disbelief.

'*Oui, monsieur*, Montpellier . . .'

She said something else, adding another word or two, but minor shell-bursts and the clatter of non-existent trains on the line drowned the rest.

What on earth had they gone to Montpellier for? The slightest trifle made him suspicious. He made up his mind to ring her again tonight. If she sounded just the minutest bit odd, he wouldn't go to Millau.

There was still a little daylight when he arrived in Vichy. He asked the cab-driver for a very good hotel and was taken to a fine place, all gilded and rococo and every single one of its rooms taken. Another large tip – but perhaps even more the fact that he intended to rest only a few hours – resulted in getting a large apartment, booked many months ahead, its rightful owners due to arrive tomorrow midday by a train called 'Le Bourbonnais' . . .

'*Naturellement*,' the concierge explained, 'the apartment is all ready now and the *femme de chambre* would have to get it ready again tomorrow . . .'

Another twenty francs took care of that, too. As soon as he was alone, he called Helen again. This time her astonished voice answered.

'This is Helen Taylor speaking.' It sounded much closer than the lady this afternoon.

'It's Karl,' he said.

'Karl!' she cried. This gasp couldn't be an enemy's. 'What's it like in Zürich?' She was convinced he was phoning from there. 'It's fabulous here. Was it you who called this afternoon? You must have got your lolly!'

'Who told you that?'

'You wouldn't call from all that distance if you hadn't. Daphne!' she shouted. 'Karl's got his money in Zürich!' She turned her attention once again to him. 'Why don't you come and visit us? The weather's super!'

'I might,' he agreed readily. 'Where were you when I called you?'

'Oh, Daphne took me to a fantastic place! You've never seen anything like it. Come here and we'll show it to you. It's marvellous!'

'The lady who spoke to me said you went to Montpellier. That's eighty miles from Millau.'

'Rubbish. Daphne! How far is that Chaos place we went to? Daphne says it's no more than four miles, that's all. It's called "Old Montpellier". In French, of course. You'll be thrilled, I promise you!'

'I'll be with you tomorrow morning.'

'Don't be silly . . .' Suddenly she had a fantastic notion. 'Karl! You haven't bought a car?'

'No. I'm coming by train. The same train you took from Paris. Arriving five to nine tomorrow morning.' He heard her reporting this to Bagshot, asking for her car, and then reporting back to him.

'I'll fetch you at the station. If I'm late, wait for me. And I've got more news for you!'

'What news?'

'I'll tell you when I see you.'

'Tell me now.'

'It's about Dan and Eve. I'll tell you tomorrow. My God, you *can* wait till tomorrow!'

'See you tomorrow then.'

He lay in his bed of polished-brass magnificence, unable to sleep. Young voices drifted up from the street through the open window, boys laughed and a girl's voice soared above their laughter. He had never before associated Vichy with young people.

What was he going to tell Helen?

He seemed too exhausted to pull his wits together and too overtired to sleep. He dressed and went down for a walk. There were still a great number of people about. Instead of elderly hypochondriacs and hospital-cases pushed about in wheel-chairs (as he expected to see) the majority of the people were young as at any holiday place at this time of the year. He followed a group to a pavilion gaily lit like an open-air bar. It turned out to be one of the numerous fountains where pretty girls in white overalls served unadulterated Vichy water. You could see it bubbling up in glass tubes from a great depth, still balmy from the womb of Mother Earth. The name 'Vichy' conjured up for him not an association of mineral water but war-time France and a tired old soldier who governed Vichy France from here, drinking – no doubt – lots of Vichy water without getting visibly invigorated by it.

But when Braun had drunk several glasses of it, he felt (whether it was his imagination or its beneficial effect) refreshed. Suddenly he knew, too, what he was going to tell Helen.

'Come and sit down, I want to talk to you about some-thing very serious, something that concerns my safety, possibly my life. You have heard of those trials of war criminals now going on in Germany? Well, there are still a number of those war criminals at large. I happen to know some of them, some of the worst of them. I'm one of the few who could recognize them. Consequently they are looking for me. Don't repeat any of those stories I told you. They could give me away. Those men are criminals and killers. I implore you not to tell anyone. Not even your best friend. Will you promise?'

He walked back to his hotel, reminded the concierge to wake him up and to make sure about the car.

He slept like a log.

CHAPTER EIGHT

1

IF HE HAD missed her on the platform when he arrived
in Millau he would have known that this was her car by
virtue of her parking it: its nose on the pavement, its back-
side sticking out into the busy road.

But she was there when the train drew up, her face
scowling as if she had not believed for a single moment that
he would be on it. When she spotted him, her eyes lit up, she
waved and sprinted towards him.

'How did you do it?' she asked. 'Daphne says it's
impossible to get here from Zürich overnight.' She kissed
him on both cheeks and said: 'This is how the French do
it. How long can you stay? There's no room in our hotel
but Daphne has talked to Madame, and she's got you one
here in Millau for three days. After that we might get you
into our mews.'

'Who's Madame and where's the mews?'

'Madame and Monsieur own our hotel which is called
La Mews and the family also owns the best hotel in Millau.'

'La Muse,' he corrected her and laughed. 'I have to be
off tomorrow.'

'You're joking.'

'I'm not.'

'Then I have to show you the Chaos today. You must see it, Karl. It's fabulous! That's where we were yesterday when you phoned. I tell you what. I'll phone Daphne from your hotel. If she doesn't need the car we'll have a picnic in the Chaos. We'll buy things here, food and drink. Now that you're rich you can treat me to a super picnic. There she is! Isn't she a darling?'

She meant the car. Although the station clock showed only nine, the metal of the car already felt burning hot from a flaming sun.

She had no idea how to find the hotel; he had to ask several times. They found it on the main square, a square that could be in any small town in France. A bulky vehicle sprayed water on the hot asphalt causing a fine vapour-cloud to rise from it with a faint rainbow quivering in it as it moved after the vehicle. It added up to a summer morning to remember.

She indicated a road sign: 'Chaos de Montpellier-le-Vieux'. 'That's where we are going!' She almost missed the hotel.

While he verified the booking of his room, she went into the lobby and joined two small boys who stood by the large and ornate fish-tank in the centre. There were a great number of live trout swimming in the tank, the children chasing them with nets provided for the purpose. He saw her lecturing the children who gaped at her and did not understand a word. He guessed rightly: she was telling them off for worrying the fish. She showed them the sign above the tank, convinced that it said: 'Patrons are requested not to pester the fish!' when, in fact, it said: 'Patrons can catch their own trout to be cooked according to their own wishes.' When he asked her what she thought of Daphne's husband who fished for trout the whole blessed day (and sometimes even before the sun rose), she replied:

'In the river it is different. The fish can get away and they get caught only because they're greedy.'

She went up with him to see his room, a large, old-fashioned bedroom with two beds, several large windows on to the square and a door which led to an enormous bathroom. She phoned Daphne and obtained her sanction to keep the car. She asked also how they would find the spot where they went to picnic yesterday. He gathered the land-mark had something to do with a giraffe, but when he asked her, she only said: 'You'll see!' For a moment, he thought of mentioning the purpose of his coming here and now. There might not be much chance later. He gathered from *her* part of the conversation that the plan was to join the Bagshots for dinner, after which the whole lot of them would drive back to Millau for coffee and a drink. She tried to arrange everything and to sound efficient as if she had already spent weeks in the district and not barely twenty-four hours.

'All's settled! Now we'll buy things for our picnic!'

And he postponed talking to her until he had another chance.

2

'A penny for your thoughts!' she called as she drove up the steep mountain-side.

'They're not worth it.'

'I bet you're thinking of that vintage red wine you bought. Right?'

'Wrong.'

'Food?'

'No.'

'You must be starving. You had no breakfast. There's no food to be had on that train. Did you know that the famous cheese-place . . . Now, what's the name of that smelly French cheese?'

'Camembert?'

'No. The other.'

'Brie.'

'No, Karl. The one that looks slightly rotten, you know!'

'Roquefort?'

'That's it. Did you know that Roquefort was very near here? About an hour's drive. We'll go there one day this week. Why don't you stay and come with us? Everybody says it's terrific. Cheese everywhere. Right inside the mountain. Eight floors deep and cheeses on every floor. Millions of them. You're very silent. How was Hermann?'

'Who?' He sounded so astonished that she turned her head and for a moment lost control of the car. To him the name 'Hermann' implied Hermann Schmiede. But she meant, of course, his mythical rich friend in Zürich.

'That was a narrow shave!' she gasped, horrified that she had all but damaged Daphne's car.

In a hollow near the top, she parked the car among many others. Crowds of people kept arriving.

'How big is this place?' he asked.

'Vast. Colossal. It has three stars.'

'What are the stars for? I thought only restaurants got stars.'

'Famous places get them, too.'

At the entrance there was a farm. It sold refreshments and tickets. For an entrance fee of one franc you were entitled to a primitive, duplicated map with the positions of the most famous spots marked on it. There were two routes marked: a short one which could be completed in less than half an hour and a much more ambitious one.

'We'll see Queen Victoria first,' she insisted as they entered. She had not exaggerated when she had praised the strangeness and size of the place. It seemed as though they had landed on another planet. Enormous rock formations, huge boulders, giant crags, rose above tortured scraggy trees. As far as the eye could see thorny brushwood covered the ground, growing out of cruel, stony soil. Although the place must have been swarming with visitors, not a soul could be seen. Occasionally, distant voices reverberated from rock to rock – no one could tell where they came from. The path descended, wound about, then climbed once more, marked out with red paint on shining, worn-out stones. It glistened like unclotted blood.

The fantastic rock formations were called 'Elephant', 'Camel', 'Sphinx', 'Giraffe', 'Cyrano's Nose' and the 'Head of Queen Victoria'. With a little imagination, you could recognize them, too.

'Well?' she whispered as if she were afraid of offending some evil spirit.

He had to admit he had never before seen anything like it, and firmly believed that this foreboding silence was due to everybody whispering as she did.

'Would you like to be lost here?' she asked softly and shuddered in spite of the heat.

'No fear,' he said. Quoting one of her favourite expressions dispelled her uneasiness.

'I'll show you the perfect picnic place. We have to turn off the path as soon as we are level with the "Old Giraffe and His Son". There they are!'

'How do you know he's his son? Perhaps the little one is a girl and the tall one her brother.'

'Daphne knows them. She comes here every year.'

He wouldn't have believed that there could be a spot for two people to sit down, but she found the place shown to her by Daphne the day before and described again on the phone this morning. The ground was even – just a few square yards of it – covered with soft green moss. He dropped the large paper-bag full of provisions. She sat down on a flat stone (part of the grown-up giraffe's left hoof); its head protected her from the sun. She spread several large paper napkins on the moss, collected two insects crawling over the napkins and transferred them to the rock.

'You go *that* way,' she ordered them and they did.

While she arranged the food, he pulled the cork from his 'vintage' bottle, dismissed her objection to drink with the importance of the occasion and the genealogy of the wine and was just about to begin telling her about the purpose of his coming, when she forestalled him.

'Karl! I want your advice.'

He filled the paper cups – altogether unworthy of the wine he had acquired for this special occasion. He raised his cup to her, waited for her to drink, then emptied his own cup, a little cross because of his lost chance.

'I'm listening,' he said.

'Dan's coming.' She took another sip to avoid his startled gaze.

'Where to? When?'

'Towards the end of next week. Bringing Eve. It's Daphne's doing. She calls it a *coup d'état*. You know what a *coup d'état* is? This is a fabulous wine. What is it called?'

'I thought you didn't see each other any more, you two.' (The wretched little bitch, he thought. Going to Paris with me and all the time plotting how to get back to that fellow, Dan . . .)

'Of course not. That's why I'm asking you. You're much older than I am . . .' She checked herself. 'Much more experienced . . . What am I supposed to do? I can't run away because of Eve. I don't want him to think that I'm afraid of him either. Give me some more wine, please. Couldn't I mix it with water?'

'I left the mineral water in the car.'

'You don't want to get me sozzled, do you? I've got to drive, you know. Go and fetch it, please. I shouldn't have alcohol on a hot day like this, I told you.'

She gave him the key and he went. He found the path with the red markings. He was striding now, fast, angry, like a deceived husband who had just found out that he had been cuckolded. 'The little hussy! . . .'

When he opened the car, the stuffy hot air hit him like the blast of a furnace. The bottle of mineral water felt boiling. He left it where he found it and decided to buy a cold one at the farmhouse. ('I come here, all the way from Zürich, and the first thing she tells me is that she wants to take up with her divorced husband again . . .') He bought a bottle of mineral water for her and an ice-cold beer for himself. The wine he had bought this morning (the best in the shop!) had lost all its appeal to him. He asked the woman to open the beer and drank it right there, at the bar. There was no hurry. He was aware that he was behaving unreasonably towards her and downright stupidly as far as he, himself, was concerned. But instead of calming down, he got hotter and hotter under the collar. By the time he had finished a second beer and the woman behind the counter gave him his change, the water had got lukewarm again and she offered to change it for another straight from the ice-box. He turned down the offer. It would do.

He had no difficulty in finding the place. It was her pink scarf he spotted first, sprawling on the green moss. Then the white of her skirt, her flushed face, the red skin of her leg. She was fast asleep. The two pork chops, the sliced silver-side, the half open tin of *foie gras* were swarming with insects. Large emerald flies buzzed over them, the heat melted the fat, the whole lot looked sticky. She looked sticky, too, under the flaming sun. The pistachio and orange ice-creams trickled in green and ochre-coloured rivulets with their confluence under her handbag. In his absence the shadows had receded before the conquering midday sun. The heat and the wine did the rest.

He withdrew a little and stayed at a safe distance so that he wouldn't wake her. He tried to argue the case on its merits. She had a proneness to heat hyperpyrexia. He certainly could not be made responsible for that. She had an attack of it years ago, when he didn't even know that she existed. He went to get a bottle of mineral water – he held it still in his hand. The woman would remember him. What he had to do now was to go back to the farmhouse and tell them that he had lost his way, he couldn't find her. He would ask them to help him to locate her. He would remember, somewhere they had turned off the path, after perhaps ten to twelve minutes' walk. It was to the left, he remembered that, too . . .

He walked slowly until he reached the path. Once on it, he changed the pace. He would have to stay here a day or two to dispel any suspicion. But he wasn't safer anywhere than here. He would stay a couple of days. It would be worth it.

There were a number of customers in the farmhouse. He apologized, pushed his way through and told the woman about his trouble. As he expected, she was too busy to worry about such trifles and to organize a search-party just now. People got lost daily. All of them would turn up before the day was out. Mademoiselle would hear people talking, would join up with them. She'd probably walk in here any moment. The proper thing was for him to sit down, have another beer, and wait for her. Much more sensible than wandering about the Chaos and perhaps missing her.

This made sense and suited his book. He said he would leave a note in the car in case she went there first. The woman and several others who had been listening to his plight, concurred.

Just before he got to the car, a sight startled him. It was so unexpected that it caught him completely off his guard and paralysed his limbs and paralysed his mind. He just stood there staring, stunned by it. A big car came up the dirt road and as it drew up among the parked vehicles, two men stepped out of it. One was short with thick glasses under his bushy eyebrows. The other was a giant, his skin tanned, dressed in a fawn-coloured gaberdine suit of American cut. Braun had stopped a few yards short of the open space cleared for visitors to park their cars. His immobility saved him. The two men asked a question of the attendant and hurried towards the entrance. Had he stayed in the house, or had he left a few seconds sooner, they couldn't have missed him. This lucky turn in his ill-fortune woke him up. First he thought of taking the car, but the sight of the parking attendant made him change his mind. He would have liked to leave the key in the car but there was no time for that. He saw an open van coming from the farm, loaded with crates of empty bottles. He raised his hand. The van stopped. It had never happened to him before, but he couldn't manage to switch to French from English and he gabbled in English to the driver.

'Take me to Millau, please.'

The driver, who had strict instructions not to pick up strangers, hesitated. In view of doing his bit for the declining tourist trade, he relented, though, and got a surprisingly large tip for his sagacity as he deposited the stranger at the corner of the Avenue Jean Jaurès and the Place du Mandarous.

Braun asked for his bill and went upstairs to fetch his suitcase.

How did they manage to find him? It couldn't be a coincidence, not even intelligent anticipation of a well-run organization. Yesterday, they traced him to Zürich and today they had tracked him down in Millau, hundreds of miles away. It must be Helen. Or Daphne and her husband. All three most likely. It was impossible otherwise.

He had to move fast. But still he had to decide where to go and by what means. Trains remained his best bet. There was one to Béziers in three-quarters of an hour's time, at 13.30, and another in the opposite direction a quarter of an hour later which went all the way to Paris. It did not matter which. He'd decide at the station. At this moment the telephone rang.

He waited before he answered it. It kept on ringing. Hopefully he said to himself: it's the clerk; he wants to tell me my bill is ready. He knew, though, it had nothing to do with his bill. There were two men downstairs who wanted to see him, who had told the concierge they were old friends. As often before, a spark soared up from all the burnt-up cinders in his mind: Call the police! Scream for help! Tear open the window and yell! But how could he dare to do it? They would arrest him, too, shave his head; he would be handcuffed, prosecuted; they would confront him with witnesses, he would stand in the dock all alone, everybody out for his blood. In a way it seemed to him even more horrible than the alternative of those two downstairs.

He could escape both alternatives. Others had done it before. He would give himself one more chance. He would prepare himself for the worst and then answer the phone. It could still be just a harmless call. He opened his suitcase, took from it the little brown box and went with it to the bathroom. The telephone stopped ringing. But as soon as he returned, it started again. He shoved the brown box under his shirts and closed the suitcase. His mouth felt very moist. His teeth, on to which he forced the unused bridge, ached. He picked up the receiver and found his voice sounded foreign, either due to his nervousness or – more likely – because of the new set of teeth. He told the concierge he had been in the bathroom. The concierge said:

'Two gentlemen are here to see you. They say they are friends.'

The spark in his mind nose-dived like a shooting star and went out. He felt with his tongue the edge of the new front teeth. They were too tight. It would take weeks to get used to them. He would have to pull them back now, with his tongue. Should go quite smoothly. There was a knock on the door, a discreet, soft tap. A soft and discreet voice called:

'Herr Doctor! Herr Doctor!!'

He advanced his tongue as far as he could, between upper lip and his teeth and tried to shift the teeth back on their tiny hinges. It took an eternity before they obeyed.

'Herr Doctor! . . .' came from the door with more urgency. It arched as strong shoulders heaved against it.

At last, the little gate moved and a minute capsule dropped in his mouth. He needed great willpower to keep it there, for it felt sticky, the membraneous envelope bent and gave, inflating the ends slightly as tongue or tooth touched it. What if it had lost its efficiency? He bit through it, tasted its sweetness and knew that it worked.

Now he didn't mind the door lock yielding. He stepped back so that a bed stood between him and the intruders. He saw the worried look on their faces and wondered why.

'Herr Doctor!' the slighter of the two said. 'Thank God we have caught up with you. I'm Ansaldo, formerly Rudolf Salter.' He pointed at the big man who closed the door and guarded it. 'This is Herr Lang. I tried to contact you in London. We missed you in Zürich . . . We were afraid we might miss you here, too, and then we wouldn't have known where to look for you. It was Herr Lang's idea that you might call on Mrs Taylor after Zürich. I got her address from the office where she works . . .'

'Who are you?' Braun asked. It occurred to him for the first time that something was terribly wrong.

'We've been sent by the Brothers, after poor Hein's death, to persuade you to join us. He wrote that he had found you, that he was just about to meet you . . . Did he? . . . Herr Doctor, is anything wrong? Herr Lang, come! Help me!'

They laid him on the bed. He seemed in very poor shape. He could still talk, but it needed a great effort. He tried desperately to be a doctor, gave orders, but it wasn't easy to understand what he meant. He was sinking fast.

'Get some hot water from the bathroom and some cold . . . Strip me! . . . Strip me and sponge my heart . . . I have taken something . . .'

As Herr Lang hurried to the bathroom and ran the hot-water tap to make the water come hotter, Ansaldo pulled off Braun's jacket and shirt.

'Would you like me to call a doctor?'

The sick man's breath became slower, his lips began to turn blue.

'It is too late for that,' he whispered.

'Herr Lang, hurry!' Ansaldo shouted. His bushy eye-brows and his little moustache bristled with excitement. 'Is there anything we can do, Herr Doctor?'

'Get quickly some . . .'

'What?' urged Ansaldo. 'What should I get?'

Braun could have sworn he said: 'Get quickly some mustard!' But they didn't hear it. Mustard would make him vomit. It was essential. He also thought: they are very clumsy. They should sponge my chest alternately with hot and cold water. But they were doing it together. He could hear Ansaldo say to Lang:

'Call a doctor!'

'Is that safe?' Lang asked.

Go! Go!! Don't stay with me, Braun thought. It's no use staying with me!

Lang picked up the receiver but had his finger on the fork. He said:

'Do you think he's got the money with him? The Brothers need it. I don't think *he*'ll need it.' He dropped the receiver back into its place. Braun wished they would take the money. He willed them to do it with all the power left to him. He tried to smile when they did take it, but his blue swollen lips wouldn't obey.

Suddenly, instead of Ansaldo, he saw Hermann Schmiede hovering over him. He knew it was Schmiede, he heard the Prosecutor calling him by name to give evidence in the case of Federal Republic versus Dr Otto Reitmüller, alias Karl Braun, alias B. Karl. 'Vain, ruthless, self-centred' repeated Schmiede. There was no use denying it now, after what he did to Helen Taylor at Montpellier. The High Court wasn't as grand as the one that the accused had been tried and acquitted at so often before. Just a simple, makeshift court, called together at short notice in an emergency, as it were. The prosecutor explained to His Lordship, that the young lady in question would reach the Court soon. She was on her way from Montpellier and by 'Montpellier' he meant not the township, but some place called the 'Chaos of Montpellier-le-Vieux'.

And Chaos it was . . .

3

On the small island called 'Little Venice' two swans were fighting. Through the wide-open window, Lilian could hear the thuds of their strong wings bashing away at each other.

'Oh, Mr Parsons! They'll kill each other!' Lilian moaned.

The junior partner – for a moment quite oblivious of the swans and Lilian Hall – looked up from the mountain range of his mail, arranged into peaks, hills and valleys, according to their importance.

'What? Oh, the swans. Don't worry about those bastards, Miss Hall. They've got no other worries than who's debauching who. Take a letter to Camberley and Houston, Cardiff. Concerning your order . . . You get the date from Jack.' He waited and heard his secretary sighing. 'What's the matter? Anything wrong with you, Miss Hall?'

'No, of course not.'

'Your mother all right?'

'Yes, thank you. She's rather busy. It's the season, you know.'

'Your love-life in good order?'

'Really, Mr Parsons!' She patted her locks which, to his surprise, were not slightly greying as he remembered them, but mousy like the rest.

'Have you dyed your hair?' he asked.

'I don't know what you mean, Mr Parsons. A woman must look after her hair.'

'True enough, Miss Hall. On second thoughts, call our solicitors. I'd better talk to them before I answer this. And get me the Camberley-Houston file, please.'

She went to her office and found an inspector from Scotland Yard waiting for her. They had been here before to inform the firm that one of their employees had committed suicide in a small French town called Millau. Mr Parsons, Jr, greatly relieved that their call had nothing to do with his purchase of that villa in Sardinia, proved himself most helpful and Lilian shed a few tears. Both stressed what an excellent and reliable employee Mr Braun had been.

'None better!' the junior partner emphasized. Neither he, nor his secretary, could even guess the reason for his death. Braun of all people! . . .

'Such a gentle man,' Lilian said.

'He loved birds,' Mr Parsons, Jr, added. 'Especially swans!' He turned to his secretary for confirmation and got it.

This time another inspector came to clear up a little matter which had nothing to do with the firm. In the morgue in Millau, a small wreath of flowers had been delivered for the deceased. It came from London, via Interflora, an institution that transferred flowers from one country to another as banks transfer money. The cheque for the flowers was signed by Miss Hall.

Lilian blushed.

'Is there any law against remembering a fellow-employee?' she challenged the inspector.

'No, madam. But there are new developments and we have reason to believe that Karl Braun lived a clandestine life and was a much more dangerous citizen than just a piano-tuner.'

He wouldn't divulge any more and left Lilian with more question-marks than she had ever typed on her typewriter.

4

If Karl Braun had ever hoped to avoid coming face to face with Hermann Schmiede in this world, he pulled it off only partially. For when the authorities, baffled by reason and the circumstances of the man's suicide, explored all avenues, only to find a dead end to every single one, it was Schmiede who offered the solution.

'It is my friend and former boss, Dr Reitmüller. I recognize him from the pictures in the newspapers.'

The head of the War Criminals Investigating Bureau in Ludwigsburg, who reluctantly granted a special hearing to Schmiede, was sceptical. But after he had spoken to Schmiede, he issued new directives to those concerned and, as word reached him from eye-witnesses who professed to have encountered Braun (or someone very much like him), the Chief State Prosecutor packed his bag and proceeded to Millau.

Braun was reported to have been in Paris, travelled from there – sitting up all night – to Zürich. A railway official at Zürich (Enge) saw him at 7.30 a.m., a ticket clerk sold him a ticket (this time first-class!) to Geneva and ever since he had spent four hours in Zürich, he seemed to have been rolling in money. As the bank kept silent, it just increased the investigators' puzzlement. How did he get the money and why did he kill himself?

A Mrs Daphne Hollywell reported that two men had called at her hotel, in Le Rozier, who wished to contact Mr Braun urgently. She told them where Helen and Braun had gone, she even described how to find the spot where the two were most likely to have a picnic. Those two friends did go to Montpellier-le-Vieux and did find Helen, fast asleep and alone. They woke her up, thus probably saving her life, poor thing . . .

The hotel in Millau supplied a detailed description of those 'friends'. When the concierge announced them to Mr Braun he hadn't objected to seeing them. The two men came downstairs shortly afterwards and vanished. They must have split up – one had been seen on the train between Perpignan and the Spanish border, but the witness was not very reliable. They had gone and could be anywhere by now. Whoever they were, they were not after Braun's money. He still had about 10,000 Swiss francs in his wallet.

Meanwhile, the suspicion that Karl Braun was none other than the infamous Nazi brain surgeon had got into the papers. Simultaneously, plain-clothes men, police officers in France, C.I.D. men, Scotland Yard detectives in England, Interpol agents and consular officials in many other countries, visited a great number of individuals, took statements, arrested and released people in order to piece together the whole story of the life and death of Karl Braun or, possibly, Dr Otto Reitmüller.

In London, Jaroslav Kolm, who had lately returned from a disappointing excursion into his past, had told the police that his journey to Prague had no connection with the clandestine life of his fellow-lodger. He admitted sending Braun a picture postcard, but the cryptic words on it: 'There's no Prague ham in Prague' were not a communication in code. They meant exactly what they said: all the famous product of the city of his birth was sent for export, none was left for home consumption.

Strohmayer complained to the officer that he himself suffered an actual financial loss, since he had bought provisions for Braun for his impending home-coming, obtained for him also a couple of concert tickets (the most expensive kind); furthermore there was also a dry-cleaning bill awaiting settlement . . . The officer regretted but couldn't help. When he had gone, Strohmayer and Kolm sat in the kitchen and discussed the case well into the night.

'Imagine, Jaroslav! If he *is* Reitmüller! . . . I could have earned all that money!' Strohmayer sighed. Kolm was brewing coffee. He looked up, mildly interested.

'What money?'

'The reward.' He sighed again, even deeper this time.

Kolm, the Wise, realized that Strohmayer was much more affected by the case than he cared to admit. Strohmayer fancied himself as a 'keen observer of human nature' and got a little worried how genuine this talent of his really was.

'A murderer next door!' Kolm said. 'Mrs Felton will have a job to let that room.'

'You're wrong, Jaro. You'll see! People will *want* to live in the room of the famous Nazi doctor who killed dozens of his patients for scientific experiments. Sending them into gas-chambers was different. That was just downright, unsophisticated murder.' He pondered for a long time before he asked: 'If you'd been told: Jaroslav Kohn, you've got the choice: either you join the others and proceed into the slaughter-house now – or you could enter the hospital where there will be food, clean sheets, for as long as three to four months. Either you'll be exterminated like vermin tonight, or, I, the famous researcher working to solve the secrets of the human mind, will carry out some experiments on you. *Which* would you have chosen? I know which I would have! The hospital, any time – the food, the three months' grace. Hell! The war might be over in three months! Hitler could be assassinated in three months! The most unexpected things might happen in three months!'

'Leslie, my friend! Taking a human life is a monstrous crime! So infinitely monstrous that there is no measurable difference whether it is taken today or in three months' time. Whether the corpse is well-fed, or a starved skeleton.'

'But was he guilty, Jaro?' Strohmayer asked. 'What did he do? He took a few starved people from the gas-chamber, fed them, made them feel like human beings again, gave them a little dignity . . .' He paused, pursuing a new train of thought. 'Let's say he had done what he had done. But he could have put it like this: I saw all those wretched people, destined to be butchered. I couldn't save them all. But I could throw a lifeline to *some*. I could get *some* out – two–three at a time. I, would bring them over to my special compound, feed them, talk to them. You should have seen those poor wretches starved to skeletons, snatched from certain death ... You should have seen the gratitude in their eyes. Of course I had to do some surgery on them. That was my alibi. Without it I couldn't have survived for a day ...' Strohmayer got quite excited, convinced that this time he had shaken the opposition. But the opposition shook its head.

'The kind of man you are describing belongs to the most common and most dangerous kind of criminals. They are the scourge of the human race. Those who can explain everything. Who commit their crimes in the name of Science, the Fatherland, Religion, for the sake of Love, Culture, for Progress ...'

5

The German gentleman who came all the way from Ludwigsburg near Stuttgart, was soft-spoken, middle-aged, almost a father-figure. Or so he seemed to Helen when he came to call on her, accompanied by a local gendarmerie officer, in the hospital in Millau. They were her first visitors. She wouldn't have allowed anybody to see her, not even her own baby daughter, and certainly not her divorced husband, both of whom had arrived a couple of days ago and were staying at the Hôtel La Muse, in a small village, only a few miles away. Her whole body had been bandaged; the young doctor called her 'the youngest mummy we ever had in this hospital', which meant quite a lot, since the hospital swarmed with mummies, most of them not bandaged at all.

The kindly gentleman from Germany carried a bulky attaché case, spoke English, and said he wanted her to help in establishing the identity of the deceased Dr Otto Reitmüller.

'Who is Doctor Whatshisname?' she wondered, and the German expressed surprise that she had never heard of him.

'You have known him as Karl Braun,' he explained.

'Oh, Karl!' she gasped. Her doctor had told her about the shocking news concerning her friend. 'Isn't it sad about Karl! Why did he do it? And why do you say he might have been Dr . . . whatever you've just said?' She added quickly: 'I blame myself. If I hadn't sent him to fetch something from the car, he might still be alive. And with him there, I wouldn't have fallen asleep and wouldn't be here, either.'

Her visitor said:

'There is reason to believe, Mrs Taylor, that Karl Braun was a Nazi war criminal. I came here to speak with you and try to establish the truth.'

'Karl, a criminal? Never!' She shook her head vigorously.

'Did he ever speak of his past? The times *before* he came to England? Of his family? His friends? His job?'

'He never had a family, I know that.'

'Really?'

'Oh, no. And I know what he did. He used to be a photographer.'

'Photographer? That's very interesting. Very helpful.'

'News-photographer. He carried on for a while *after* he left Germany. He worked as a photographer in Paris.'

'When did he go to Paris?'

'In 1933 or '34, I believe. After Hitler turned up, you know? I'm not very good at politics.'

'Did he ever tell you about Paris?'

'*Did* he!'

'Tell me, please.'

'You're not spying for Michelle's husband, are you?'

'No. Who's Michelle? Wait a minute – wasn't she married to somebody who managed a night-club?'

'How do you know?' She seemed completely flummoxed and he became suddenly very grave. Something told her that she was betraying Karl, even if this man had nothing to do with Michelle's husband. 'I'm not going to tell you any more,' she said firmly.

'Please,' he pleaded. 'It is desperately important.'

'Who do you work for? You're not an investigator, are you?'

'I am.'

'What are you investigating then?'

'The murder of scores of innocent people in Nazi concentration camps.'

'What has Karl to do with it?'

'He did it.'

She shook her head.

'I don't believe it.'

'Will you help me if I prove to you that he was lying to you? That he had never been a photographer and certainly not in Paris? It is most likely that he had never been in Paris before he went there with you.'

She again shook her head in desperation. He looked out of the window into the hospital garden, the deck-chairs on the lawn, the nurses pushing patients in invalid-chairs under the trees.

'Do you like animals?' He didn't wait for an answer. 'Look at that cat in the garden. What would you do if somebody caught it, cracked open its head, chopped up its brain . . .'

'Please don't!' she implored, but he went on.

'If he waited till it had healed and then did it again!' She buried her face in her hands, but it wasn't enough to barricade herself from it. He said: 'There's a Society for Prevention of Cruelty to Animals – I'm working for a Society for Prevention of Cruelty to Human Beings.'

'You must be wrong.' She began in a low voice but, as she went on, it gained in strength. 'I know positively that he did live in Paris. We met people there that he used to know many years ago. We went to places he knew so intimately; only someone who had been there could know. We met the porter of a little hotel. Karl reminded him of his childhood. Of boyhood pranks. Of his brother. The man remembered everything. I saw with my own eyes an apartment where he used to live. Karl knew the layout of every room. He told me of things that happened in Paris, people would remember them – a robbery, when bandits snatched the takings at the Brasserie Lorraine and were caught in the tube . . . He was there when, at midnight, the cabs came out on strike . . . All these things can be looked up in the papers, I suppose . . . I can show you where he lived . . . I can tell you how he left Germany and with whom, back in '33. You must be making a mistake. Nobody can invent all these things . . .'

'He hasn't invented them,' the kind gentleman said quietly. He drew his pot-bellied attaché case closer, snapped the catch open and pulled out a thick manuscript from it. It looked like the typescript of a book. On top, there was a filing number. The title said: *Dr Otto Reitmüller: Diary and Case Histories, 1940–1945. (Verbatim Translated.)*

'Have a look!' he challenged her and put it on her blanket. In the lower right-hand corner, she could read: 'Property of War Criminal Investigation Bureau, Ludwigsburg.' She hesitated to touch it, but he insisted: 'Open it! Go on! Open it, anywhere!'

She put her hand on it. It burnt like the fire of hell. But she couldn't draw her hand away. She opened it somewhere in the middle. The heading of the page caught her eye. It read: 'The Glass Pearls.' Underneath, in quotes, it went on: 'It was the first party in the new flat in the Rue Quentin-Bochart. We had invited three girls. I remember their names: Simone, Monique and Babette. We bought a barrel of oysters, the little green ones, called "Portugaises". Frank stood for hours watching the leather-aproned oyster-man opening them. I had the idea of buying half a pound of glass pearls, washed them carefully under the tap, lifted the flesh of the largest oysters and inserted a glass pearl between oyster and shell. It was great fun watching the girls' behaviour . . .' On the edge of the page, there were marginal notes: 'Third experiment. Date: 22.1.1943. Sixty-one days after second surgery. 142 days after first surgery. Patient sufficiently recovered from last experiment. Breathing: normal. Temperature: slightly rising. Speech: unsteady, but intelligible. Re two previous surgeries, see pages III and 67, also photographs and pen drawings, marked . . .'

'What are you reading about?' the German asked. She turned the manuscript towards him, so that he could see the heading. 'Did he ever mention it to you?' She nodded. He said: 'You'll find it all there. The love-affair with the nightclub manager's wife, the shooting in the club . . . Did he tell you about the one-legged Frenchman who profited from his missing leg to get ahead in queues? It would be funny, if it were not so tragic.' After some time she asked, pointing at the diary:

'Who was the man?'

'A poor young Jewish photographer. He managed to escape from Germany in '33.' He indicated the manuscript. 'It tells you how he got across the border, how his hands were shaking when the Gestapo examined the passports in the train. He was caught, though, in Paris when France was overrun. They carried him off to Wittau concentration camp.'

She tortured her brain for the proverbial last straw.

'Perhaps it was *he* who got caught? Perhaps all that horror he went through made him keep silent . . .'

'No,' he said. 'This man died – somewhere on page 183. After the third operation.'

She tried to grab the straw but, as she watched the man's face, it drifted out of her reach.

AFTERWORD
by Kevin Macdonald

A couple of years ago I went to the Berlin Film Festival to see a newly restored version of Powell and Pressburger's classic *The Life and Death of Colonel Blimp*. Prior to the screening I spoke to Michael Powell's widow, Thelma Schoonmaker-Powell, and she told me how nervous she was. What would the Berlin audience make of what was essentially a propaganda film – made in 1942 at the height of the Second World War?

She needn't have worried. The audience was smitten. There was more laughter than any seventy-year-old film should rightfully receive – the warm laughter of recognition and a joke shared. Here was a film made during the bloodiest period of the war, featuring many German characters, that was adored by the 'enemy' nation, perhaps because it showed decency and foolishness on both sides, even as it insisted on the unquestionable evil of Nazi ideology. How many parallels are there for that, not just in films from the Second World War but even in today's cinema? Are there any films about the Iraq or Afghan wars that would evoke a similar response in the 'enemy'?

The writer of *Colonel Blimp*, my grandfather Imre (Emeric) Pressburger, was born in Miskolc, Hungary, in 1902, into a culture that was unabashedly Germanophile.

He was Jewish, but grew up reading Goethe, playing the great German composers on his violin, admiring German engineering and coveting a German education. He attended the German university in Prague (Kafka's alma mater, and the first university to offer Einstein a professorship), followed by the University of Stuttgart. Then, after some terribly difficult and poverty-stricken years during which he relied on the kindness of strangers, living hand-to-mouth on the streets of Berlin, he found his foothold in the film industry at the famous UFA studios. The city he wrote about with such affection and humour in *Colonel Blimp* was a place he knew intimately. It was to him – as to many Europeans at the time, Jews and Gentiles – the most exciting place to be in the world.

Given all this, it is perhaps not so surprising that when Hitler took power in 1933 and Emeric was forced to flee soon after to Paris and then London, he brought a complex and humane view of Germany and the Germans with him. In his own mind he was clear that 'Germans' and 'Nazis' were not the same thing and that there were many Germans who rejected the aims and methods of Hitler and his mob.

What is perhaps more surprising is that over the following years – right through the war – he persisted in lacing the films he wrote (many of them made with an overt propaganda intent) with sympathetic German characters. Perhaps the most nuanced of these was Anton Walbrook's characterisation of Theo Kretschmar-Schuldorff in *Colonel Blimp*. His speech about how, when he has lost his two sons to Nazism, he starts to yearn for the beauty of the English countryside, is a deeply affecting appeal to all that is best about Britain, but simultaneously a bitter recollection of what Germany has lost.

But even that is on a whole different level from what Emeric did twenty years later in *The Glass Pearls*, his second (and last) published novel. It is written from the point of view of a concentration-camp doctor who, like Joseph Mengele, has experimented on his unwilling 'patients'. Although this character, 'Karl Braun', is presented as capable of great evil, we are encouraged to sympathise with him on a personal level – to understand his loneliness, his yearning for love. Even more bizarrely, Emeric went so far as to imbue the Braun character with certain traits of his own; such that, to some degree, Braun is a self-portrait.

What makes this even more extraordinary – even shocking – is that, as he only found out at the war's end, Emeric's own mother Katarina had been sent to her death in Auschwitz, together with many of his cousins, aunts and uncles.

Until his dying day I think Emeric felt guilty for not having brought his ageing mother to England when he still could. In his declining years, as his mind corroded and senility set in, he was forever haunted by the thought of being chased by Nazis. When, delirious after a bad fall towards the end of his life, he was taken to hospital, he fought against the ambulance crew, thinking they were taking him to the gas chamber.

In my opinion, all of this makes *The Glass Pearls* not just a significant and overlooked part of Holocaust literature, but a thematically coherent capstone to a long and remarkable writing life. Since it has endured fifty years of neglect

I couldn't be more pleased that Faber are now making this entertaining, enigmatic and – it has to be said – troubling novel available again.

Kevin Macdonald is the director of documentary feature films including One Day in September *(2000),* Touching the Void *(2003) and* Marley *(2012), and of dramatic features including* The Last King of Scotland *(2006),* State of Play *(2009),* How I Live Now *(2013) and* The Mauritanian *(2021). His biography of his grandfather,* Emeric Pressburger: The Life and Death of a Screenwriter *(1994) is published by Faber.*

Maud Martha

by Gwendolyn Brooks

With a new foreword by Margo Jefferson

Maud Martha Brown is a little girl growing up on the South Side of 1940s Chicago, where she dreams: of New York, romance, her future. Soon, she falls in love, decorates her kitchenette, gives birth. But her lighter-skinned husband has dreams too: of the Foxy Cats Club, other women, war. And the 'scraps of baffled hate' – a certain word from a saleswoman; that visit to the cinema; the cruelty of a department store Santa Claus – are always there . . .

'I loved it and want everyone to read this lost literary treasure.' Bernardine Evaristo

'An exquisite portraiture of black womanhood by one of America's most foundational writers.' Claudia Rankine

'Reveals the poetry, power and splendor of an ordinary life.' Tayari Jones

'One of the most spatially poetic novels ever . . . Awesome.' Eileen Myles

'Alive, reaching, and very much of today.' Langston Hughes

FABER

EDITIONS

FABER

They

by Kay Dick

With a new foreword by Carmen Maria Machado

This is Britain: but not as we know it. THEY begin with a dead dog, shadowy footsteps, confiscated books. Soon, the National Gallery is purged; dissidents are captured in military sweeps; violent mobs stalk the countryside destroying artworks – and those who resist. Survivors gather together as cultural refugees, preserving their crafts, creating, loving and remembering. But THEY make it easier to forget . . .

'Creepily prescient . . . Insidiously horrifying.' Margaret Atwood

'A masterpiece of creeping dread.' Emily St. John Mandel

'The signature of an enchantress.' Edna O'Brien

'Delicious and sexy and downright chilling. Read it!' Rumaan Alam

'A masterwork of English pastoral horror: eerie and bewitching.' Claire-Louise Bennett

EDITIONS

Mrs Caliban

by Rachel Ingalls

With a new foreword by Irenosen Okojie

Dorothy is a grieving housewife in the Californian suburbs. One day, she is doing chores when she hears strange voices on the radio announcing that a green-skinned sea monster has escaped from the Institute for Oceanographic Research – but little does she expect him to arrive in her kitchen. Vegetarian, sexually magnetic and excellent at housework, Larry the frogman is a revelation – and their passionate affair takes them on a journey beyond their wildest dreams . . .

'Still outpaces, out-weirds and out-romances anything today.' Marlon James

'Genius . . . A broadcast from a stranger and more dazzling dimension.' Patricia Lockwood

'So curiously right, so romantically obverse, that it creates its own terrible, brilliant reality.' Sarah Hall

'A feminist masterpiece: tender, erotic, singular.' Carmen Maria Machado

'Like *Revolutionary Road* written by Franz Kafka . . . Exquisite.' *The Times*

Palace of the Peacock

by *Wilson Harris*

With a new foreword by Jamaica Kincaid

A crew of men are voyaging up a turbulent river through the rainforests of Guyana, led by a domineering captain. But their expedition is plagued by tragedies and haunted by drowned ghosts. As their journey into the interior – their own hearts of darkness – deepens, it assumes a spiritual dimension, leading them towards a new destination: the Palace of the Peacock . . .

'A magnificent, breathtaking and terrifying novel.' Tsitsi Dangarembga

'The Guyanese William Blake.' Angela Carter

'A masterpiece.' Monique Roffey

'One of the great originals . . . Visionary.' *Guardian*

'Staggering . . . Brilliant and terrifying.' *The Times*